W9-BDE-479

STARTER

VILLAIN

OTHER TOR BOOKS BY JOHN SCALZI

Agent to the Stars
The Android's Dream
Fuzzy Nation
Redshirts
Your Hate Mail Will Be Graded: A Decade of Whatever, 1998–2008
The Kaiju Preservation Society

THE OLD MAN'S WAR NOVELS

Old Man's War
The Ghost Brigades
The Last Colony
Zoe's Tale
The Human Division
The End of All Things

THE LOCK IN SERIES

Lock In
Head On
Unlocked

THE INTERDEPENDENCY SEQUENCE

The Collapsing Empire
The Consuming Fire
The Last Emperox

EDITED BY JOHN SCALZI

Metatropolis

STARTER VILLAIN

JOHN SCALZI

TOR PUBLISHING GROUP
NEW YORK

This is a work of fiction. All of the characters, organizations, and events portrayed in this novel are either products of the author's imagination or are used fictitiously.

STARTER VILLAIN

A Tor Book
Published by Tom Doherty Associates / Tor Publishing Group
120 Broadway
New York, NY 10271

www.tor-forge.com

Tor® is a registered trademark of Macmillan Publishing Group, LLC.

The Library of Congress Cataloging-in-Publication Data is available upon request.

ISBN 978–0–7653–8922–0 (hardcover)
ISBN 978–0–7653–8923–7 (ebook)

Our books may be purchased in bulk for promotional, educational, or business use. Please contact your local bookseller or the Macmillan Corporate and Premium Sales Department at 1-800-221-7945, extension 5442, or by email at MacmillanSpecialMarkets@macmillan.com.

First Edition: 2023

Printed in the United States of America

0 9 8 7

This book is dedicated to:

Everyone who could make someone else's day worse, but tries to make it better instead.

Thank you. It's more important than you think.

Also, to Sugar, Spice, and Smudge, my current set of cats.

You are all a real pain in my ass, and I love your stupid furry faces.

CHAPTER 1

I learned about the death of my uncle Jake in a deeply unexpected way, which was from the CNBC *Squawk Box* morning show.

I had *Squawk Box* on from force of habit; when I was a business reporter for the *Chicago Tribune* I would turn it on in the mornings, in rotation with Bloomberg and Fox Business, while I and my wife Jeanine got ourselves ready for our respective days. These days I had less need of it—substitute teachers do not usually need to be kept up on the state of the Asian markets in order to babysit a bunch of students in a seventh-grade English class—but old habits, it turns out, actually do die hard.

Thus it was, as I was preparing my peanut butter on toast, I heard the name "Jake Baldwin" from the iPad I had running on the kitchen island. I stopped mid-peanut-butter spread, knife in hand, as cohost Andrew Ross Sorkin announced that my uncle Jake, reclusive billionaire owner of the third-largest chain of parking structures in North America, had died of pancreatic cancer at the age of sixty-seven.

"Are you hearing this?" I said to my breakfast partner, who was not my wife Jeanine, because she was no longer my wife and no longer living with me. She was now back in her hometown of Boston, dating an investment banker and, if her Instagram account was to be believed, spending most of her time being well-lit in enviable vacation spots around the globe. My breakfast partner was Hera, an orange-and-white cat who, after I had retreated to my childhood home after the divorce and layoff, had emerged from the backyard bushes and informed me through meowing that she lived with me now. Hera's breakfast was Meow Mix; she was eating on the center island and was watching *Squawk Box* with me, presumably to decide if Andrew Ross Sorkin was a prey animal she could smack around.

I had not known my uncle Jake was sick with anything, much less pancreatic cancer, which was the disease that had also felled fellow billionaire Steve Jobs. (My brain, on journalistic autopilot, had started writing the lede graf for my uncle's obituary; have I mentioned that old habits die hard?) To be fair, it wasn't that Uncle Jake had been hiding it from me. It was that he hadn't been in contact with me, at all, since I was five years old. Jake and my dad had a falling-out at my mom's funeral. I vaguely remember the yelling, and then after that it was like Jake simply didn't exist. Dad preferred it that way, and Jake must have too. Jake didn't come to Dad's funeral, in any event.

As for me, I didn't think about Jake at all until I was in college and started writing business-related articles for the *Daily Northwestern*, and discovered that half the parking structures in Evanston were owned by BLP, a private company majority-owned and entirely controlled by Jake. I tried to score an interview, figuring I might have an in, but BLP didn't have a PR department or even contact information on its website. When I got married, I dragged an address for Jake out of my dad and sent my uncle an invite, mostly to see what would happen. Jake didn't show, but sent a gift: berry spoons, and a cryptic note. I stopped thinking about him after that. Jake had almost no media presence and never showed up in the news, so this was easy enough to do.

Jake's lack of paper trail was giving CNBC fits, however. I watched as Sorkin and presumably his writers struggled to say anything about a man who was obviously important—

billionaires are important to CNBC, at least—but had also made his billions in the least sexy way possible. Steve Jobs had given the world the Macintosh and the iPhone and lifestyle tech like the tablet I was watching *Squawk Box* on. Uncle Jake had given people a place to park a car. CNBC solved this lack-of-drama problem by bringing on a reporter from *Parking Magazine*, the trade rag of the National Parking Association—and yes, both of those things are real.

"Oh, boo!" I said, when the reporter came on, and threw a corner of my peanut butter toast at the iPad. It bounced off the screen, leaving a peanutty smear, and landed in front of Hera, who looked up at me, confused. "It's friggin' Peter Reese," I explained, waving at Peter's obviously-being-recorded-on-a-laptop face as he explained what impact Jake's death would have on the mission-critical world of parking garages. "He's a terrible reporter. I should know. I worked with him."

Hera, not impressed, ate the crumb of peanut butter toast.

I had indeed worked with Reese, at the *Tribune*. And he was indeed a terrible reporter; I remember one of the assistant editors in the business section miming strangling him after he had bungled an important story that other reporters, including me, then had to rescue. He and I had been laid off from the *Trib* around the same time. I was annoyed with him now because, while his new perch at *Parking Magazine* was a reputational step down from the *Tribune*, he was still somehow in journalism, while I was substitute teaching in my old school district. There were reasons for that—the divorce, being broke, dad getting ill and me coming back to care for him while licking my own existential wounds—but it didn't make it any less annoying. Here was Peter friggin' Reese on *Squawk Box*, living in Washington DC, while I ate my toast in a house I grew up in but didn't technically own, with a cat as my only friend.

"Enough of that," I said, cutting off Reese as he explained that as BLP was a private company, the demise of its owner should not have a significant effect on stock prices of other publicly traded parking companies. Which probably wasn't true, but which no one, including Reese and Sorkin, actually cared enough about to dig into, and they were about to throw to commercial anyway. This was the public legacy of a billionaire and his life's work: two minutes of forgettable business reporting, and then a commercial for gastric-distress medication.

My phone took this moment to ring, an unusual occurrence in this age of texting. I looked down to see who it was: Andrew Baxter, my dad's old friend, lawyer, and executor of his estate, which was almost entirely the house I was living in. I groaned. Whatever Andy wanted from me, it was too early in the morning for it. I let the phone go to voice mail and finished my toast.

"How do I look?" I asked Hera. I was not dressed in my usual substitute teacher uniform of dress shirt, sweater vest and Dockers; I was instead in my best suit, which was also my only suit, the one I'd worn to both my wedding and to my father's funeral, and at no time in between those two events. It was actually only most of a suit, because apparently in the move back to my dad's house I'd lost the shoes. I was wearing the black Skechers I had worn to dad's funeral. No one noticed them then, and I was hoping no one would notice them today. "Would *you* give me a truckload of money if you saw me dressed like this?"

Hera gave a small chirrup and a slow blink, indicating her approval. Well, of course she approved. She had picked out my tie, my green one, mostly by lying on the red one after I had put it on the bed with the green one to choose between them.

"Thank you," I said, to my cat. "As always, your approval is the most important thing." Hera, satisfied, went back to her Meow Mix.

I looked at my watch; my appointment was twenty minutes in the future. In twenty minutes I would know the shape of my life for the next several years. Unlike my uncle Jake, it would not take billions of dollars for me to accomplish any of my life goals.

Just a few million would do.

Belinda Darroll looked at her computer. “So, Mr. Fitzer, you want a business loan for . . . three point four million dollars.”

“That’s right,” I said. I was sitting in Darroll’s office in the Barrington First National Savings and Loan building, which had been recently refurbished after its purchase by CerTrust, a Chicago-based financial company whose thing was buying local banks and then keeping the former branding so everyone in town would think they were still dealing with a local business and not some faceless financial behemoth. The building smelled of fresh paint and outgassing esters from the newly laid high-traffic carpet.

I had been slightly early to the appointment; Darroll had introduced herself when she came in. She said I looked familiar, and we determined she had been a freshman at Barrington High when I had been a senior. She remembered me getting in trouble as the editor of the school paper for running a story about Mr. Kincaid, a ninth-grade algebra teacher, being the biggest supplier of meth on campus. I got suspended for not showing the story to the newspaper faculty advisors before running it; Mr. Kincaid got six years at Big Muddy River Correctional Center for possession and distribution. I got the better end of that deal, I think.

Darroll asked me if I was still writing. I told her I was working on a novel. It’s the standard lie.

“You want the loan for a business you’ll have here in Barrington,” Darroll continued.

“Yes. I want to buy McDougal’s Pub.”

“Oh!” Darroll looked away from her computer to me. “I love McDougal’s.”

I nodded at this. "Everybody does." McDougal's had been a Barrington constant for decades, located in an enviable downtown corner while other restaurants and bars had come and gone around it. Turns out, ale and heaping plates of fries never go out of style in the Chicago suburbs.

"I had my first drink there," Darroll said. "Well, first legal drink," she amended.

I nodded again. "Everybody does," I repeated.

"Do you know why they're selling?"

"The economic downturn hurt business, plus Brennan McDougal wants to retire and none of his kids want to take over the business," I said. "This is what happens when your kids all get college educations. They don't want to run a bar."

"Don't you have a college education?" Darroll asked.

"I do, but unlike McDougal's kids, who got MDs and MBAs, I got a journalism degree," I said.

Darroll nodded. "That'll do it." She glanced at her information on the screen. "So you would take over the pub . . ."

"The pub, the restaurant next door, and the building both are in. Brennan McDougal is selling the whole thing. Everything's already up and running. All I would need to do is walk in."

"Do you have experience running a pub? Or a restaurant?"

"No," I admitted. "But McDougal's already has staff and managers."

Darroll frowned at this. "This sector is always a risk. Restaurants fail all the time. Even with experienced managers and staff. And now is an even more precarious time for these businesses."

"Sure," I acknowledged. "But you said it yourself: Your first legal drink was at McDougal's. It's a Barrington institution. People here want it to be here. I want it to be here for them. I'm not saying there isn't risk. When I was a reporter for the *Trib* I did the local business beat for a couple of years. I know how it goes for restaurants. But McDougal's is as close as it gets to a sure thing. Heck, I'm not even going to change the name."

Darroll clacked at her keyboard and then was silent for a moment, reading what was on her monitor. "The Zillow listing has the building for sale for three point four million," she said. "You're asking for the whole amount of the business."

"I am."

"You're not putting down a percentage from your own assets?"

"I would like to have a margin," I said, "for unexpected contingencies. There's always something that comes up at the last minute that the seller didn't disclose and that the inspection missed."

Darroll pursed her lips at this but said nothing. I had an idea what that meant; she was now thinking she might be smelling some bullshit on my part. She clicked onto another window. "You have your home listed as collateral."

I nodded. "Yes, 504 South Cook Street. It was my parent's house. I live there now. Barrington First National used to own the mortgage on it, a long time ago. Before my dad paid it off." I didn't volunteer that Dad paid off the house with the life insurance policy on mom after her car accident. This wasn't *America's Got Talent*; I didn't want to share a sob story. "Since you already have Zillow up you can see that they currently estimate its value at about eight hundred thousand."

Some more clacking from Darroll. "I see the house is currently administered by a trust."

Well, crap, I thought. She had shifted off Zillow to find that bit of information.

"Family trust, yes," I said.

"And you administer the trust?"

"I'm a beneficiary."

"A beneficiary."

"There are also my older siblings."

"I see. How many of them are there?"

"Three."

"And they've agreed to allow the house to be used as collateral?"

"We've discussed it and they seem positively inclined," I lied.

Darroll caught the long explanation of something that should have been answered with "yes," which was not in my favor. "I'll need documentation of that from the trustee of the estate, notarized and preferably with the signatures of your siblings," she said. "Do you think you can get that to me in the next couple of days?"

"I'll get on it."

Darroll noted this not-quite-affirmative response. "Will there be a problem getting that?"

"My sister Sarah is on vacation," I said, and who knows, that might have actually been true. Sarah loved her vacations. "One of the smaller Hawaiian Islands. A resort that takes your cell phone when you arrive."

"That actually sounds kinda great to me," Darroll said. "But it does complicate things for you right now." She put her hands down on her desk with a finality I didn't think was great for me. "Mr. Fitzer, I'm going to be honest with you, here. Barrington First National has a new owner—"

"CerTrust," I said. "I used to cover them at the paper." Which was true. I didn't hold a terribly high opinion of them. CerTrust didn't achieve Wells Fargo levels of financial fuckery, but it wasn't for lack of trying.

Darroll nodded at this and continued. "The loan policies at CerTrust are more stringent than they were here before the buyout. We want to encourage local business ownership, but we also have to keep a tighter eye on the fundamentals. You're asking us to approve a multimillion-dollar loan with no percentage of the amount put up by you personally, backed by an asset that you don't possess sole ownership of."

"So you're saying that's a no," I ventured.

"It's not no. I'm saying it's tough. I can't approve a loan this size myself. I have to bring it up to our loan committee, which meets on Thursdays. If you can get that letter to me from your trustee in the next couple of days, that'll help. But even then it'll be tough. And after that, if our loan committee does give it a thumbs-up, it'll have to go through another layer of approval at CerTrust."

"They don't trust your judgment here?"

Darroll smiled thinly. "They have different criteria for consideration, is how I like to put it."

"So not no, but probably no, and it'll take a week to say it."

Darroll opened up her hands apologetically. "It'll be tough," she repeated. "I owe you that honesty."

"Well," I said. "I can't fault you for being honest."

"I know it's not what you want to hear," Darroll said. "Is there anyone you can get to come in as a partner with you?"

"You mean, who doesn't have the same financial situation as I do?" I snorted at this. "Most of the people I know are ex-journalists like me. They're either working as bartenders or substitute teachers."

"Which do you do?"

"The latter for now. I was hoping to upgrade to the former."

"What about your siblings or another family member? Maybe one of them will help you."

"I think my siblings would think offering the house as collateral would be enough involvement," I said, which was about as euphemistically as I could phrase that. "I have an uncle. Jake. He's rich."

"A rich uncle isn't a bad thing," Darroll said. "He might be looking for an investment opportunity."

"It's a nice thought," I said. "Unfortunately he just passed away."

"Oh, no," Darroll said, looking graciously distraught. "I'm so sorry."

"Thank you."

"Are you all right?"

"I'm fine," I said. "We weren't close. He's been out of my life since my mother passed away when I was a child."

"Not to be indelicate, but . . . do you know if he left you a bequest?"

"It would be . . . surprising," I said, using another euphemism.

"I'm sorry," Darroll repeated. "It's unfortunate you couldn't have seen if he was interested before he passed on."

"It would have been an awkward moment," I said. "I mean, how is that going to look, me coming in and saying 'Hey, Uncle Jake, sorry I haven't seen you in person in almost thirty years, oh and by the way, can you cosign a three-million-dollar loan for me.'"

"You never know."

I shook my head. "I'm pretty sure I do. Anyway, I don't have too many positive feelings for him. The last time I had any contact with him at all was on my wedding day. He sent a pair of berry spoons as a gift, and a note that said 'three years, six months.'"

Darroll frowned. "What did that mean?"

"I didn't know at the time. I figured it out three and a half years later when my wife filed for divorce."

"Holy shit," Darroll said, and then put her hand to her mouth. "Sorry."

"Don't be. That was basically my reaction, too. So, yeah. The good news is, I kept the berry spoons after the breakup, so there's that." I stood up.

Darroll stood up too. "You'll get that letter from your trustee to me," she said.

"I'll get on it," I lied to her, one last time.

"Good luck on your novel," she said, as I left her office. She didn't mean that as a final stab in the kidneys, I'm sure. I felt the knife slide in anyway.

CHAPTER 2

I had walked to the bank from my house because it was not far, and it was a nice day, and because it was debatable that my dad's 2003 Nissan Maxima would have made it the quarter mile from my garage to the bank parking lot. I was walking home, and had just got onto Cook Street, when my cell phone rang.

I groaned and answered the phone.

"I'm not selling the house," I said to Andy Baxter. It's what he'd been wanting from me, as executor of Dad's estate, for more than a year now.

"Hello to you too, Charlie," Andy said. "I know you're not selling the house. *You* can't sell the house. Only I can sell the house. What you can do is tell me you finally *agree* to sell the house, like all the rest of your siblings have."

"I'm not going to do that."

"And why not?"

"For one thing, I live there."

"I know you do," Andy said. "Rent free, while you're at it."

"Per my father's wishes, set out in the will, with tenancy so long as I keep up with the bills and property taxes. Which you *know*, because you helped him make that change to the will."

"Since you bring that up, you should know he did it to help you get back on your feet after your divorce and layoff. He didn't intend for you to squat in it forever."

"He did it because he was already sick and knew if he didn't, my loving siblings would use their three-to-one majority in the trust to punt me out onto the street as soon as they could," I said. I avoided the part where I had to admit that I wasn't, after probably too long a time, what anyone would call "back on my feet."

"That doesn't change my point," Andy countered.

"I'm not squatting in the house anyway," I said. I paused at the corner of Cook and Lincoln to make sure this little phone conversation didn't cause me to blithely walk in front of a vehicle carrying Amazon deliveries or a Barrington matron back from Pilates, as tempting as that might be at the moment. "I'm paying the bills and the property taxes. That's the deal."

"You were late on those property taxes this year," Andy noted. "And you're late on the bills. Often."

Well, Andy wasn't wrong about that. I was again deeply annoyed at the fact that all the bills and taxes on the house were in the name of the estate, so Andy, and by extension my siblings, knew when I got around to paying them, and when I was delayed. "They still get paid."

"They do get paid, eventually," Andy agreed. "But I can't help notice these delays are getting longer, Charlie."

"Substitute teaching is not the lucrative endeavor you appear to think it is, Andy," I said. No trucks or SUVs were coming to put me out of my misery, so I stepped off the curb and continued my walk.

"You could try to get another writing job."

I smirked at this, not that Andy could see. "Yes, well. I can tell you the *Trib* and *Sun-Times* aren't exactly hiring these days. The people they got there are clinging to their jobs like barnacles."

"So move to the dark side," Baxter said. "Go corporate. Chicago has a lot of companies. They need a lot of publicists. Or a trade publication. You probably know some people who went that route."

"One or two." I thought of Peter friggin' Reese on *Squawk Box* that morning and tried not to grind my teeth over it.

"So there you go."

"I'll take that under advisement," I said. The truth was I was more than taking it under advisement. I'd been scouring the online job sites, applying for writing jobs in Chicago and the suburbs. Substitute teaching wasn't what you would call a passion for me. It was a job that gave me a little bit of money while I cared for my dad when he was sick. When dad had passed on and I didn't need to be nearby to look after him, I'd tried getting into any job that would let me use my writing skills.

The problem was, journalism was hanging on by its fingernails—even the trade journals—and the other jobs that need writing were largely split into three categories: jobs I was told I was overqualified for, jobs I was told I didn't have the skill set for, and jobs that paid eleven dollars an hour ghostwriting social media posts for would-be influencers and/or OnlyFans models.

And, look. I wasn't too proud to take the last of these. But at thirty-two, it's possible I might be too old for those gigs, a fact that filled me with an almost existential terror. I'm not saying I started looking at McDougal's Pub as a viable career option because I felt the icy finger of death in the idea I had aged out of typing bubbly nonsense for nineteen-year-olds pretending to be excited about questionable skin care products they'd been sent for free. But I'm not saying I *didn't*, either.

"You *should* take it under advisement," Andy said. "You've been spending a lot of time in neutral recently."

"You're not my dad, Andy," I said to this.

"I know I'm not your dad, Charlie. I also know your dad would tell you what I just said."

He had a point there, which I did not want to concede. So I said, "Look, Andy. It's not that I'm not looking for better things. I *do* actually still have ambitions."

"Like that pub."

This made me stop on the sidewalk. "How do you know about that?"

Andy sighed. "Come on, Charlie. We're Facebook friends, remember? I saw where you posted a picture of the pub and said 'Big plans.'"

I closed my eyes. *Fucking Facebook,* I thought. "I forgot I friended you."

"Well, I don't post much, it's easy to forget," Andy said. "Call it my cautious nature. I saw what they're asking for the pub. More than you can afford from sporadic substitute teaching, I think."

"I've been made aware of that." I started walking again.

"The good news is I know where you might be able to get that seed money."

"If I agree to sell the house."

"That would be the way, yes."

"It's not enough," I said. "Even if we sold it at market value, it's split four ways. Me and Sarah and Bobby and Todd."

"You could get them to go in with you."

I snorted at that.

"Yeah, all right, fair," Baxter admitted, hearing the snort. "Gotta say I don't understand why you all don't get along."

"*They* get along just fine," I said.

"Maybe it's a generational thing."

"Maybe." My siblings, Sarah and Bobby and Todd, were actually my half-siblings. I had a different mother than my siblings, a younger one, who our father had married after a less-than-congenial divorce, the details of which were never explained to me and which, I admit, I never really wanted to pry into. The youngest of my siblings, Todd, had already been a teenager when I was born, so the age gap was always going to be difficult to navigate.

The gap was made wider by the fact none of my siblings lived with me growing up. The three older kids had lived with their mom in Schaumburg. Outside of holidays and occasional, increasingly forced family vacations, the older siblings were their own group, and I had always been on the outside.

Which was fine. I didn't really mind being an only child with three siblings most of the time. At the moment, with them wanting to punt me from my home, it was less great.

"No matter what, your father gave each of you an equal share of his estate," Andy said. "Most of the value of which is wrapped up in that house."

"They're not exactly hurting, Andy," I said. My siblings were various sorts of high-end professionals, living comfortably one percent lives. "They need the money they'd get from the house less than I need someplace to live."

"I don't disagree, Charlie, but that's not the point," Andy said. "Your dad didn't slice up his estate into four equal parts because you all have an equal need. He did it because he wanted to make the point that you all had his equal love. You staying in that house is keeping them from accessing that representation of his affection. You're reminding them that in many ways, you were his favorite kid."

I stopped again, on the corner of Cook and Russell, one street and a couple of houses away from the home in question, to take in what he had just said to me. "So you're saying I should be homeless so a trio of financially secure middle-aged people can put to rest their psychological issues with their father."

"I wouldn't put it like that. But it's not wrong, either."

"Therapy would be cheaper," I noted.

"You wouldn't be homeless anyway. A couple hundred thousand dollars pays for a lot of rent. And would give you time to get your life back together, for real this time."

"Your concern for my future feels less sincere than it was previously, I have to say, Andy."

"I'm sorry it's coming across that way, Charlie. It's actually not insincere."

I was about to respond to this when a small but insistent meow came from the hedge of the yellow house on the corner of Cook and Russell. "Hold on a sec, Andy," I said. I put my phone in my pants pocket, still on, and peered into the hedge.

The hedge meowed again.

"Come on out," I said.

As if understanding me, a small orange-and-white kitten emerged from the hedge, looked up at me, and meowed quite insistently and indeed, one might say, demandingly.

This felt familiar. An orange-and-white cat coming out of bushes and meowing demandingly is how I had met Hera. That had worked out well for her.

"Déjà cat," I said to the new kitten, and reached down for it.

The kitten walked into my palm, and then immediately scaled up my suit arm to attempt to perch on my shoulder. I shifted my weight around so it wouldn't fall and scritched the kitten on the head, which caused it to purr as loud as a jet engine.

"Hello?" Baxter said, from my pants.

I secured the kitten and retrieved the phone. "Sorry," I said. "I've been found by a kitten."

"Another one?" While dad had been alive Andy had been to the house a bit to visit his friend, my dad. He had heard the story of how Hera came to live with us.

"You make it sound like it happens every day," I said.

"Doesn't it?"

"Not *every* day."

"Is this one orange and white, too?"

"As a matter of fact, it is."

"Somewhere in your neighborhood an orange-and-white spotted tom cat is getting a lot of action."

"You're probably right," I said. "Listen, Andy, I'm going to go. I've got to see if anyone's missing a kitten."

"Your siblings are going to want to know what you said about selling the house."

"You can tell them I'll think about it."

"Okay," Andy said. "And *are* you going to think about it?"

"Sure."

"That's not a very convincing 'sure,' Charlie."

I grinned at this. "Goodbye, Andy," I said, and hung up. "I am absolutely *not* going to think about it," I said to the kitten. The kitten, purring contentedly, seemed not to care.

I couldn't just abscond with the kitten; kitten pilfering is morally and probably legally wrong. I am not a monster, or not that kind of monster, anyway.

I checked around to see if anyone was missing their kitten, starting with the owners of the house with the hedge. The people inside informed me that not only was the kitten not theirs, the owner of the house was horribly allergic to cats. I tried the house next door to the yellow house on the corner, and then the two houses across from them on Cook Street. No answers at two of them, not unusual for a weekday morning, and a no at the third.

"Well, that's enough," I said to myself. When Hera had showed up, I'd suspected she might be someone else's cat as well, so I had taken a picture of her with my phone, made a "Found Cat" flyer, and posted copies on the telephone poles up and down the street. After a week of no one responding, we owned a cat. I had a pretty good feeling something similar would be happening with this little ball of fluff. "Why don't we go meet your sister," I said to the fluffball. The fluffball seemed content to do so.

I didn't need another cat. At this point in my brilliant career as an itinerant educator I could barely afford to feed myself. But then, no one ever needs a cat these days. That's not why we have cats. We have cats because they amuse us and because otherwise our clothes would lack the texture only cat hair can provide.

Besides, when a kitten walks up to you and makes demands, what are you going to do? Say no? I repeat: I am not a monster.

The home Andy Baxter was trying to get me to move out of and sell—my home—was only a couple of houses away once

I crossed the street. It was a pastel blue Cape Cod two-story, with a porch at the front. It was neither large nor small for the neighborhood, and had nothing especially noteworthy about its construction or architecture. A Realtor might call it "cozy" or "a great starter home," depending on the income and ambition of the people she was showing it to.

For me, however, it was just home. The house I came home to after I was born, the house I lived in for all my childhood, where Dad and I roughed it out after Mom died, where I came back to for holidays once I went to college in the far-distant land of Evanston.

There were a few years I *didn't* live there, the years where I was married and building my career as a reporter and journalist. But then came the year of layoffs and divorce and Dad's illness. So I came back to the little Cape Cod on Cook Street.

And here I was, alone except for a cat. Maybe two cats, now.

As I came up to my house I noticed a car on the street in front of it: a black Mercedes S-Class. Its wheelbase was stretched out slightly in the way that let you know that whoever owned it didn't drive it; they had people for that. I knew this sort of car from my journalism days in the business section. It was a CEO taxi. A smug wagon.

I wondered who it might belong to and why, of all the places in Barrington that they could have parked, in front of my house made the most sense to them. I didn't assume they were there to see me. The executive class of the Greater Chicagoland Area was not exactly breaking down my door to have me ghostwrite their memoirs these days. I tried to peek into the back of the Mercedes as I walked past it, but the windows had the shades up. In the journalism trade, we called those "peasant blockers" and were absolutely envious of them.

But as it turns out, the car *was* in front of my house for a reason. On my porch, sitting in the swing on which my dad had spent many a summer night, especially at the end, was a woman.

She was about my age, and even from the distance of the small walkway to my porch I could tell she was dressed in the sort of business couture that suggested she did not spend her time tooling around in, say, a nearly broken-down 2003 Nissan Maxima. She was using her foot to lightly kick the swing into motion. She sat on that swing like she owned it, and the house, and possibly most of the street.

"Make yourself comfortable," I said to her, as I walked up to my porch.

"Thank you, I did," she said, and then nodded at the kitten on my shoulder. "Interesting accoutrement. Do you always wear one of those?"

I petted the kitten, who was now simultaneously napping and purring on my shoulder. "They're just terribly comfortable," I said. "I think everyone will be wearing them in the future."

The woman looked at me, wryly.

"That's a *Princess Bride* reference," I explained.

"No, no, I got it," the woman assured me.

"Not to be rude," I said, "but who are you, and why are you on my porch?"

"I'm Mathilda Morrison. I'm on your porch because before this moment, you weren't here, and at the moment, you haven't invited me in."

"I see. And why would I invite you in?"

"Because I need to tell you something, and then I need to ask you something."

"And you can do neither on the porch?"

"I could, but I think you'll want to be sitting down for them, and I don't know you well enough to invite you to sit on this swing with me."

"It's my swing," I pointed out.

"Technically, it's your father's estate's swing," Morrison said, and then caught my expression. "Ah, a sore spot."

"Just a little," I admitted.

"My apologies. I'm not here to irritate you."

"Then why *are* you here?"

"I'm here on business for your uncle."

"No you're not," I said.

"Well, you certainly seem sure about *that*," Morrison remarked.

"I only have one uncle, and Uncle Jake is dead."

"Ah. So you've heard."

"I have access to CNBC, yes."

"I thought their segment on him was underwhelming," Morrison said. "Whoever that reporter was talking about him should be thrown out a window. He was spouting absolute nonsense."

I smiled despite myself. "*Thank* you," I said.

"And yes, your uncle is dead. My condolences."

"Thank you. Although if you know my uncle, then you know we weren't close."

"I did know that. If it means anything to you, Charlie, it was something that weighed on him."

"I will have to take your word for that," I said.

"Actually, I can give you proof," Morrison replied.

"If you're going to tell me he left me exactly three point four million dollars, I'm not going to lie, that would be tremendous."

Morrison cocked her head. "That's a very specific number."

"I have a very specific purpose for it."

"He did not leave you exactly three point four million," Morrison said. "He did leave you something."

"What is it?"

"Something you'll like," Morrison promised. "He also has a request."

"There are strings attached," I said.

"There are strings on everything, Charlie. But these particular strings are pretty slack." From the swing, Morrison waved idly with her hand. "Do you want to discuss it here on your porch, with a kitten on your shoulder? Or should we go inside?"

CHAPTER 3

Inside, an orange-and-white cat was waiting for me. She meowed as I came through the door.

"Hello, Hera," I said. I plucked the kitten from my shoulder and brought it down to Hera's eye level. "I've brought you something." I set the kitten down in front of her and waited.

If Hera was surprised or irritated at the sudden intrusion of a kitten, she gave no hint of it. Instead, she considered the kitten for a moment as it chirruped at her. Then she started grooming it, both of them purring as she did so. Peace achieved. I went to the kitchen to get both of them food.

"You went the goddess route," Morrison said, as she closed the door behind her.

"What is 'the goddess route'?" I asked.

"When people name cats, they usually do it in one of three categories: food, physical characteristics or mythology," Morrison explained. "So, you name your cat Sugar, or Smudge, or Zeus. You went with mythology."

"What about people who name their cats for characters in fantasy books?" I picked up Hera's food bowl from her mat, and got a smaller bowl for the kitten. "Gandalf. Sauron. That sort of thing."

"Covered under mythology."

"That feels like cheating," I said.

"It's not," Morrison said. "Gandalf and Sauron were Maiar."

"What?"

"Maiar. You know, like gods in the Tolkien mythos. Or angels. So still applies."

"You have officially outnerded me," I admitted. I filled the bowls with cat food and set both bowls on the mat, and then slapped my thighs to get the cats' attention. They both padded over. Hera went to her bowl, and the kitten, without hesitation, went to the smaller one. No arguments over food. A good sign.

Morrison pointed to the kitten, who was now snorkeling through the food in its bowl, purring as it did so. "Is that one Athena, then?"

"Maybe," I said. "I was thinking maybe Persephone, though. Less used. Deeper cut. Unless it turns out to be a boy, in which case maybe Apollo."

"You seem perfectly willing to take in a stray regardless."

"It's not the kitten's fault it's a stray. And anyway it came up to me, asking for help."

"It knew a sucker when it saw one," Morrison said, smiling.

"Probably," I said. "Maybe I'm just better with cats than people, and cats seem to know that."

"That's the toxoplasmosis talking."

"I'm sure it is." I waved at the fridge. "Can I get you a drink?"

"Thank you, I'm fine." Morrison motioned to a chair in the den, the one that had been Dad's favorite. "An actual Eames chair?" she asked.

"You mean, from Herman Miller and not just a cheap knockoff?" I opened up the fridge to get myself a beer.

"That was what I was asking, yes."

"It is." I grabbed a beer—Michelob Ultra, I'm not proud—and twisted off the top. "A first-anniversary gift from Mom to Dad. She knew he'd always coveted one, and she surprised him with it. He always said it was the actual chair and not a knockoff, and I took his word for it. Please, sit."

Morrison sat in the chair and felt free to avail herself of the ottoman. "Definitely the real thing," she said, after a moment.

"You would know better than me; I've only ever sat in that one."

"Not a cheap first-anniversary gift," Morrison ventured.

"I never thought about how much it cost, it was just always here," I said. "Although now that you mention it, I don't know if my mom could have afforded it on a dental hygienist's salary. Maybe Uncle Jake helped her out on it."

Morrison nodded at this. "Jake was fond of Lizzie," she said, mentioning my mother's name.

"You don't seem old enough to know that from personal experience," I said. I ventured out of the kitchen and back into the den. I aimed myself at the couch.

"I know from the personal experience of him telling me."

"And it was a frequent topic of conversation?"

"You might be surprised."

"Speaking of which, how *do* you know my uncle? How did you know him, I mean." I sat on the couch, sinking into my particular spot, where the cushion had deformed, just so, to my ass.

"I was a stray, and I came up to him asking for help," Morrison said, nodding in the direction of the kitten, who was still snorkeling through its food.

"I'm sure there's more to it than that," I prompted.

"There is, but that's the basic version."

"You're not a cat."

"No, I'm not."

"So, there are a lot of ways that could go, a young woman asking a much older man for help," I said. I took another swig of my beer.

Morrison made a face. "If that's what you think, then you don't know your uncle very well."

"Well, that's just it, isn't it?" I said. "I *don't* know what to think, and I don't know my uncle very well. The last time I was in the same room with him was when I was five. I knew he existed, but other than that he's a total blank to me. He didn't seem to have much of an interest in me, either."

"That's not quite true," Morrison said. "Your uncle and your father had a falling-out over your mother's death. Your father told him to stay away from his family. Your uncle . . . honored that request."

"I don't know anything about that," I said. "Including whether it's true."

"I don't imagine your dad spoke much about your uncle Jake."

"Not at all. Not in a good way or a bad way. His existence just never came up, with Dad or anywhere else. Well, except for that wedding gift." I took another sip.

"The berry spoons," Morrison said.

I choked at this. "You *know* about that?"

"I do," Morrison confirmed. "That was around the time I started working closely with your uncle."

"Do you know about the note that came with the spoons?"

Morrison nodded. "Yeah, I do. Sorry about that. I told him not to put it in. He wouldn't listen."

"It was a real asshole move, making a bet on how long my marriage would last."

Morrison pointed at me in agreement. "That's what I said to him. His reasoning was he thought you should know, so at least you could plan ahead."

I coughed, still clearing the beer out of my upper lungs. "It didn't help me plan ahead. I didn't even know what it meant until I was clearing out my stuff from our apartment and I came across the box with the spoons."

"You didn't take the spoons out of the box?"

"Of course we didn't take the spoons out of the box," I said, annoyed. "When were we going to use berry spoons? We lived in a one-room basement apartment in Ukrainian Village. Not exactly the place for high-end entertaining." I pointed to the kitchen. "They're still in the box, right now. No card. I threw it away when I figured out what it meant."

"Sorry," Morrison said again.

"What I really want to know is how he pegged the time so accurately. The card said 'three years, six months,' and three and a half years later, there I was, hauling away my berry spoons."

"Your uncle knew people."

I gave Morrison a doubtful look. "Apparently not well enough to know that a divorce prediction might not be welcome on someone's wedding day."

"There were gaps, yes," Morrison agreed.

"And anyway, how *could* he know me? Or Jeanine?" My mouth felt odd shaping the name of my former wife, who I'd met at Northwestern and who, when I was twenty-four and standing at the altar of Saint Michael's Episcopal Church with her, I'd been certain I would love and be married to the rest of my life. This turned out to be overly optimistic by a considerable margin.

"He kept tabs on you," Morrison said. "Discreetly. From a distance. In a way that wouldn't antagonize your father."

"Well, that doesn't sound creepy at all," I said. My lungs had cleared enough for another swig of beer.

"It wasn't meant to be creepy. Your mother meant a great deal to him, like I said. He was curious about her son."

"Not so curious he would come to say hello."

"I already explained about your father."

"Okay, but Dad's been dead for a while now."

"The last few years there have been other reasons for him not to be in contact."

"Is this where we blame pandemics or something?"

"That's one," Morrison agreed. She took her feet down from the ottoman and leaned forward in the Eames chair. "The pancreatic cancer is another. Look, Charlie. I'm not here to explain your uncle Jake, or to excuse him. I am perfectly willing to stipulate he was not the best uncle he could have been to you. He was a flawed human being at the best of times, and the last few years were not the best of times for him. I'm sorry that what you have of him is a hole in your memory."

"It's not your fault," I said, after a minute of taking in what she said.

"It's not, but your uncle isn't here to apologize, so I'm doing it for him."

"Thank you."

"You're welcome. Whatever his sins may have been toward you, one of the last things that he did on this earth was to ask me to come here. To talk to you. And to ask you for a favor."

"What's the favor?" I asked.

"Your uncle was a successful man, financially, but he had no family of his own," Morrison said. "He never married, and he never had any children. His parents, your grandparents, passed away before you were born. Your mother was his only sibling. You're her only child."

"You're saying I'm his only family."

"Unless you want to count a pair of third cousins once removed who live near Leipzig, and your uncle Jake was inclined not to count them, yes."

"Well, now I want to know about these third cousins, once removed," I said.

"Both very odd shut-ins," Morrison said. "One collects Hummel figurines. The other has seventeen cats. That's currently. The number fluctuates."

I glanced over at my now two cats, who were finishing up their repast. "Not the greatest family resemblance."

"You're fine. Two cats are nowhere near crazy cat-person level."

I smirked at this. "Thanks."

"Because you're his only family, your uncle Jake would like you to represent him at his memorial service, which will be here in Barrington, at the Chesterfield Family Funeral Home. You know it?"

"Of course." It was literally the only funeral home in Barrington, a few blocks up and over from the house. It had been the location of the memorial services of both Mom and Dad. I suspected Morrison might have actually been aware of this.

Morrison nodded. "It will be this Saturday at three. Your job is to show up, welcome mourners and accept their condolences, and then, after the visitation, be present for the cremation. Everything's been arranged. All you have to do is be there."

"Why here?" I asked.

"Why Barrington?"

"Yeah. Uncle Jake has no roots here. I mean, Mom wasn't from here. She grew up outside Pittsburgh, so I assume Uncle Jake did, too. But at least she lived here. Uncle Jake doesn't even have that. And if the CNBC reports are to be believed, he's rich. Not just Barrington rich, like, *actual* rich. Billions rich. Like 'he could have a memorial service in a massive cathedral with thousands of mourners' rich."

Morrison smiled at this. "He did all right for himself."

"See, that's what *really* rich people say." I pointed at Morrison. "Or what their people say in their place. No offense."

"None taken. Your uncle had his reasons for wanting his service here," Morrison said. "One is sentimentality. He wanted his service at the same place his sister had her service. He said it would give him a sense of closure with her. The other is no matter how rich your uncle was, he wasn't extravagant. Not in the usual ways. A large memorial service would strike him as a waste of money."

"Does he not have friends?"

Morrison shook her head. "Not so much. He didn't like that many people, and not that many people liked him."

"Did *you* like him?" I asked.

"Yes," Morrison said. "But I had a high tolerance for his quirks."

I smiled at this. "That was artfully put."

"You have *no* idea. In any event, the memorial service attendance will be relatively small."

"Well, the funeral home here is small, so that works out."

"Also, as I understand it, the home gave him a really nice package deal on the service and the cremation."

I was glad I did not have beer in my mouth for that one. "He's not planning to take all his money with him?" I said, archly.

"No, he had other things he wanted to spend his money on instead," Morrison said. "Which brings us to the matter of your compensation."

"Ah. I do this favor for my dead uncle, then you give me the thing he left me."

"Yes, that's the deal."

This is where I took another swig, to give me a moment to frame my thoughts. "That seems almost unbearably cynical," I said, after I swallowed.

Morrison nodded. "I understand. Maybe think about it this way: For all your life your uncle Jake was told to keep you at an arm's length, or further. This will be compensation for everything that you could have had between you in all that time. Minus the berry spoons."

"All right, so, what does my uncle Jake propose to give me for my time?"

Morrison waved, encompassing the house. "This."

I glanced around. "This is already my house."

"It belongs to your father's estate, which you share in equally with your three siblings, and they want you out of it so they can get their hands on what it's worth. Your uncle knew about the tenancy agreement in your father's will, and he also knew you've come close to failing to live up to that agreement—through no fault of your own."

I frowned. "How did he know that?"

"Like I said, he kept tabs on you."

"That's even creepier now than it was before," I said.

Morrison ignored this. "If you do this service for your uncle, in both senses of the word, then one of your uncle's more discreet real estate holding companies will make a private offer on your house to your estate trustee, for more than the current market value," she said. "You can surprise your siblings by agreeing to go along with the offer, and take your quarter of the sale. Then, once the sale is closed, the holding company will sell it back to you at a deeply discounted price, one you can easily afford, and cover the taxes that will accrue by selling it to you below market value. You'll own it free and clear, and you won't have to bother with your siblings anymore. That, and at closing, you'll receive an additional cash payment. Low six figures. Not a lot, but enough to give you some options about what to do next."

I thought about a world where "low six figures" was "not a lot," and decided to table that for now. "And you'll put this in writing," I said, to Morrison.

"Of course, if you like," she said, amused. "Why? You don't trust your uncle, Charlie?"

"I don't know my uncle," I reminded her. "Didn't know him, I mean."

"I assure you that if he had wanted your house, there were less complicated ways of getting it than dying first. It's a Barrington Cape Cod. They aren't thin on the ground."

"Are you aware when you're rude? Or does it just sneak up on you?"

"I'm not saying that to be rude," Morrison assured me. "Just that, if it's all right, I would like to stay on topic."

"What happens if I say no?" I asked. "To representing the family at the memorial service, I mean."

"Well, I'm not going to go to the Hummel collector next, if that's what you're asking," Morrison said. She shrugged. "If you don't do it then I suppose the funeral home staff will take care of it."

"What about you? Are you going to be there?"

"Your uncle asked me to take care of other things for him during the service," Morrison said. "We've already said our goodbyes."

There was a meow at my feet. Hera had come up and wanted

lap time. I set down my beer on the coffee table and patted my leg. Hera leaped up and after some positioning, flopped down.

"She likes you," Morrison observed, as I petted my cat.

"I told you I was better with cats than people."

"You seem to be doing all right with me."

"You don't have to live with me," I said.

"Fair enough," Morrison said, and then looked at the watch on her wrist. "Speaking of which, I need to be on my way. So. Will you stand for your uncle at his memorial?"

I thought about it. "It feels weird to do it," I said. "To be the representative of someone I don't know, just because he was my mother's brother."

"Then think of it as a kindness to a stranger," Morrison said. "A stranger who has no one else to do it."

I thought about it that way, and for the smallest of moments felt sad for my billionaire uncle that apparently there really was no one else to do it.

"All right," I said. "That I can do."

"Good," Morrison said, stood, and immediately motioned at me. "Don't get up. Your cat just got comfortable."

"So what do I do now?"

"I'll call Chesterfield today and let them know to expect you. I have your number, I'll text you the details later. If you want to call or go by before the service to get instructions from them, that's fine; otherwise they'll get you up to speed when you arrive on Saturday. Arrive a little early." She glanced down at my suit. "What you're wearing should be fine. Although . . ."

"Although what?"

"Maybe find better shoes." She smiled, nodded at me, and at my cat. Then she let herself out before I could say anything else.

CHAPTER 4

I got better shoes.

I took dad's Maxima and drove it to Kildeer and its outlet mall for them. They were black wingtip oxfords. They were uncomfortable and they pinched my toes, but they were on clearance and the other, nonclearance shoes I was looking at were more than I wanted to spend. I had a small but profound existential crisis deciding whether a dead uncle I hardly knew warranted full-price shoes over clearance rack oxfords. Then I remembered my electricity bill was on its second notice. Clearance rack oxfords it was.

The Maxima almost died twice on the twelve-mile round trip to Kildeer and back, so when Saturday finally rolled around, I decided to walk to the Chesterfield Funeral Home. It wasn't that far, and it would give me a chance to break in my cheap oxfords. On the day, I dressed again in my best and only suit and once more let the cats choose the tie. Hera picked the red one. Persephone the kitten pounced on the red one and tried to disembowel it with a rabbit kick. The red one it was. They accompanied me downstairs and watched from the window as I started my way down the street. It's nice they cared.

There were a few ways I could get to the funeral home; I chose the one that walked me by McDougal's. Now that I would soon own my house outright, there was a real possibility that I could go back and actually get that business loan with the house as collateral. And then I could own McDougal's, and become a bartender/small businessman in my hometown.

I wanted to own McDougal's to try something new, and to actually talk to people who weren't my cats or middle-school students, but there was another reason as well. Before Dad died, he and I would head to McDougal's and settle in, drinking beer and eating fries and watching Premier League football we didn't care about just to have something to do out of the house. Those were good memories, and some of the last good ones I had of Dad.

Maybe it was odd to want to own a pub to keep alive a connection with one's parent. But this is where my life was at the moment. Jeanine had gotten most of our friends in the Great Post-Divorce Sort, and the friends I had kept, the ones in journalism, I didn't see much of. They had mostly gone on with their lives, while I was marinating in Barrington, living in my dad's house and substitute teaching.

Owning McDougal's wouldn't make me any new friends, probably. But at least people would be where I was, and wanting to be there, if only for beer and fries. And I could invite my old friends over and not be a complete sad, lonely bastard. That would be worth making an effort for.

A few minutes later, as the Chesterfield Funeral Home rose into view on the left side of County Line Road, I had two thoughts rise into my consciousness. The first thought was the fact that, thanks to the walk, my feet had sent a memo that they hated both my shoes and me, that I should have paid for the full-price shoes, and that they were now forming blisters to punish me for my life choices. I had at least three hours to go in these shoes. I decided that I would be barefoot for the walk back.

The second thought was to wonder who would be showing up to Uncle Jake's funeral, and what they might have to say to me about my mysterious, and now dead, relation.

"Let's see how lonely you really were, Uncle Jake," I said, and opened the door to the funeral parlor.

The funeral home was how I remembered it from Dad's service, and I guess from Mom's, for what little I remembered of that one. There were cream-colored hallways and walls. Carpets of green. Doorways of polished wood. Serenity, or at least, the absence of tension, flooded the space. Calm music played as quietly as possible to be heard. The building had a smell that I, at Dad's service, had described to my siblings as "Floral Neutral." They had not been amused.

I looked right, to the doorway that led into the funeral home's primary gathering room, where the guests would congregate and where any service, if held on site, would be. Beyond that room was the viewing room, which could be accessed by a hallway to the left, or by sliding back a partition in the gathering room to expand the space.

Somewhere back there was my uncle Jake. Who I had not seen since I was five.

"Mr. Fitzer?"

I looked over to see a man in a suit coming down the stairwell to the right. It was Michael Chesterfield, the managing funeral director. He had just taken over the job when Dad passed away; he had told me at the time it had been one of his first services in the position.

"Hello," I said. We shook hands.

"My condolences to you," Chesterfield said.

"Thank you. I was told to be here a little early. I figured an hour before would be appropriate."

"Yes, that's fine," Chesterfield said. "Actually, more than fine."

"Is everything all right?" It finally registered on me that Chesterfield, who at Dad's memorial exuded an almost Vulcan-like calm, was right now acting out of character.

"With your uncle, yes, everything's fine," Chesterfield said.

"He's in our viewing room. There are other things I need to discuss with you."

"Okay," I said. "Such as?"

"The floral arrangements."

"What about them? Have they not been paid for?" I had no idea how the service was being paid for, or if I was responsible for any of the charges. If I was expected to pay for anything, it was going to be a very short, hilariously bare memorial service.

"Money is not the issue," Chesterfield said. "Everything's been paid for. It's not the floral arrangements that have been paid for by your uncle's estate that are the problem. It's . . . the other ones."

"What other ones?"

"Very often, other mourners at a service will pay for flower arrangements to be delivered."

"Yes, I know that. Is there a problem with the flowers?"

"The flower arrangements are beautiful. The sentiments attached to the arrangements, less so."

I frowned at this. "What do you mean?"

"Well, one of them says 'See you in Hell.'"

"What?"

"'See you in Hell,'" Chesterfield repeated.

"Is . . . that a joke?"

"I'm pretty sure it's not."

"Why do you say that?"

"Because, Mr. Fitzer, it's not the only one that says something like that. It is, however, one of the nicer ones."

"Well, you were right," I said, to Chesterfield. "The flowers are beautiful."

All the flowers were gorgeous, in fact. The ones with "See you in Hell" emblazoned on the sash were white roses, Asiatic lilies, football mums, carnations and blue delphinium, or so Chesterfield told me when I came up to it to get a better look. Another standing spray featured hot pink roses and carnations, orange lilies, yellow sunflowers, lavender stock and green Athos poms, as well as the sentiment of "Not soon enough." I have to say I was especially taken with the basket arrangement of lavender daisy poms, mums, white roses, snapdragons and Monte Cassino, with the words "Suck it, motherfucker" lovingly engraved onto the base of its gorgeously ornate vase.

There were others, but these were a representative sample.

All of the floral arrangements were currently in Chesterfield's office on the second floor of the funeral home. He had been, understandably, reluctant to set them out without checking with me first. The office was a riot of floral beauty, and rotten sentiment.

"Your uncle appears to have provoked passionate responses in his acquaintances," Chesterfield said.

"I appreciate how you chose the nicest possible way to say that they hated his guts," I said.

"Yes, well, tact is part of the job," Chesterfield allowed.

"What sort of person actually sends these sorts of things to a funeral?"

"I have opinions, Mr. Fitzer, but they aren't very tactful."

I waved at the flowers. "And the local florist didn't have a *problem* with any of these."

"They weren't locally made," Chesterfield said. "They all arrived by courier of some form or another this morning. I did use our usual florist for our own arrangements. There are no particular sentiments on those."

I smiled at this and then motioned to a standing spray that featured red roses and lilies, with "Dead? LOL okay" and a smiley-face-with-a-tongue-sticking-out emoji. "At least *this* one isn't one hundred percent awful."

"It's not, but it seems to suggest the sender is not entirely convinced your uncle has passed on," Chesterfield said.

"Has he?"

"Passed on?"

"Yes."

"He was dead when he arrived here," Chesterfield said.

"Do you expect that condition to change?"

"It would be unusual if it did."

I smiled again and studied the flowers for a few moments before looking back to Chesterfield. "The sashes and cards can be removed, right?"

"Yes, of course."

"Remove them before putting the arrangements into the visitation area, please."

Chesterfield nodded and then pointed to the "Suck it, motherfucker" vase. "And this?"

"Do you have another vase you can repot the flowers into?"

"We do. It might mar the flower arrangement when we transfer them."

"I think the sender lost the right to a perfect arrangement when he engraved 'Suck it, motherfucker' onto the vase, don't you?"

"Just so," Chesterfield said, and hesitated. "What do you want us to do with the original vase?"

"Why? Do you want it?"

"When clients choose not to take floral arrangements to the gravesite or home with them, I sometimes keep the vases and stands for later use."

"And you think you're going to find a use for this vase at another memorial service?" I'm not going to lie, I found the thought of the "Suck it, motherfucker" vase being used at some very proper old-money funeral amusing.

"Probably not," Chesterfield admitted. "But if you don't mind, I might share it on a private funeral director's site I visit. We live for this stuff."

I gave permission to Chesterfield to keep the profane vase,

and he and his assistants stripped the floral arrangements of their sentiments and started moving them out of the office. I stepped into a corner of the room and got out my phone to text Mathilda Morrison.

What the hell is up with my uncle? I sent. *People are telling him to fuck off in flower arrangements.*

That's amazing, Morrison texted back. *Get pictures.*

What did he do to deserve this? I texted, instead of taking pictures. *Is parking actually this cutthroat?*

In his line of work he competed against some very strong personalities, Morrison replied.

You mean assholes, I sent back.

That's the word, Morrison agreed.

Are any of them going to show up to the service? I asked.

They might, Morrison texted.

How will I know? I asked.

Believe me, they will announce themselves, Morrison replied.

CHAPTER 5

I didn't see the knife until the dude was just about to stab it into my uncle's corpse.

More accurately, I did see it. But my brain didn't register it as an actual, no-bullshit, holy-shit-that's-actually-a-knife knife until the dude, who had produced it from an overcoat pocket, cocked back his arm in a windup to drive the frankly *rather substantial* blade into my uncle's already cold and lifeless heart.

In fairness, it had already been an extremely odd service.

Forty minutes back in the timeline, Chesterfield and his associates had funneled the mourners into the main seating area, and announced that they would open up the viewing area soon. The mourners were exclusively male, in their late thirties to early forties. They all stood in a manner that suggested that at some point in their lives they had spent a lot of their time at parade rest.

The men arrived mostly in pairs or trios, and kept to their own groups, with little to no cross-conversation. What conversation was being had was kept low and murmuring. Every once in a while one or two of the men would glance briefly at me and then look at something else. I was being noted and registered.

None of the men went out of their way to offer me condolences, or to speak to me about my uncle, or the service, or, well, anything.

They were all just . . . *waiting*.

"Well, this is weird as hell," I muttered to Chesterfield, after half an hour of this. The duos and trios of men were still clumped and mostly silent, and all of them were conspicuously not sitting.

"Your uncle kept interesting company," Chesterfield said, equally quietly, back to me.

"This is your tact thing again, isn't it?"

"It is."

"I like it. Keep it up."

"What would you like us to do now, Mr. Fitzer?"

I looked back at the door to the funeral home. No one new had entered in the last few minutes. This was as good as it was going to get for attendance. "Let's go ahead and start the viewing."

"All right," Chesterfield said. "Would you like to say anything before we start the viewing? Or would you prefer to wait until afterward?"

"I'm supposed to say something?" I asked. Morrison hadn't informed me that this was something I was meant to do.

"Family members often speak a few words."

I glanced at the assembled men. "I don't think anyone here is waiting on a speech from me," I said.

"You may be right," Chesterfield allowed. "In which case, I'll announce that we'll be opening up the visitation room in five minutes. Why don't you go ahead and position yourself to accept condolences. That'll also give you a little time to say your own goodbyes."

"Thanks," I said. I left the seating room to go down the hall to the visitation room. A funeral home assistant was there, guarding the entrance. She recognized me from earlier, when they were stripping the floral arrangements, and let me in.

The floral arrangements, denuded of their asshole sentiments, now surrounded Uncle Jake's casket, complemented by the funeral home's own arrangements and sprays. The casket itself was simple, and made entirely of wood and natural fibers so that it could be placed into Chesterfield's on-site crematorium directly after the viewing. The casket was open, and Uncle Jake, presumably, was in it, resting.

I walked up to Uncle Jake and, finally, took an up-close look at him for the first time in almost three decades.

It took a minute, but eventually my brain synced up the man in the casket to the man I had vaguely remembered as a five-year-old, who I had last seen in person, as it happens, here at this very funeral home. In my memory of him, my dad had pulled him into a hallway right before the ceremony and was speaking to him quietly but emphatically. I remember looking up at them from the visiting room hallway, not hearing what was being said but knowing it wasn't good. At one point Jake turned his head, and looked at me head-on. The older version of that face was in the casket now.

Jake had been four or five years older than my mom, his sister. In death, Jake looked his age, but in a wealthy way, if you know what I mean. He had the sort of look you get to have when you've had access to the top doctors, the top aestheticians and the top trainers all looking after your health, your weight, your diet and your overall being. Jake looked like he'd been in glowing shape right until the moment he dropped.

And he probably had. I mean, why lie, Jake looked better right now, dead, than *I* did, alive. Certainly less stressed. I imagined that if I checked behind those stoppered lips of his, Jake's teeth were perfect. I didn't actually try to check, however. I wasn't that curious.

Jake's face reminded me of my mom's, both in my memory and in the photographs that Dad kept around the house. They had the same nose, same cheekbones, same ridges. It didn't arouse any great emotion in me to note it. Mom died when I was young, and all the grief I had about that was worked through long ago. Jake looking like Mom reminded me that I ended up looking more like Dad, which I think made Dad wistful. Dad would have been happy to have seen more of the woman he loved in their only child.

"You look great, Uncle Jake," I assured his corpse. Uncle Jake said nothing, which, mind you, was only in keeping with what he did when he was alive.

The folding partition opened, and the presumed mourners began to come through. I stationed myself at the far end of Uncle Jake's casket. The idea was that mourners could come up, pay their respects, and then offer condolences to me, if they had any. I figured it would be more efficient than asking them to pay their respects before they got to the casket, and would eliminate any awkward pauses if someone lingered by the body before moving on.

After a minute, the mourners began to queue. The first two mourners to the body were stocky, bald men who hadn't bothered to rid themselves of their overcoats, which, as I looked around the room, seemed to be a recurring theme. They glanced over at me briefly, then returned their gaze to Jake's body. They muttered to each other in something that sounded vaguely Slavic to me, and then one of them reached into the casket, to Jake's neck, as if to take a pulse.

"Excuse me?" I said to the pulse-taker. "Are you serious?"

He looked up at me but said nothing, then closed his eyes, as if to focus. The other got out a phone, opened up the camera, and started taking pictures.

After a few seconds of this, the first of the men opened his eyes and looked directly to me. "Sorry for your loss," he said, Slavically.

"Thank you," I said, dumbfounded, and then looked at the man taking photos. "Please don't take selfies."

The photographer chuckled at that, and took a couple more shots. He said something to the palpator, who grunted out a chuckle, then turned and took a picture of me. They both removed themselves from the condolence line before I could ask him why they'd done what they did. I turned back to my uncle, which is when the stabber had come up to do his party trick.

I yelled and launched myself at the stabber. Almost immediately, and yet too late, I realized that was a not-at-all-smart thing to do. The stabber was taller and more muscular than I was, and had the sort of close-cropped hair and almost-fashionable stubble that made me think of some of the more active yet less legitimate secret services out in the world. I pushed this man, and as I did I had the terrible sense that the man was deciding whether or not to *allow* himself to be pushed, or to deflect me and drive me into the carpet.

That infinitesimal moment lasted forever. Then the stabber chose to let himself be pushed. He stepped back, insultingly casually, from the casket, his knife still at the ready for additional stabbing.

"What the actual hell are you doing?" I yelled. I decided that the man might gut me like a fish, but until then, there was no upside to backing away now.

"I was about to stab your uncle," the man replied, calmly. "I may still."

"Why the *fuck* would you do that?"

"Because your uncle has faked his death before," the man said. "I was told to confirm it had taken this time around."

I stared at the man uncomprehendingly, and then looked around the room.

The room was now filled with men all staring back, waiting to see what was going to happen next, all of them looking not unlike the man in front of me. I realized now that if I had pushed any one of them, they too would have had to decide whether to take the push or slam me to the floor.

It was not clear to me whether all of them would have made the same choice the stabber had.

I collected myself and tried to pretend I wasn't about to wet myself in the visitation room. "Let me guess," I said to the stabber. "You're the asshole who sent the floral arrangement with the 'Dead? Lol okay' message on it."

"That's not me," the stabber said. "It might have been my boss."

"What?"

"My boss," the stabber repeated.

"You don't know my uncle, then."

"Not personally. I've seen him before from a distance. I know him by reputation."

"So you're not here to pay your respects."

"No," the man said. "I'm here to stab him."

"To make sure he's dead."

"That's right. So, if you would be so kind," the stabber said, hefting the knife again.

"No!" I held up my hand, and then looked around the room, at the room full of probably-assassins. "Do *any* of you know my uncle personally?"

No one responded.

"How many of you are here to make sure he's dead?"

All the hands went up.

"And you were all going to stab him?"

"I was going to inject him," one man said.

"With *what*?"

"Nothing. Just air. Into his carotid. If he wasn't dead, he'd be then."

Another man held up a swab in a plastic wrap. "I'm just here to get DNA. To make sure it's him."

The syringe man snorted. "Can be faked."

"At least *I'm* not murdering anyone with three dozen witnesses, air boy," swab man replied.

"Everybody shut up," I said. The two men quieted. "I want to be sure I'm getting this right. *None* of you know my uncle. *All* of you are here just to make sure he's dead. And you've all been sent by someone else. Do I have that right?"

There were general nods around the room.

"What the *fuck* is wrong with all of you?" I asked.

"It's not personal, Fitzer," the stabber said.

"Clearly it's not personal," I shot back. "None of you actually give a crap about Uncle Jake. But why do your *bosses* care?"

"We don't care why our bosses care," syringe man said. "We were told to be here. We were told to make sure he's dead. That's it."

I looked over to Michael Chesterfield, who was standing by the partition between the rooms. He seemed amazed at current events, which, fair. "Will you please give your professional verdict on my uncle's current state?" I asked him.

"I personally drained his body of its fluids and replaced them with embalming solution," Chesterfield said, clearly, to the room. "If he wasn't dead before I did that, he was dead after. You don't come back from formaldehyde and methanol."

"Thank you," I said. I turned to the stabber. "Stabbing is not required."

"Sorry," the stabber said. "Your friend here could be lying. I have to make sure."

"No."

The stabber considered me for a moment. "Why do you care, Fitzer?" he asked me. "You never knew your uncle. He means nothing to you, and you sure as hell meant nothing to him. In life, he never went one inch out of his way to help you. What do you care if I stab him, or George here pumps air into his vein, or Kyle swabs the inside of his cheek? If he's dead, it won't matter. And if he's not dead, then he's played you for a fool. Either way, there's no reason to stand in our way." He stepped forward to the casket again.

I got in his way. "I said no."

"You can't actually stop me," the stabber said, mildly.

Which I knew was true, but on the other hand, fuck this dude. "You'll have to go through me," I said.

The stabber smiled. "You know, I wouldn't mind."

"Enough," said one of the Slavic men, the one who had palpated Jake's neck. "He's dead."

The stabber didn't break eye contact with me, but addressed the Slav. "And you know this how?"

"I was medic in Chechnya," the Slav said. "I know dead."

"And I have thermographic camera," said the other Slav. He pulled out his phone and showed a multicolored photo. "Corpse is corpse temperature. You see Andrei's hand for contrast."

"He's dead," the Slav named Andrei repeated. "If it's good enough for us, it's good enough for our boss, and it's good enough for you."

"And who is your boss?" syringe man asked.

"Dobrev," said Andrei. This got a mutter in the room.

Stabber, who had never once broken eye contact with me, smiled in a deeply unnerving manner. "You should have led with that, Andrei," he said. "Saved us all some time." He backed away from me. "We're done here," he said, and put away his knife.

"We're done," I agreed. "Everyone out. All of you."

They all began to depart. I caught the eye of Andrei the Slav, who I suppose might have been Russian or Ukrainian. "Thank you," I said.

"Don't thank me," Andrei said. "My boss sent 'Suck it, motherfucker' vase." He left, the man with the thermographic camera directly behind him.

In two minutes the funeral home was empty except for me, Chesterfield and his assistants.

"Holy shit," I said, when the last of the men was gone. I turned to Chesterfield. "I have to tell you I almost wet myself on your carpet."

"One of the more memorable visitations I can recall," Chesterfield replied.

"Still with the tact."

"It comes with the job," Chesterfield said. "Now, Mr. Fitzer.

Your uncle paid for the option of you being a witness to the cremation if you like. But after the events of today, I think you might be ready to go home."

"You would be right," I said. All the adrenaline of the last several minutes was dissolving away, and all I had left was being shaky and tired.

Chesterfield nodded. "In that case, let us handle everything from here. I'll call you tomorrow to arrange the pickup of your uncle's ashes."

"Thank you," I said. "Honestly. For everything."

"Of course, Mr. Fitzer," Chesterfield said. "This is what we do. For the dead. And for the living."

I was carrying my torture shoes and stepping up barefoot to the curb for the southwest corner of Cook and Russell when I heard meowing that sounded like Hera. I glanced down the sidewalk but didn't see her, then looked down the rest of the street. Hera and Persephone were both sitting in the driveway of the Gunderson house, right across the street from mine.

I crossed the street and came up to them. "Okay, what are you doing?" I asked Hera, as I crossed the street to them. I didn't actually expect an answer. Hera was a cat. I tried to keep her inside most of the time, for her safety and so I could have a conscience clear of bird murders.

That said, I knew that she could get out somehow; I'd caught her in the backyard when I hadn't let her out. I suspected a loose window in the basement but had never bothered to check. But it was still rare when she was out that she would deliberately let me see her. "Why did you think it was okay to leave the house?"

Hera looked up at me, meowed loudly, and then looked, quite deliberately, at our house across the way. I followed her gaze.

There was someone visible in one of the upstairs windows, the one for my bedroom.

"What the actual hell?" I reached into my pocket for my phone, to call 911.

The person in my room turned, looked out the window, and saw me. They disappeared from the window.

"Shit," I said.

I was in the act of crossing the street when my house went and exploded itself all over it.

CHAPTER 6

"Burned to the *ground*," Andy Baxter said to me, over the phone.

"Yes." I was sitting on the Gundersons' curb, although this time it wasn't just me and the cats; the whole neighborhood had come out to watch the spectacle of my house turning into ash. There was a full complement of fire and police services to boot. It was a regular hootenanny here on Cook Street. "Well. Exploded first. Then burned to the ground. With a dead body inside."

"*Whose* dead body?"

"That's a really good question," I said. "I don't know, and neither do the police or the fire department. The money is on burglar or arsonist. Considering that the fire went through the house much faster than it would have without help, 'arsonist' has the lead at the moment."

"That's not great."

"It's worse for the arsonist. He didn't get clear of his own handiwork."

"But *you're* fine," Andy said.

"I wouldn't say that," I said. "I'm physically fine. I wasn't in the house when it happened."

"Where were you?"

"At a memorial service for my uncle."

There was a pause here. "Jake. Your mom's brother."

"That's the one."

"He died?"

"There was debate about it with the mourners, but yes."

"I didn't know you were close to him."

"That's all right," I said. "Neither did I."

As I was talking to Andy, I was once more taking in the scene on the street, and the smoking hole in the neighborhood where my house used to be. The explosion had wrecked the house and made it easier for the fire to catch hold. But other than strewn glass and some cracked windows at the next-door houses, there was no major damage to any other house on the block. The fire department was on the scene in minutes, and the threat of fire spreading was contained. That was a small mercy. After the day I'd had, I didn't want anyone else's misfortune on my conscience.

I had given my report to the cops, and the firefighters were now finishing up their work, and an ambulance had come for the poor, crispy probably-arsonist and had carted him away. Everything that was going to happen had happened, and the neighbors were now heading back to their homes, because they still had them. A couple of them nodded to me on the curb in sympathy. I nodded back, but I was glad to be on the phone because I didn't really want to have a conversation with any of them right now.

"I'm glad you're physically fine," Andy said. "What about the rest of it?"

"Well, my house and all my possessions have burned up, I have no place to live and nowhere to go, and in the immediate future me and the cats will be living in dad's Maxima," I said. "So I could be *better*."

"You need a place to stay."

"I agree. Are you offering?"

"I'll call the insurance company," Andy said. "They can probably set you up with a hotel for a few days at least. They'll need the police and fire reports, and they'll probably send their own investigators, seeing that there's a dead body and the possibility of arson."

"Right."

"Charlie . . ." There was a definite tone to Andy's voice here.

"Oh, *here* we go," I said, and looked to the heavens. Hera, perhaps sensing I was about to get irritated, gave me a reassuring headbutt. I reached down to pet her.

"It sounds like you know what I'm about to say, but I'm going to say it anyway," Andy said. "You gotta know the police and fire department are going to be looking at you for this."

"Come on, Andy. I'm not going to burn down my childhood home."

"I'm not saying you did or would. I'm saying that they're going to eventually figure out that you don't own the place outright and your residency is hanging by a financial thread. *Was* hanging. They're going to figure out that your siblings wanted you out of the house, and that you don't have the best relationship with them. They're going to figure out that you need money. Two of the biggest reasons for arson are revenge and insurance fraud. You're going to fit that profile."

"Is this conversation covered by attorney-client privilege?" I asked, because that seemed suddenly relevant.

"That's a good question," Andy replied.

"If they're going to look at me for that, they need to look at Sarah and Bobby and Todd, too," I said, continuing despite the rather-shaky privilege of our communication. "If *they* burn the place down, they get to split the insurance money and they don't have to deal with me ever again. The house is our last thread of mutual obligation."

"I'm sure they will look at your siblings," Andy said. "But they'll look at *you* first and most. And if they think you hired someone to burn your house down, you're maybe on the hook for what happened to him, too."

I stopped petting Hera and put a hand to my head. "Are you trying to make my day *worse*, Andy?"

"What I'm saying is you might look into getting a criminal lawyer. Did you talk to the police or fire department people?"

"Of course," I said. They asked me what happened (I didn't know), whether I rented or owned (it was complicated), where I had been (Uncle Jake's service), who the person in the house might be (no idea) and where my shoes were (in the street, left there when I fell back on my ass after the explosion). They were the ones who surmised the person inside the house might be a burglar or arsonist. I told them I had no idea why either would target my house. They took my report and I gave them my cell phone number. They promised to be in touch."

"Okay, so don't talk to them anymore without a lawyer," Andy said.

"You're a lawyer."

"I'm not *that* kind of lawyer."

"How the hell am I going to afford a lawyer?" I asked, exasperated. "I don't have any money. Everything I have literally just went up in smoke."

"When I talk to the insurance company I'll see if I can get them to give you a little something in advance."

"That will be a fun conversation," I said. "'Hey, do you mind giving the person the police think burned down his house some money so he can hire a lawyer to beat the rap?'"

"I won't phrase it like that when I ask."

"I mean, please *don't*."

"Let me get on this," Andy said. "I'll be in touch soon."

"Okay."

"Sorry, Charlie. I know this is a mess."

"Thanks, Andy." I hung up and looked at my cats. "Well, *that* was a delightful conversation," I said to them. Hera gave me a slow blink in sympathy. Persephone padded over and meowed to be picked up. I complied with the request.

"Excuse me," someone said, behind me. It was Kayleigh

Gunderson, the across-the-street neighbor's teenage kid, on whose curb I was currently sitting. She was holding a small serving bowl.

"Hey," I said.

"Here," Kayleigh said, thrusting the bowl at me. "It's cat food. You know, uh, for the cats."

I took the bowl, which had a plastic top on it to keep the kibble from escaping, with the hand not currently occupied by a kitten. "Thank you. That's very kind of you."

"I'm really sorry about your house," Kayleigh said.

"Thanks," I said. "So am I."

"Are you going to be okay?"

I smiled at this. "I guess we're going to find out," I said, and lifted the bowl of cat food. "This will help. My cats say thanks."

Kayleigh smiled at this and went back into her house.

My well-trained eye identified the kibble as Meow Mix, and I wondered if the Gundersons already had it in the house, or if they'd sent Kayleigh out to get some. I don't remember the Gundersons having their own cats. But then I'd never been to their house, despite them having lived across from me for years now. That was on me, I suppose. I could have made an effort to be more neighborly.

By this time the cats had figured out there was food about, so I cracked open the bowl, and set it down on the grass by the curb. Hera started nibbling, and Persephone hopped down from my hand, straining to get her fluffy little head over the lip of the bowl.

"Well, at least *you* won't starve," I said to them. "Not yet, anyway." I looked back to the shell of my house.

I'm not going to lie, here: I was screwed. The house was a ruin, everything in it was a ruin, if not from fire then from water damage from the firefighters. As of this moment, my entire set of assets were me, the cats, my suit, my awful shoes, my phone, and my wallet, which contained twenty-three dollars in cash, an

ATM card that would allow me to access a similar amount in my checking account, and a maxed-out Visa.

Oh, and dad's Maxima, as well as a lawn mower and whatever other gardening tools were stored in his house's detached garage, which did not burn down with the rest of the house. I wasn't lying to Andy; if the insurance company didn't put me up in a hotel, I'd be sleeping in the garage, in the car, and eating from the rotating hot dog cooker at the Circle K. At least, until the money ran out.

Which it *would*, because here's the other thing: My "reward" for standing up for Uncle Jake at the funeral, the ownership of my house, had literally just gone up in flames. I'd get nothing for my efforts there, because there was nothing to sell, save the land the burned house was on. Even if Jake's company bought that and gave it to me, I couldn't afford to build a new house on the property, even with what his people were going to give me at closing, if they were even going to do that now, because there was no house to hand over.

There was nothing. I had less than a hundred dollars to my name, in cash and credit.

A hundred dollars, an old suit and uncomfortable shoes.

I turned to the cats. "I'm going to need you to hunt for me," I said. "Good bet I'll starve otherwise." The cats, still busy eating, said nothing.

Pretty sure this was the actual low point of my entire existence to that moment.

My phone buzzed.

Heard about the house, Mathilda Morrison had texted. *Sucks.*

Thanks for the sympathy, I texted back. *It will comfort me when I sleep in the back seat of my car.*

I think we can do better than that, Morrison texted.

I'm listening, I replied.

The phone rang. It was Morrison. I picked up.

"I'm still listening," I said.

"Great," she said. "Follow your cats."

"What?"

"Follow your cats," Morrison repeated.

"What is that supposed to mean?"

"What part of 'follow your cats' is hard to understand?" Morrison asked.

"All of it, honestly," I said.

"Look, don't overthink it, Charlie," Morrison said. "Tell Hera I told you to follow her. She'll take it from there. I'll see you later tonight. We have things to discuss." She hung up.

I stared at my phone for a minute, and then looked over to Hera, who had apparently just finished eating, and who was now looking at me expectantly. Persephone was still scarfing away.

"I feel really stupid for even saying this out loud," I said to Hera, "but Morrison said I should follow you."

Hera *fucking meowed at me* after I said this, and then turned and chirruped at Persephone. The kitten took one last bite of kibble and then stepped away from the bowl. Then the two of them started walking north on Cook Street. I watched them for a few seconds, absolutely dumbfounded. Then Hera stopped, turned her head back to me and meowed loudly, as if to say, *Well, are you following me or not?*

I put the lid back on the bowl, picked it up, and followed my cats.

Hera and Persephone walked up Cook to Russell, and then made a right, heading east. They walked unhurriedly, tails up, Hera clearly knowing where she intended to go and Persephone happy to follow.

When Hera walked us to Grove Avenue, she looked both ways before crossing the street and then headed down the far side of the road.

At 611 South Grove, there was a smallish, well-maintained white Cape Cod, set in a plain but well-manicured yard. Hera walked up to the porch, to a door that had a cat entrance set into it. She looked back at me, meowed again, and went in. Persephone followed.

"What the hell?" I said. I knew of cats who time-shared owners, but it didn't make sense that Hera would be doing that. She was home every night, even if she snuck out during the day.

And yet, Hera walked into 611 South Grove like she owned the place, and Persephone had no problem following her. And here I was, standing in the walkway, gawking like a fool.

I walked up onto the porch and stood at the door. Honestly, I had not the first clue what I was going to do next. Whoever was in there clearly thought they owned Hera, and possibly Persephone, and from their perspective I was probably a catnapper.

That doesn't explain why Morrison told you to follow your cats, or how your cats actually took you here, my brain said to me.

You're not wrong, brain, I thought. Whoever was on the other side of this door would have some explaining to do about how they trained their cats to understand that phrase "I should follow you," and to know it meant leading me to this particular door.

I looked down at the side of the door and saw a doorbell there.

"Oh, what the hell," I said, and pressed the thing.

There was a flat tone, followed a couple of seconds later by a buzzing that I remembered from apartment living. I was being buzzed in.

I turned the doorknob, pushed, and entered the house.

The inside was dim from shaded windows and the lack of artificial lighting. The furniture was sparse, and the walls were festooned with cat stairs and cubbyholes. Whoever lived here was clearly much more involved with their cats than I ever was. Maybe a little *too* involved.

"Hello?" I said.

From around a doorway, Hera popped her head out and meowed at me, then disappeared. I went where she had gone.

I imagine the house floorplan would have told me I was in the living room. In here, there were more cat beds and trees, a couch, and a desk of odd dimensions, on which rested a large monitor and a sprawling keyboard of a sort I'd never seen before. The more I looked at it, the more it reminded me of a mutant, overgrown stenography machine—those things that were used in court to record the proceedings.

What I didn't see were the people who had let me in.

"Hello?" I said, again.

This is the part of the movie where people get ax-murdered, my brain said, unhelpfully.

"Shut up, brain," I said out loud.

Hera came out from behind the desk, meowed at me, and then hopped up onto the desk. As I watched she pressed a button on the keyboard, which turned on the monitor and woke up the backlighting on the rest of the keyboard. Hera hopped onto it, and used all four of her feet to chord the buttons there.

Words popped up on the lit screen.

HELLO, CHARLIE, they read. SORRY ABOUT YOUR HOUSE. WELCOME TO MY OTHER HOME. I HAVE A ROOM WAITING FOR YOU UPSTAIRS.

CHAPTER 7

Mathilda Morrison's S-Class drove up to my cat's house and stopped at the curb just long enough for Morrison to get out of it, then drove off again. It occurred to me that I had not actually seen the driver of the car. At this particular point, I was not entirely sure there *was* a driver. I wasn't feeling sure about a lot of things.

I watched as she walked up the small path to the porch, on which I was sitting.

"Let me guess," she said, stopping in front of me. "Sentient cats a bit overwhelming."

I stared up at her, not speaking. She took that as an affirmative, which it of course was. "If it makes you feel better, I felt the same way the first time I met one," she said.

"My cat types and has her own house," I said.

"Yes."

"And you *knew*."

"Yes."

"And you were going to tell me my cat owns a house *when*?"

"Actually the house is owned by one of your uncle's real estate corporations. Technically it's an Airbnb. Good cover for what appears to be a mostly vacant house in an upscale neighborhood."

"But she *is* actually typing," I said.

"Oh, yes. That's definitely her."

"How?"

"The short answer is 'genetic engineering.' The long answer requires a PhD."

"And why?"

"Because sentient cats are useful to your uncle's business interests."

"He owned *parking garages*."

"He did," Morrison agreed. "But I think you've probably already guessed by now that's not the whole story."

I opened my mouth to say something else when an entirely different S-Class Mercedes Benz rolled up to the curb and a man stepped out of the passenger door. I recognized him immediately.

"It's the stabber," I said to Morrison.

She looked at me, confused, as he walked up to us.

"He tried to stab Uncle Jake's corpse," I explained. "I stopped him."

"Why did you do that? Tobias could have killed you."

"You *know* him?" I gaped.

The newly named Tobias grinned from the footpath.

"Stay behind me," Morrison said. She turned and put herself between me and Tobias the Stabber.

He stopped and nodded at Morrison. "Hello, Til," he said. "Nice of you to put your boy up in an Airbnb. Considering what happened to his house." He stepped to get past her to me.

"Don't you even," Morrison said. She shifted her weight in a way that I realized meant she was getting ready for a fight.

Tobias appeared to recognize it too. He took a step back. "Relax. If your boy was supposed to be dead, I'd have knifed him at the funeral home. That's better than others can say." He looked past Morrison to me. "Condolences on your house, Fitzer. And your uncle. Seeing that he *is* actually dead and all."

"Thanks," I said.

"Don't talk to him," Morrison said to me.

"Sorry."

"You should get used to her telling you what to do," Tobias said to me, then looked back to Morrison. "Bit of a family tradition, that."

"Are you here for a reason?" Morrison said, ignoring the provocation.

"You mean, if I'm not here to end your friend right on the lawn?" Tobias smiled. "I come with an invitation."

"For whom?"

"Well, if it were from me, it might depend, wouldn't it?" Tobias said. "But since I'm just the messenger, it's for your new friend here. I'm going to reach into my coat now."

"Do it slow," Morrison said.

"Of course. I remember that's how you like it, Til." He reached into his coat—slowly—and extracted an envelope from a coat pocket. The envelope looked bespoke—made from heavy, handmade paper—and was sealed with wax and a cord. "See? Just an envelope." He reached out to hand it to me.

"Don't take that," Morrison said to me.

"I already told you I wasn't here to kill him," Tobias said to Morrison.

"It's not you I'm worried about," she said. She nodded to him. "You open it."

"You think it's going to explode?"

"If it does, I want it to be your fingers on the yard."

"I don't remember you being this paranoid before your employer kicked off," Tobias said.

"Less talk. More fingers," Morrison said.

Tobias shrugged, got a better grip on the envelope, and yanked at the cord. It bisected the wax seal, and the flap of the envelope popped open. I flinched despite myself. Tobias noticed and gave me a wry smile. "You're going to need more of a spine than that, Fitzer," he said.

"Take the invite out," Morrison said to Tobias.

He did, showing elegant writing written with what was undoubtedly a very expensive fountain pen.

"Lick it," Morrison said.

Tobias lost his smile. "The fuck you say."

"Lick it," she repeated, "both sides."

"You have plain lost your mind," Tobias said.

"And you're wearing gloves," Morrison said. Which stunned me. I had been looking at Tobias this whole time and simply had not noticed. But he was: If they weren't literal kid gloves, then they were still of some sort of tremendously expensive leather, dyed to a color matching his skin tone.

Tobias, acknowledging Morrison's observation, held up the invite in front of his face. "Only for you," he said to her, stuck out his tongue and ran it across the card, first one side and then the other. "Not dead yet," he said, when he was done.

"I'm willing to wait," Morrison replied.

"That's nice," Tobias said. "I'm not. I have other places I need to be." He put the card and the envelope into one hand and thrust them at her. "Take these."

"No."

"Fine. Then how about I hold it up, and you take a picture of the damn invitation with your phone. Then I can say I delivered the invite, and we can all go on with our lives. Deal?"

Morrison considered it. "Charlie, take a picture of the invite with your phone," she said, never taking her eyes off Tobias.

"You're not going to do it yourself?" Tobias asked Morrison.

"I want to keep my hands free," she said.

"Now you're just putting on a show for your boy," Tobias said. Morrison didn't answer this.

I got out my phone and zoomed in to the invite before taking the photo. "What is this for, anyway?" I asked, as I was putting my phone away.

"Let's just say it's a confab for the industry you're joining,"

Tobias said, to me, then turned his attention back to Morrison. "Which you really need to catch him up on."

"I don't need your advice."

"You've made that clear enough. So, no advice, just a reminder. Now that he's got the invite, you know he has to show up for it. If he doesn't, it's not going to end well for him. Or for you."

"I thought you had other places to be," Morrison said.

"I'm going," Tobias agreed. He looked over at me. "Good luck, Fitzer. You're going to need it."

"Leave," Morrison said.

"Good to see you too, Til." Tobias nodded to me as he walked back to his Mercedes, invite still in his gloved hand.

"What did he mean, that I have to accept the invitation?" I asked, after he was driven away.

"I'll explain it to you later," Morrison said.

"He called you Til," I observed.

"Yeah."

"That seems . . . friendly," I said.

"We dated briefly."

"You dated a stabber?"

"Do *you* really want to get into failed relationships with me right now?" Morrison snapped.

"No," I said, taken aback. "I suppose not."

"Good," Morrison said.

We were silent for a couple of seconds. Then I asked her, "Did you really think there was poison on that invite?"

"No."

"Then why did you make him lick it?"

Morrison looked at me. "It would have been nice to be wrong."

"Don't take this the wrong way, but I don't know how to feel about you right now."

Morrison nodded at this. "I get that a lot." She motioned with her hand. "Let's go inside, Charlie. We have lots to talk about. We shouldn't say it in the open air."

Hera was at her desk when we came inside. Morrison went to her and greeted her with a scritching. Persephone the kitten was also on the desk, next to Hera.

"How long have you two known each other?" I asked. I maneuvered myself over to the couch.

"This is only the second time we've met," Morrison said, giving Persephone a scritch as well. The kitten arched her tiny back for it. "The first time was the other day at your house, but I couldn't say anything then."

Hera went to her keyboard. WE EMAIL A LOT, she typed, to me.

"How is he doing?" Morrison asked Hera, about me.

HE'S HAVING A LOT OF COGNITIVE DISSONANCE, Hera typed.

"Fair," Morrison said. She noticed where I was and made a motion with her hand. "Sit, Charlie. We have a lot to cover."

"Can we start with the cat?" I asked, sitting.

CATS, Hera typed. PERSEPHONE IS MY INTERN.

Persephone looked at me and mewed.

"Paid internship, I hope," I joked.

OF COURSE, Hera typed back. WE'RE ANIMALS, NOT MONSTERS.

I paused. "Do you actually get paid?" I asked my cat.

YES.

"How much?"

MORE THAN YOU.

"I suppose I deserved that for asking," I said. I turned to Morrison. "You said sentient cats are useful to my uncle's business."

"I did," Morrison said.

"How?"

"Intelligence gathering," Morrison said. "Human and electronic intelligence gathering are difficult. No one suspects a cat."

I eyed Hera, who, to be fair, looked like an ordinary cat, except for the fact she was sitting at a keyboard ergonomically designed specifically for her species. "And this matters in the parking garage game," I said to Morrison.

"More than you might think," Morrison said. "But as I mentioned outside, there's more to your uncle's business than parking garages."

"But I'm not part of any of it," I said. "Jake wasted a cat." I turned to Hera. "No offense."

NONE TAKEN.

Morrison shook her head. "Not a waste," she said. "Charlie, after your mother died your father told Jake to keep away from his family, so Jake kept away. Still, Jake always kept an eye on you. Not always with cats. But also, with cats."

"Why?"

"You're your mother's son, and he wanted to know you were okay for that reason alone. You're his family, Charlie. His only real family. And also, to keep you safe."

"What does *that* mean?"

"It means that in your uncle's line of work, there's an unwritten rule that family not directly involved in the business are not to be targeted," Morrison said. "Turns out, not every one of your uncle's competitors was what you would call ethical."

"This explains my house blowing up," I said.

Hera started typing. NO. YOU STOOD FOR YOUR UNCLE AT HIS FUNERAL. THEY THINK YOU'RE FAIR GAME NOW.

"What?" I looked at Morrison. "You didn't tell me that."

Morrison made a half-shrug. "Sorry."

"*Sorry?* They blew up my house! With themselves in it."

More typing. THEY BLEW UP SOMEONE ELSE, ACTUALLY. THERE WAS AN EARLIER PAIR OF VISITORS. I HAVE VIDEO.

"Show it to him," Morrison said, before I could ask my cat how she had video. Hera typed, and a window popped up on the monitor showing the interior of my house from the point of view of several cameras that I was not aware had been in my house.

On one of the cameras, two men had entered the house through the back. The men were dressed as plumbers or electricians, carrying work bags. Hera and Persephone came up to them, curious. The men ignored the cats and made their way through the house, first wandering about spraying something and then heading to my bedroom, where among other things my laptop was, and doing something by the door to my room. "Setting a bomb," Morrison said. "It'll arm when someone enters the room, go off when they try to leave. They were probably spraying accelerant earlier."

Hera fast-forwarded the video for a while as the two men exited, and then slowed down again a while later when a new person entered the house, also by the back door. This new person also looked around the house before heading up to my bedroom.

It was at this point the cats left the house.

The new person, in my bedroom, spied my laptop, fiddled with it for a moment, and then caught me looking up at them from the street and decided to leave, taking the laptop with them. As they passed the threshold of my doorway, the bomb planted by the others went off, flinging the new interloper down the stairs and visibly breaking their neck as the fire raced around my home. The video cut off.

"Who are these people?" I asked, shaken.

LOOKING INTO THE BOMBERS, Hera typed. WE THINK THE PERSON WHO BLEW UP WAS CIA.

I blinked at this. "Excuse me? A CIA agent died in my house?"

MAYBE FBI, Hera amended.

My phone rang. It was Andy Baxter.

"Should I answer that?" I asked Morrison. She shrugged again.

I answered. "Hi, Andy," I said.

"Charlie, I have okay news and I have less-than-okay news," Andy said. "Tell me what you want first."

I rubbed my forehead. "Give me the okay news and work your way down."

"The okay news is the insurance company is going to cover a hotel for a week. They have you at the Bainbridge Express Inn. You know it?"

"I know it." The last time I had been at the Bainbridge Express Inn was on the night of my junior prom, when I had rented a room in the hopes that Vicki Harrington and I might have a personal afterparty. But then Vicki ditched me shortly after we arrived at the hotel to have drama with her only-sort-of-ex-boyfriend, and all I got out of the Bainbridge was a case of bedbugs. All things considered I'd be better off in my dad's Maxima. "What's the less-than-great news?"

"The FBI just dropped by my house asking about you."

"The FBI." I looked over to Morrison, who arched her eyebrows, but said nothing.

"They wanted to know when I last spoke to you and where you were right now."

"What did you say?"

"I told them the truth. I talked to you a couple of hours ago, and I had no idea where you were. Where are you?"

"At a friend's," I said, eliding the fact that my friend was a cat who could type. "Still in Barrington. Don't worry, they'll probably find me at the Bainbridge, if they haven't already got a warrant for my phone and are triangulating where I am from this phone call."

"Allow me to again suggest you get a criminal lawyer," Andy said. "This is not a personal assessment of your character, Charlie. You're a good kid. But it's the FBI."

"I'm going to get right on that," I promised.

"Can I do anything for you? In my capacity as your noncriminal lawyer?"

"Thank you, Andy," I said. "I'm all right. Thank you. For everything."

"Take care of yourself, Charlie."

"I will." I hung up and looked over to Morrison.

"Wanted by the FBI, are we?" she said.

"Apparently when a federal agent burns up in your house, they have questions," I said. I held up my phone. "I expect they know where I am by now."

Morrison nodded. "So what do you want to do?" she asked.

"I have options?" I said. "I'm broke, homeless and the feds are looking for me. My house burned down, so I'm guessing the deal we had went up with it. Unless you have a better idea I'm planning to sit on the curb until the FBI roll up and then see who the Federal Public Defender Office can roll out for me."

"We can do better than that," Morrison said. She turned to Hera. "Where's Charlie's go bag?"

DESK DRAWER, Hera typed. Morrison looked over to me and motioned for me to check the drawer. I opened it up and found a toiletry bag inside. I unzipped it and looked in.

Inside was two thousand dollars in assorted bills, debit and credit cards, a driver's license and a passport. I took out the passport and opened it.

"Desmondo Jose Ruiz?" I said, looking over at Hera.

YOU GO BY DES, Hera typed.

"Absolutely no one is going to buy that."

"Sure they will," Morrison said. "It's not a fake passport. It's real. Des Ruiz has been in the system almost as long as you have. Des and his family emigrated to the United States when he was two, and he became a citizen when he was fifteen. Mother Cecelia was a homemaker, father Juan was a private investment counselor, and Des followed him into the trade. Des has done very well and pays his taxes every year. He has excellent credit and a large bank account. He's got a condo in Schaumburg and a vacation home in the Outer Banks of North Carolina. He's as real as it gets, as far as the United States government is concerned, and you're him."

"This doesn't make any sense," I said.

"It makes perfect sense if you believe that your uncle has been watching out for you."

"For what?"

"To have an escape route if you needed one," Morrison said. "Which now you very much do."

"But that doesn't explain why he *cared*," I pressed.

"He cared because you're family," Morrison said. "And because, if Hera and I decided you were up to it, he had a job for you, and he needed you alive for that."

"Excuse me?"

"There was a reason he wanted to have you stand up for him at the funeral, Charlie. He knew what sort of person would be there and what they would try to do. He wanted to know what *you* would do. What you did was stand up for him."

"You had cameras at the funeral home too, I suppose," I said.

THE FUNERAL HOME HAS A STREAMING OPTION, Hera wrote. I PAID EXTRA FOR IT.

"You stood up for him when you didn't have to and when you had all sorts of reasons to do only the bare minimum of what was asked of you," Morrison continued. "And that's what we wanted to see."

"And you wanted to see that, why, exactly?"

SO YOU COULD TAKE OVER YOUR UNCLE'S BUSINESS, Hera wrote.

"Parking garages," I said, stupidly, all things considered, but things were moving fast at this point.

Morrison smiled. "Yes. Parking garages, Charlie. But I was thinking more about his *actual* business."

THE ONE WHERE HE CREATES TYPING SPY CATS, Hera wrote.

"Your uncle is in parking garages because they fund his more important work," Morrison said. "Which is to seek out, fund and create the sort of technologies and services that bring disruptive change to existing industrial and social paradigms, and offer them, on a confidential basis, to interested businesses and governments."

"That's a great mission statement," I said. "But it doesn't say what he actually *did*."

HE WAS A VILLAIN, Hera typed.

I stared at what she had written and looked back at Morrison.

"We don't use that word in public, and also, yes," she said.

"And this meeting that the stabber had that invite for?" I asked.

"Villain conference," Morrison said. "Think of Davos, except they don't pretend they're helping people."

"And I'd be going there."

"Yes. After we visit the volcano lair. We have some business there first."

"Volcano lair," I repeated.

"There's a good reason why we have one. It's not just for show."

I looked back at Hera. She slow-blinked at me.

"So," Morrison said. "You want in, Desmondo?"

CHAPTER 8

The volcanic island of Saint Genevieve lay in the southern Caribbean, roughly five miles north of the island of Grenada and five miles west of Ronde Island. It's small—about two thousand acres—but used to be twice as large, until 1784, when a massive volcanic eruption destroyed about half the island, killing three hundred souls. The volcano subsequently remained active, both above the waves and below it, and caused the British government to declare it, and the seas immediately surrounding it, off-limits to the locals. For the next 150 years it remained officially uninhabited and unvisited, save for the occasional pirate, rumrunner or ambitious naturalist.

In September of 1940, British Prime Minister Winston Churchill ordered the Royal Navy to occupy the island and to create an outpost where the United Kingdom could work on scientific and military innovations critical to the war effort, far from prying eyes and spies and the threat of German bombing or invasion. Within a year "Marlborough Park" was up and running, the scientists and military and British intelligence staff taking advantage of the abundant geothermal energy provided by an active volcano to make the outpost entirely self-sustaining.

In August 1942 the British were joined at Marlborough by members of the newly formed United States Office of Strategic Services. The Americans and their staff vastly expanded the size and scope of the base, adding a vast subterranean network of rooms and tunnels as well as establishing a service port that could accommodate a Gato-class US submarine. By the end of the Pacific stage of World War II Marlborough had created, or assisted with the creation of, dozens of "spy toys" and clandestine military weapons.

After the war, the United States intelligence services took over Marlborough entirely, leasing it from the British and renaming it Donovan Station. From Donovan, the CIA carried on research and development of spy technology and kept tabs on the southern Caribbean for nearly fifty years, finally vacating the base in 1992 with the dissolution of the USSR and the end of the Cold War.

In 1993 the entire island, including the infrastructure of Donovan Station, was bought by a group of real estate and entertainment investors, the Genevieve Development Partners, who had the idea of turning Saint Genevieve Island into a themed tourist destination and Donovan Station (now renamed Jenny's Bay) into a high-end hotel, casino and amusement park with moorage for cruise ships and yachts. The partners approached Universal Pictures with the intent of licensing their famous animated characters for the amusement park, showing off plans for a Woody Woodpecker rollercoaster (made of wood, obviously) and a Chilly Willy toboggan ride.

Within a couple of years the plans for a tourist destination devolved into chaos, riven by competing visions, out-of-control development costs and graft. By the turn of the century the various investors of the Genevieve Development Partners sold their interests, sometimes for pennies on the dollar, to one of the smallest initial investors, Allegheny Hospitality, LLC. As the new millennium dawned, Allegheny Hospitality was the sole owner of the property and development rights for the entire island of Saint Genevieve, and had become so for roughly the same amount of money as you'd have to pay for an Upper West Side penthouse in Manhattan, or a hillside compound in Malibu.

Rather than continue to develop Saint Genevieve as a tourist destination, however, Allegheny Hospitality took the island back to research and development, refurbishing the former intelligence base with new equipment and power systems, and inviting science and technology companies to enjoy the advantages of clean energy, relative solitude and a certain regulatory laxity to give them a jump on competitors. Within a year, several companies had relocated some or all of their R&D departments to Saint Genevieve, working on fields as disparate as biotech, security software and hardware, satellite development and alternative power.

All of these companies were privately owned, as was their landlord, Allegheny Hospitality. And all of them were owned, directly or through intermediary companies, by the same company: Baldwin Holdings, LLC.

Which was owned by one man: Jake Baldwin.

My uncle.

Who, in his wisdom, decided to put me in charge of all of it.

"Good news," Morrison said to me. "You may have burned up in a fire."

The two of us, and the cats, were standing on the deck of the *Jennifer Lawrence*, a utility boat that ferried passengers and cargo between Saint Genevieve and Grenada, or, rather less frequently, between Saint Genevieve and the island of Saint Vincent. The *Lawrence* was one of three utility boats operated by Allegheny Hospitality for the use of Saint Genevieve's tenants, all of them named after actresses; there was also the *Jennifer Tilly* and the *Jennifer Lopez*. The *Lawrence* was now making its way into Jenny's Bay; we would soon be disembarking.

The trip to Saint Genevieve had been almost suspiciously incident-free. From Barrington we (me, Morrison and the cats) were driven to Schaumburg Regional Airport, where we boarded a corporate jet owned by Baldwin Holdings, my uncle's umbrella corporation. Its presence was not coincidental; Uncle Jake's body had arrived in it, to be transported to the Chesterfield funeral home. Morrison had accompanied the body on the way out; arrangements had been made for his ashes to be sent later. My driver's license was checked by the pilot as a matter of course; nothing was said about it. Inside the plane was a change of clothes and new shoes for me. I gratefully got out of my suit before takeoff and put it into a trash bag provided me by the flight staff, who threw the suit to waiting ground staff from the door. Good riddance.

From Schaumburg Regional Airport we were flown to Mobile International, where a private charter took us to the Caymans. On the plane I was asked for my passport. I gave it and got it back, no questions asked. Des Ruiz was a real boy now. By this time it was well past my bedtime. I slept on the plane, Persephone purring in my lap.

We landed in the Caymans in the early morning for a refuel and then flew straight on to Grenada, where a car and driver were waiting for us right off the runway. A short time later we were on the water and steaming toward Saint Genevieve. It was still morning, in the low eighties (high twenties, I corrected myself; we were in a metric part of the world now), and there was a lovely breeze flowing across the deck. My uncle's island, whatever else it might be, looked like a tropical paradise from what I could see of it so far.

I don't know how other people got on being a fugitive from the FBI, but for me it was going pretty great.

"*May* have burned up," I said to Morrison, returning to the subject of my possible death. "Why the uncertainty?"

"You might need to be alive later," she said.

"So the FBI can add evading them to my potential charges?"

"We'll get that cleared up before then."

"Really," I said. "How?"

"Don't worry about that right now," Morrison said. "Just know you have excellent representation, alive or dead, in the form of your uncle's personal lawyers, who are now your lawyers."

"Where did I burn up?"

"The Bainbridge Express Inn."

"You burned up an entire hotel?"

"Not the entire hotel. Just a wing."

"I never checked in."

"Sure you did. Wearing that suit of yours, too."

"And if they check with the hotel staff? Or a surveillance video?"

"You were wearing a mask when you checked in. People still do that."

"Not really."

"You were coughing at the time."

"What's the excuse for the fire?"

"Faulty wiring. Which the Bainbridge absolutely has—they've been cited and fined for it."

I thought about this for a moment. "There's a body?"

"It was a pretty intense fire."

"I'm sorry, I was unclear in my line of questioning," I said. "Did you put, or cause to have delivered, a body, either living or dead, into the room in order to give the impression I burned up in it?"

"Do you think I would do that?" Morrison asked.

"You worked for a villain and dated a stabber," I said. "I *absolutely* believe you would do that."

Morrison smiled at this. "No. No bodies, living or dead, were in the room when it went up. Your suit was, however. And to answer the next question you will have, no, no one else who was staying at the hotel went up with it. Everyone survived the conflagration. Except you. Maybe."

"You have experience with this sort of thing," I said.

"There's a reason everyone at your uncle's funeral was trying to make sure he was really dead," Morrison replied.

"None of Uncle Jake's so-called business associates think I'm dead, do they?"

"Absolutely not. And even if you were, they'd still have your corpse attend the meeting."

"It's that important?"

"It's that important to them, yes." There was a thrumming; the *Lawrence*, which had been slowly maneuvering itself toward a dock, was now settled in and being secured.

"Is it important to *us*?" I asked.

"Not as important as what you're doing here," Morrison said.

"And what is that, exactly?"

"Your uncle was sick for a while. For most of the companies he owns, this didn't matter. They all have their own C-suites and staff, and he left them alone to do their thing." Morrison motioned in the direction of land. "This place was what he cared about. Where he did his real work."

"Being a villain," I said.

"I told you, we don't use that word in public."

"I don't see why not. It's a perfectly good word."

"For public use it's reductive," Morrison said. "Privately it offers some advantages. Which you will be finding out soon. But *you* won't be doing much overt villainy anyway. You're needed for something else entirely."

I nodded. "Useful idiot."

"I was going to say 'administration.'"

I chuckled at this. "You know the last time I was in charge of anything I was the editor of my high school newspaper," I said. "I ended up getting suspended."

"No one's going to suspend you now."

"No, they just might kill me instead."

Morrison nodded in the direction of the shore. "Harder to do here."

"I would have preferred if you had said 'impossible.'"

It was Morrison's turn to chuckle. "Occasionally someone would make an attempt on your uncle. They would rarely make it past the dolphins."

"The dolphins," I said.

Morrison waved out into the water. "They patrol the waters around the island. Not much gets past them."

"So we have smart dolphins."

"I mean, the dolphins were always smart. They just work with us now." Morrison looked at me. "You've met typing cats, Charlie. Don't act like smart dolphins are such a leap."

"What are they like?"

"The dolphins?" Morrison asked. I nodded. "I'm going to let you find that one out for yourself. I wouldn't want to ruin the surprise." She looked down the jetty to where a man, and a cat, were walking toward the *Lawrence*. "Come on," she said, tapping me on the arm. "Our welcoming party is here."

Five minutes later we were off the *Lawrence* and heading toward the man and the cat. Hera and Persephone walked ahead and greeted the approaching cat, a black-and-white shorthair. Hera and the new cat did a brief head tap, and then the three of them headed back toward land. I was about to call out to Hera when Morrison shook her head.

"Let them go," she said, and nodded toward their retreating forms. "That's the head of the Feline Intelligence Division. Hera and Persephone have to be debriefed."

"You understand how weird this is for me," I said. "Still."

"You've had a whole day," Morrison said. "Deal with it."

"Tough love, I see. Very effective."

"You'll have more to freak out about soon," she promised. Then she smiled, yelled, and held out her arms toward the man coming toward us. He reciprocated the smile, raised his own arms, and the two of them fell into a hug.

"Charlie, this is Joseph Williams," Morrison said to me, after they stopped hugging. "And aside from being the best dancer on Saint Genevieve, he's also the general manager for Allegheny Hospitality here. That means he runs the place."

"Well, now," Williams said. "We both know that's not true. I don't run the place. I'm just responsible for all of it."

"He runs the place," Morrison assured me. "Don't let him tell you otherwise. Joe, this is Charlie."

"Mr. Fitzer," Williams said. "Welcome to Jenny's Bay and Saint Genevieve. And allow me to offer you condolences on the passing of your uncle Jake."

"Thank you," I said. "Although it should be the other way around. You knew him. I didn't."

"I did know him," Williams agreed. "We all did. And we are all looking forward to working with you, Mr. Fitzer."

"Please call me Charlie," I said. "Being called Mr. Fitzer reminds me too much of being a substitute teacher."

Williams laughed at that. "We can't have that." He held out his hand. "Charlie. Welcome."

I shook it.

"I just told Charlie about the dolphins," Morrison said.

Williams cocked his head. "Did you now? Have you told him of our woes?"

"There are woes with the dolphins now?" I asked.

"I didn't go into detail," Morrison said. "I wanted it to be a surprise."

"Ah," Williams said, and then looked back at me. "Surprise, Charlie."

"What woes?" I repeated.

"They're thinking about going on strike," Williams said.

"Like a labor strike," I said. "Like a 'let's haul out Scabby the Rat on to the sidewalk' strike."

Williams nodded. "Again."

"*Again,*" I echoed, stupidly.

"Maybe we should give Charlie an overview first," Morrison suggested. "Let him know what he's gotten himself into before he has to deal with the dolphins."

"No, no," I said, holding up my hand. "You're trying to put me in a bunch of meetings, I can feel it. Before I have to sit in a room with PowerPoint presentations, I think I want to see the striking dolphins first."

"Are you sure?" Williams said. "You're diving into the deep end, here."

"Yes, I'm sure," I said.

Williams turned to Morrison. "I like him. He's brave."

"Sure," Morrison said. "Not very smart, but brave."

"Aren't I your boss now?" I said to her.

"You want me to be obsequious all of a sudden?" she asked.

"Maybe."

"Good luck with that, boss," she said.

I ignored this and turned back to Williams. "Just to be clear, the 'diving into the deep end' phrasing of yours was metaphorical, right? I will not actually be in with the dolphins when we talk."

Williams shook his head. "Oh, no, Charlie. Don't swim with the dolphins during a labor dispute. No matter how much they try to convince you otherwise."

CHAPTER 9

The Cetacean Division offices were a small hike from the dock, in a sheltered, partially enclosed artificial lagoon that stretched for a couple hundred meters. Within it, a substantial pod of dolphins swam and played. Most of them were moving about in an unorganized manner—or at least, in a manner that seemed unorganized to me—but near the middle of the length of the lagoon, by an interior wall, six of them gathered in two rows in the water, squeaking loudly at a woman in a wet suit. The woman did not look pleased.

"What's happening?" I asked, as we walked toward the dolphins.

"An airing of grievances," Williams said.

"What grieves a dolphin?"

"More like, what *doesn't*," Morrison said. We cleared the path and got to the landing near the lagoon. The woman in the wet suit turned and noticed us.

Confession: I had, until this point, never seen a dolphin in real life.

I take that back. I probably saw one during a field trip to the Shedd Aquarium when I was in the fifth grade or something. But I'd never gone out of my way to see one. Field trips aside, aquariums weren't my thing, and as an adult, "swimming with the dolphins" felt exploitative and creepy. I can't imagine a dolphin actually wants to spend its life being hugged by a parade of drunken podiatrists and preteen girls, and I didn't want to spend any time in a line with members of either group to do the same thing.

During our honeymoon on Maui (I know), Jeanine and I took a sunset cruise (I know) that promised dolphin sightings (I *know*), but the cruise directors didn't consult with the dolphins, and none showed up. This was the cruise where Jeanine learned she got desperately seasick on medium-sized boats and threw up three mai tais and the ship's "luau buffet" on my pants and sandals. It was not a great start to married life. I don't think seeing dolphins would have helped.

Aside from the fact that these six dolphins were arrayed in two neat rows of three, treading silently in the water directly in front of us, they looked like any dolphins one might see. I knew they must be of a particular species but had no idea what it might be; dolphin physiology was not my specialty. I did notice that one of them, front row center, was hovering near what appeared to be a microphone.

"Do they talk?" I asked.

The dolphin chittered something. "Who is *this* fucknugget?" is what came out of a nearby speaker.

"I guess that's a yes," I said.

"Fucknugget! Fucknugget!" the other dolphins started chanting in unison.

The woman in the wet suit turned to the dolphins. "It's your new boss, you thumbless cretins."

"Fuck him! And fuck your manucentric world view!"

"'Manucentric'?" I asked.

"It's not what you think," the person in the wet suit said, getting up and coming toward me. "*Manus* is Latin for 'hand.' 'Manucentric' is their new go-to word when they want to accuse us of bigotry."

"Fuck your fingers!" the central dolphin said.

"Finger fuck! Finger fuck!" the other dolphins chimed in.

Speaking of hands, the woman in the wet suit held out one of hers. "Astrud Livgren. Cetacean relations."

I shook her hand. "And how are relations?"

Astrud looked back. "About usual."

"She's an asshole!" the central dolphin said.

"So they're always like this?"

"We're right fucking here! You can ask *us*, you bipedal scrotemonkey!"

I raised my eyebrows at Livgren.

"'Scrotemonkey' is new," she said. "They mix and match insults to see what works. You get used to it." She motioned to the dolphins. "Please, be my guest."

I approached the dolphins. Their chittering died down.

"Hi," I said. "You're the first dolphins I've ever met."

"Well whoop-de-fucking-do," the central dolphin said.

For the very briefest moment I wondered about the translation software that had the capability to take the chittering of a dolphin and translate it to "whoop-de-fucking-do," but I pressed on. "I'm Charlie Fitzer."

"Hi, Charlie," the dolphin said. "I'm Who Gives a Shit, and these are my associates Don't Care, Fuck You, Fuck Off, Burn It Down, and Eat the Rich."

"Nice to meet you," I said. "I understand there's some sort of labor dispute."

Who Gives a Shit snorted. "As if you care."

"I was in a union myself," I said. "Chicago Tribune Guild."

"But you're not anymore, are you? Now you're management! A suppurating bourgeois fistula of oppression!"

"Bourgeois fistula! Bourgeois fistula!" the rest of the dolphins chimed in unison.

"Not going to lie, I appreciate your way with words," I said.

"Don't condescend to us, you ambulatory collection of skin tags," Who Gives a Shit said. "If you're just going to continue your uncle's repressive labor policies, you can fuck off right into the sun."

"Sun fucking! Sun fucking!"

I looked back to Morrison. "Uncle Jake was a union buster?" I asked.

"He was of the opinion that animals didn't have legal standing to form unions," Morrison said.

"How do the cats feel about that?"

"Most of them are in management."

"Cats are fucking class traitors," Who Gives a Shit said. "Furry little quislings is what *they* are."

"How . . ." I turned to Livgren. "How do dolphins have class consciousness in the first place?"

"Dolphin societies are complex," Livgren said. "They don't necessarily track one-to-one with human societies, but there are rough analogues, and the idea of class apparently is one that works for them. Also, my predecessor in this role read them *Das Kapital* and other economic texts."

"We have a better education than you, you smooth-brained last-gasp Habsburg," Who Gives a Shit said.

"I went to Northwestern," I said, only a little defensively.

"Oooooh, *Northwestern*," Who Gives a Shit said. "Fucking doormat of the Big Ten, you must be *very* proud."

"Doormat! Doormat!"

"You're forgetting about Rutgers," I said, but then looked back at Livgren. "Still a fairly esoteric bit of information for a sea creature."

Livgren shrugged, and pointed. "There's a laser projector and they have access to a remote control. They watch a lot of things in their downtime. American college football is one of them."

"What do they do when they're working?"

"Security and intelligence," Livgren said. "They patrol the waters around Saint Genevieve and alert us to anyone or anything out of the ordinary. And they also do information gathering on ship movements and communications."

"That's a lot," I said.

"You can't do shit without us," Who Gives a Shit said. "Shame if we had to strike."

"You've had strikes before?" I asked. Who Gives a Shit shut up and looked away.

"They've threatened before," Williams said, when I looked back toward him and Morrison. "They never follow through."

"Why not?" I asked.

"No leverage," Morrison said.

"What does that mean?"

"It means we're fucking slaves," Who Gives a Shit said.

I looked back sharply at Morrison.

"They're free to go whenever they like," Morrison said. "We don't track them. Well, we do track them when they're working, that's part of the job. But if one or more of them decides they want to leave, they can leave. But they don't."

"Why not?" I asked Who Gives a Shit.

"For the same reason you don't leave your house to go live in the jungle with a fucking tribe of bonobos, you pustulant trash fire," Who Gives a Shit said. Even through the computer translation I could hear his (her? I don't know how to gender dolphins and now was not the time to ask) heart wasn't in that last insult.

"There are drawbacks to being intelligent," Livgren said. "Or more accurately, having a more human intelligence than other members of their species." She motioned to the six dolphins. "They get bored easily. They don't integrate well with unaltered members of their species. They've seen how humans generally treat captive sea mammals."

"Fucking *Blackfish*," Who Gives a Shit said.

"They complain a lot, but they also know what the alternatives are," Livgren said. "They're well compensated for their work and cared for, and their personal and group needs are tended to. It's an equitable exchange for their labor."

"It's not just that and you know it," Who Gives a Shit said, and I think this was the first sentence without either an insult or a profanity, or both.

Before I could ask what that meant, Williams cleared his throat. "Charlie, we do have things we need to attend to."

"That's right, run the hell away," Who Gives a Shit said.

"Run away! Run away!"

"I'm going to come back to this," I said. "There's more here I need to dig into."

"Of course," Williams said, and smiled. "You're the boss now, Charlie. You don't have to do things the way your uncle did. But your uncle did things for a reason, and you should learn what those reasons are." He motioned me away from the dolphins.

I turned back to Who Gives a Shit. "Don't strike yet, please."

"Oh, he said 'please,' that makes it *all* better," Who Gives a Shit replied. The subdued moment had clearly passed.

"I'm going to look into this," I promised.

"Northwestern sucks," Who Gives a Shit replied.

"Sucks! Sucks!" went the dolphin chorus.

"Well, was that everything you were hoping it would be?" Morrison asked me, as we walked away from the lagoon.

"I don't know what I was hoping for, or expecting," I said.

"Probably not dolphins who say 'fuck,'" Morrison said.

"They did seem to use it a lot."

"If you were a dolphin without options, maybe you'd say 'fuck' a lot too, Charlie."

I paused to consider this. "Are you on the dolphins' side here?" I asked.

"I can see the dolphins' point."

"But do you *agree* with it?"

Morrison looked over to me. "It wasn't my job to agree with it or not. My job was to do what your uncle needed to be done."

"That leaves a lot of room for moral flexibility," I said, after considering what she said.

"That's a good euphemism for it," Morrison agreed.

"What's your job now?" I asked.

"It's the same job," she said. "Just now it involves you, too. Time to see how flexible your morality is, Charlie. Because you should know it's going to get a hell of a workout."

CHAPTER 10

A picture of Ernst Stavro Blofeld appeared on the screen, complete with white Persian cat. "When you think of what a villain is, you probably think of this," Eve Yang said. She was head of Allegheny's HR department on Saint Genevieve, and she was, apparently, in charge of my orientation session. "Or this." A picture of Dr. Evil popped up instead, finger by the side of the mouth. "Or even this." Dr. Evil was replaced by Thanos, no doubt fresh from his culling of half the universe, which never made sense from a scaling point of view, but there was no arguing with billions of dollars in box office, so I said nothing.

Another picture popped up, a stock photo of young, attractive and multicultural people in suits. "But in fact, they look like this," Yang said.

I nodded. "Soulless corporate automatons," I said.

Yang pursed her lips.

"I don't think that's what she was going for," Morrison said. She was in the session with Williams and Hera, who was set up at her own desk with a keyboard. I had been unreasonably happy to see my cat again.

"My mistake," I said. "Investment bankers."

"Charlie."

"Sorry," I said to Yang.

Yang smiled tightly before continuing. "They look like everybody else," she continued.

Just like serial killers, I thought, but did not say, because I could already tell my comedy stylings were not being appreciated.

The conference room we were sitting in was depressingly normal, part of a complex that was also depressingly normal. Except for the fact that it was on a small volcanic Caribbean island, and that there were talking dolphins and typing cats, it could have been the conference room of any mid-priced hotel chain anywhere in the world. There were even little water bottles, although these were made of biodegradable paper. My uncle's brand of villainy did not extend to wanton use of plastics.

"The reason that they look like everybody else is because 'villain' is not a state of mind or value judgment," Yang went on. "It's a job title." She clicked the remote in her hand; the smiling stock photo people disappeared and a new slide popped up, with the words "What Does It Mean to Be a Villain?" in yellow, on a blue gradient background.

"Do they give this presentation to all the new hires?" I whispered to Morrison.

"Executives and managers, yes," Morrison said. "Shut up and listen."

I shut up and listened.

And what I heard was that villains, at least for the purposes of this particular human resources presentation, were not bad people, and not evil people. What they were, were professional disrupters: the people who looked at systems and processes; found the weak spots, loopholes and unintended consequences of each of them; and then exploited them, either for their own advantage or the advantage of their client base. These activities, Yang explained, were neither inherently good nor bad in themselves—their "goodness" or "badness" was entirely dependent on the perspective of the observer.

"Then why call yourself a villain?" I asked.

Yang pursed her lips again. I could tell I was not her favorite person, even if I was ostensibly her new boss. "Is there something wrong with the word?"

"No," I said. "It's just the actual use of the word for hundreds of years is different from what you're saying it is here, no matter how you try to polish it up."

"What would you prefer?" Morrison asked.

"I don't know, I'm new to this," I said. "Systems exploiters? Loophole miners? Chaos arbitrageurs?"

YOU HAVE NEVER BEEN IN MARKETING, Hera typed.

"We would need to workshop the phrasing," I admitted.

Yang opened her mouth to speak, but Morrison held up her hand. "Your uncle insisted we use it," she told me. "What we do here by definition will have negative outcomes for the people whose systems and processes we disrupt. By taking the name 'villain' for ourselves, we robbed it of power when other people used it for us."

I waved toward the presentation. "Then why do this at all? Why rationalize it?"

"If I could continue my presentation," Yang said.

"Actually let's not," Morrison said to her. Yang looked upset. "The presentation is for the people who have already bought in to what we do here. Charlie's still fighting it."

"Not a great thing if he's supposed to be the boss," Williams mused. He reached for a nonplastic bottle of water.

"I'm not fighting it," I said. "I'm here, aren't I?"

YOUR ONLY OTHER OPTION WAS A QUESTIONABLE HOTEL AND NO CLEAN CLOTHES, Hera typed. AND THE FBI WANTING TO QUESTION YOU.

"All the more reason for me with get with the program," I said.

"No, I agree with Til," Williams said. "The PowerPoint is not for you."

"I just asked one question," I protested. I turned to Yang.

"You're telling me no one else asks why you call yourselves villains."

Yang looked over at Morrison, then shook her head. "By the time they get here they're already with the program," she said. "The point of the presentation here is to give them a framework to think about the term."

"To let them know it's not all maniacal laughter and plots to take over the world with a giant laser," I said.

Yang looked over at Morrison again.

"Wait, *is* there a plot to take over the world with a giant laser?" I asked.

"This is the Chac Four," Morrison said, pointing to a shipping container–sized object that stood on its own concrete pad outside a laboratory complex. At the top of the object was a series of what looked like tubes, pointing up toward the sky, in which a few fluffy white clouds lazed overhead. She and I had taken this field trip. Yang had stayed behind, presumably to prepare other materials for me to interrupt, and Williams had headed off because he ran the place and had actual work to do. Hera, a cat, was taking a nap.

"What's a Chac?" I asked, looking at the entire apparatus.

"Chac is the Mayan god of rain," Morrison said. "The Chac Four is the fourth iteration of a laser-based rainmaking machine that Regenwolke Systems, one of your uncle's smaller technology companies, is making for Mayland-Gibson under a subcontracting deal."

"Mayland-Gibson the massive government contractor," I said. I had done a story on them a few years back, about a minor accounting scandal. A company VP had used taxpayer money to buy her side guy a Tesla. It had not ended well for her.

"That's right," Morrison said, and motioned at the Chac Four. "This is part of an MG contract with the Department of Agriculture to deliver reliable rainmaking technology to the farmers in the western part of the United States. You point the lasers up there at clouds, it ionizes the water molecules in them and that helps develop rain, or something to that effect."

"And that actually works," I said.

"It works well enough that we're on the fourth version of the thing. The first version of it was the size of a barn and not very portable. This version is small enough that it can be trucked around to where clouds are. There's one tooling around West Texas now."

"Okay," I said. "So where's the villainy? Where's the plot to take over the world?"

Morrison reached into her suit pocket and pulled out what looked like her phone, tapped at it, and then handed it to me in landscape mode. On the screen was an app that showed a small, curved representation of Earth, and a large number of very small dots in a cloud above it. The dots in the cloud were moving, with some disappearing off one edge of the screen, and other dots appearing on the other side.

"What is this?" I asked.

"It's a map of every artificial satellite that's currently over Saint Genevieve," Morrison said. "Tap on one of the dots. Any dot is fine."

I tapped on one of the dots; it expanded and a little dialog box popped up to identify it as being owned and operated by the Chinese Ministry of National Defense. Another dialog box then popped up: "Tap to Track." I tapped it.

One of the tubes on the top of Chac Four came to life and swiveled. A new dialog box popped up. "Tap to Engage," it read.

"It's asking if I want to engage," I said.

"You can tap that," Morrison said. "Maybe wait after that tap, though."

After I tapped to engage I could see why she'd advised me not to go further. There were three dialog choices at this point: "Disrupt," "Destabilize" and "Destroy."

I looked over to Morrison. "Is this for real?"

"You mean, could you actually tap a button and use the Chac Four to blast a Chinese spy satellite right out of the sky?"

"Yes, that, exactly that."

"It's real," Morrison said. "Nothing would happen *right now* if you pressed any of those buttons, because Eve Yang hasn't finished putting you into the system. You have to have your own phone and biometric ID. But once you're in, yes, absolutely, you could fry that satellite. Or, if you don't want to destroy it, you could use the laser to push it out of its orbit, or mess with its communications." She reached out her hand to take back her phone. I gave it back to her, gladly. She closed out the app and put the phone back into her suit pocket. The Chinese spy satellite was safe for now.

"So we've given the ability to shoot down foreign satellites to . . . the United States Department of Agriculture," I said.

Morrison smiled at this. "The mobile version of Chac Four can't mess with anything but clouds," she said. "That's what Mayland-Gibson asked for, and that's what we delivered. Among the several other reasons their version can't shoot satellites, it doesn't have enough power in the portable batteries to get a coherent beam out of the atmosphere. But here, this Chac Four research model has different, more powerful specs. And it's drawing nearly limitless energy generated from an active volcano."

"And that's enough to zap a satellite?"

"It's enough that I could carve my initials into the Sea of Tranquility, Charlie."

"I . . . have no way to verify that," I said.

"We have a telescope if you want to check."

"So what are we doing with this ability?" I asked. "Are we blackmailing governments or companies? 'Give us money or we blast your satellites into smithereens'?"

"Trying to blackmail the US or China would be a really good way to have Saint Genevieve turned into a smoking crater,"

Morrison said. "A stupid villain threatens, Charlie. A smarter villain offers a service."

I blinked at this. "We offer satellite blasting services?"

"We have a select clientele who, for an annual retainer fee, have the option to use our ability to enact logistical challenges to their competitors. In space."

"So that's a yes."

"It's a 'we make a lot of money offering a service no one uses.' The sort of clientele we have doesn't pay us to blast satellites. They pay us to have the satisfaction of knowing they *could* blast satellites out of the sky."

"And how much is that worth to them?"

"Last year Baldwin Consultants, which is the company your uncle filtered these sorts of retainers through, took in sixty-eight million from satellite technology consulting services."

"That's a lot."

"And it's pure profit." Morrison nodded to Chac Four again. "All the research and development of the Chac technology is funded by Mayland-Gibson, who funds it through US government grants. Regenwolke Systems didn't put a penny of your uncle's money into it. We developed the tech at no cost to us, we own the underlying patents for the rainmaking but give MG an exclusive license for that particular use, and now we have a subscription model that requires us to do nothing other than to keep this one iteration of the technology in nominally working order."

"That's amazing," I said. "And also ridiculous."

"What's really amazing and ridiculous is that we have subscriptions from direct competitors," Morrison said. "So if one tells us to take down the other's satellites, we have standing orders to take down satellites from both. And the companies *know* about each other having subscriptions with us. Neither can stop subscribing to us because if they do they will be vulnerable to the other."

"It's mutual assured destruction, with a subscription fee."

Morrison nodded. "This is why we don't have to blackmail anyone, Charlie. They blackmail each other. And pay us the fee."

"It's perfect."

"It's villainy."

"I think I'm beginning to get it now," I said.

"Good, because we have a lot of shit like this and we need you on board, now."

I was going to answer but Morrison's phone rang. "Go," she said, and listened for a couple of minutes. Then she looked up. "Yes, all right, I see it," she said. I looked up and did not see whatever she was seeing. But in the far distance I heard an echoing cavitation, like an engine of some sort.

She hung up her phone and looked at me. "Come on," she said. "We need to head back."

"What's up?" I asked.

"We're about to perform another of our specialties," she said. "And this one is a little messy."

CHAPTER 11

"We've captured a CIA agent," Williams said to me and Morrison, as she and I came back to the main complex of buildings. It occurred to me that for all the events of the day, I hadn't seen my own office or quarters. I'm not sure I had either; maybe I would be given a cot in the dolphin lagoon. "He just parachuted in. Landed in the island center. I use the word 'landed' advisedly, as his chute got caught in some palm trees. Not one of our more difficult captures."

"Does this happen often?" I asked.

"The island is still largely undeveloped. Parachuting into the trees is always a strong possibility."

"Cool, but I meant are we often the target of CIA invasions."

"From time to time. Not just CIA. MI6, Mossad, French intelligence, so on and so forth. And then there are the private mercenaries and occasional criminal syndicates." Williams caught my look. "Is something bothering you?"

"I don't know, I thought we'd be more clandestine than this," I said.

Williams smiled broadly. "We're on Google Maps, Charlie. There's only so clandestine we can be. Everybody knows we're here, and they know what we do."

"They don't know *all* of what we do," Morrison said. "We keep some things for ourselves."

"Why do we do that?" I asked.

"Some things aren't ready to share yet. And some we keep as a competitive advantage."

"Spy cats," I said.

"As it happens, yes," Morrison agreed. "This was another reason we needed to get you here. If anyone figured out that the Airbnb you were staying at was a safe house run by Hera, that would have been bad for us and for a lot of our cat operatives."

"I'm still not sure why I needed to be spied on."

Morrison nodded. "Yes, that was the point, Charlie."

Williams cleared his throat. "The CIA agent," he said, getting us back on track.

"Right." She turned to me. "What do you think we should do?"

"Uh . . . what do we usually do?"

"Usually we interrogate them," Morrison said. "And then sometimes we kill them."

"Is that last one necessary?"

"You want us to keep them in a dungeon forever?"

"We have a dungeon?" I looked over at Williams.

"I don't know that we would call it a *dungeon*," Williams said. "We have lots of subterranean rooms, courtesy of the US Army Corps of Engineers. Some of them we use for detention. It's where we've stashed the CIA agent for now. But to Til's point, they're not very good for long-term storage."

"We're not set up to be a prison," Morrison said. "Prisoners are so much work. You have to feed them and occasionally hose them down to get the stink off."

"I can't tell if you're joking with me," I said.

"I'm mostly joking with you."

"That 'mostly' is doing a lot of work in that sentence."

"Why don't we go meet our CIA agent and see where things lead from there," Morrison said.

"You want *me* to interrogate him?" I would like to say that my voice didn't squeak at the end of that sentence, but that wouldn't be strictly true.

"Tell you what," Morrison said. "I'll handle the interrogation this time. You can learn how we do it around here. And then, at the end of it, you can decide what we do with the CIA agent. Death, or long-term storage."

The interrogation chamber was anticlimactic, as it was, in fact, the same conference room I had been getting a PowerPoint presentation in a little while earlier. The presumed CIA agent sat on a chair near the end of the table. He was on the younger side of middle-aged and fairly generic in appearance and wearing camo fatigues. He had been given a cup of water, which appeared mostly full, and at the moment he was fully engaged in petting Hera, who had floofed down in front of him on the table and was accepting belly rubs. Her keyboard had been stowed away or removed, leaving no trace she was anything but a cat.

"You've sent your best interrogator to question me," the man said, of Hera, as Morrison and I entered the room. "But she didn't get me to crack." He was joking.

"Trust me, if she wanted you to crack, you would have cracked," Morrison said. She was not joking, not that the CIA man knew that. She took out her phone and opened an app. "Ready to verify?"

"What happens if I get the code wrong?" the CIA man said.

"The cat kills you," Morrison said.

"Ooooh," the CIA man said, not knowing that it was probably true. "Ready."

"Treble Treble C Bass," Morrison said.

"Mozart Schönberg Adams Bach," the CIA man said.

"You mispronounced Schönberg."

"Umlauts always give me trouble."

"Okay," Morrison said.

"That's it?" I said, disbelieving. "An easily cracked code that's like something from World War Two?"

"Adams is a postwar composer," the CIA man said.

"And that wasn't the code," Morrison said. She pointed to Hera. "She's the code."

"Hera the cat?"

"If I saw a cat, I was supposed to comment about it," the CIA man said. "Depending on what I said, she was supposed to respond, and we go from there. Everything up to 'okay' was the code."

"It's still crackable," I said.

"That's why we ran his face through our database as soon as he came through the door," Morrison said. "If he dropped in and wasn't on the guest list, things would have gone differently, no matter if he had the code. The code was just confirmation."

I stared stupidly. "You knew he was coming."

"Not him in particular, but someone from the CIA, yes."

"But—"

"But you're supposed to kill me," the CIA man said.

"Well, yes."

The CIA man turned to Morrison. "You can tell he's new," he said.

"Don't give him shit, I can still have the cat end you," Morrison replied.

"I'm deeply confused," I admitted.

"One of our services is identity destruction and reconstruction," Morrison said. "He's here to fake his death and get a new identity."

"The CIA can't do that themselves?" I asked. "This seems like a natural for them."

"They can, but sometimes they want it done out of their system."

"For what reason?"

"For their own reasons," Morrison said. "We don't ask and they don't tell. But we figure sometimes they want someone so off the books that no one at Langley can look up the fact they're in deep cover. Secrets are harder to keep these days than you might think."

"And this works in an era of facial recognition and biometrics," I said, waving at the soon-to-be-fake-murdered man.

"Well, you got out of the country, didn't you, *Desmondo*?" the CIA man said. He looked over to Morrison. "We caught the reference from *The Fugitive*, by the way."

"Then you can assume you were meant to," Morrison said. "We had other identities ready to go if we wanted to be sneakier. Now, Mr."—she glanced at her phone—"Evan Jacobs, analyst from the CIA. Interrogation time. You have some information for me."

"I do," Jacobs said. "The first bit involves Desmondo here. You should know he's been let off the hook in the murder investigation of a federal agent. The home security video your lawyer so helpfully provided clears him entirely."

I glanced at Hera at this; she flopped about on the table and chirruped. Jacobs petted her absentmindedly.

"That's good news," Morrison said.

"For the sake of not making more work for everyone, we're going to ignore the forged government documents, which by the way are absolutely a felony that will get you up to twenty-five years." Jacobs looked at me here. "Do us all a favor, Mr. Fitzer, and bury Desmondo in the backyard. If he pops up again several different branches of the United States government will be obliged not to ignore him."

"Got it," I said.

"Thank you."

"Who were the people who planted the bomb that killed your guy?" Morrison asked.

"We don't know yet. It happened domestically and lord knows your old boss had enough enemies among US citizens, so the FBI is taking the lead on this investigation."

Morrison made a dismissive noise at this.

"I'm sure they will do fine," Jacobs said. "On our end we are checking in with our people who we have embedded in the circles your boss existed in, but so far we're not coming up with anything." He looked back to me. "Whoever wanted you dead is being quiet about it for now."

"I can't think that's good," I said.

"It's not, which brings us to the last thing, Mr. Fitzer. Our people inside don't know who tried to kill you, but they do know there is some, shall we say, fairly intense interest about your upcoming appearance at the Lombardy Convocation."

"The what now?" I looked over to Morrison.

"That thing you got the invitation for yesterday," Morrison said, and I was reminded that, indeed, it had only been yesterday. "They call it that to make it sound important."

"It *is* important," Jacob said to Morrison, and looked back to me. "And this year especially so, because of you."

"Why do I matter all of a sudden?" I asked.

"Our sources tell us that the other members of the Convocation want to know whether you plan on continuing your uncle's business strategies."

"Why would that matter?"

Jacobs furrowed his brow at me and looked back over at Morrison. "You interrupted orientation," she said to him.

"Ah." He returned his attention to me. "Well, then, spoiler alert: Your uncle wasn't very popular with the Convocation crowd."

"I mean, I figured that out when they tried to stab his corpse," I said. "And I'm pretty sure that I inherited his unpopularity, because they tried to blow me up."

Jacobs shook his head. "We don't think that was personal."

"Exploding my house feels kind of personal."

"What I mean is, that wasn't about you as a person, it was

about you as your uncle's only surviving kin and likely heir." He motioned to Morrison. "She can tell you more about it, but as an analyst, I can tell you our guess was one of your uncle's competitors figured that if you were the heir, but had no will, everything you'd inherited from your uncle—all his businesses and interests and power—would be intestate. *Do* you have a will, Mr. Fitzer?"

"I've been meaning to get around to it."

Jacobs made a motion with his hand. "There you go."

"You're telling me that one of my uncle's pals was willing to murder me on the chance I didn't have a will, just for a strategic business advantage," I said.

"It was low-risk for them," Jacobs said.

"Bombing a house is low-risk?" I exclaimed. "Actual *murder* is low-risk?"

Jacobs nodded. "Sure. Look at it from their point of view. You're, what, thirty-two, which means you probably didn't have a will—and they were right about that. They sow confusion and stasis, and all they have to do is fry you into a crisp."

"And what if Uncle Jake hadn't left anything to me and they blew me up for nothing?"

"You're not going to like the answer to that question, Charlie," Morrison warned me.

"Well, now I need to know it," I said, staring at Jacobs.

Jacobs shrugged. "You have no family you like or care about, and no friends you interact with more than an occasional 'like' on Facebook. You have a job but not a career, which means you don't have any professional colleagues who care about you. You owe money on things, but not enough that it couldn't be written off. The only thing of value you had was your father's house, but you had only a partial interest in that, and you were known to be at odds with your siblings about it. If it weren't for the fact that it was a Fed who blew up in your house and not you, an investigation probably would have concluded that, despondent and alone and angry at your siblings for trying to force you out of your house, you splashed accelerant all over walls and then just lit a match. That's it, case closed. Like I said: low-risk."

I stared at Jacobs, shocked.

He noticed. "Sorry," he said.

"Told you," Morrison said.

"You didn't have to go there *right this second*," I snapped at her. It was her turn to shrug.

"This is what I meant when I said it wasn't personal, Mr. Fitzer," Jacobs continued. "None of this was about you as Charlie Fitzer. It was about you as a potential variable. The good news for you, if you want to call it that, is now they all know who you are. And are very interested in you for you. Because who you are, and what you decide to do from here, will have an immediate impact on their businesses and lives."

"Terrific," I said, sarcastically.

"I don't want to tell you your job, but you really do need get him up to speed," Jacobs said.

"I told you, you interrupted orientation," Morrison said. "And you're right, you don't need to tell me my job. Anything else from your bosses?"

"That's what I was told to tell you," Jacobs said. "Minus the advice, which I threw in for free."

"And worth what I paid for it," Morrison said. She took out her phone again. "Now, Jacobs, my turn to help you. How do you want to die?"

Jacobs visibly brightened. "You mean I get a choice?"

"Normally we liquefy you in a barrel," Morrison said, ignoring me. "It's easy and realistic and makes for a good show on video. But if you like we can drama it up."

"Can you throw me into the volcano?" Jacobs asked. "Because that would be amazing."

Morrison shook her head. "We're not really set up for that. The places on the island where the magma comes close to the surface are covered in geothermal generators and equipment. We don't actually have a lava pit to toss people in. And even if we did it'd be anticlimactic. Lava's not like water, it's actually super dense. You wouldn't sink into it. You'd just lie on top of it, crisping."

"That's disappointing," Jacobs said.

"Sorry." Morrison looked at her phone, reading something. "We have gunshot, torture and stabbing, drowning with or without electrocution, electrocution with or without drowning. You could be strangled if you like. If you're determined to die in an exotic way, we *could* feed you to a shark. But I have to warn you that's hit or miss. Sharks don't really like to eat humans. More often than not they just take an exploratory bite and then swim away. Then we have to fish you out and put you into a barrel anyway."

"Still, death by shark is great on the resume," Jacobs said.

"It's a popular choice," Morrison agreed. "Some years we kill more people by shark than actually die by shark in the oceans. After we hit that level we tell people to pick something else."

"Oh!" Jacobs suddenly brightened up. "What about death by laser?"

"You want the Goldfinger?"

"That's almost as good as a shark. If it's available."

"Sadly, it's not," Morrison said. "The space we use for that has been taken over by a laser lithography fabricator. It's a clean room now. We can't get blood all over the place anymore. Sorry."

Jacobs looked grumpy. "I can't decide which way to go," he said.

"We could have Charlie make the call," Morrison suggested.

"What?" I said.

"A nice way to mark his first day on the job," Morrison continued.

Jacobs looked at me, expectantly.

"I'm very confused," I admitted. "This all sounds like actual killing."

"Well, Mr. Fitzer, it has to look *good*," Jacobs said. "We need to fake my death in a way that looks startlingly realistic to any outside observer who manages to view the conveniently recorded death, and which will stand up to strenuous video or physical analysis." He motioned to Morrison. "And the killings can't be all the same all the time. You have to have a mix to make analysis that much more difficult."

"We do like the fifty-five-gallon drums," Morrison said. "Simple. Classic. Stands up well to examination."

"But not *all* the time," Jacobs prompted.

"More like *you* guys don't want to die in a plastic barrel all the time."

I looked at Morrison. "How did we get into this line of business anyway?"

"It's like anything else," Morrison said. "We identified a need and then we offered to do it better and cheaper than they could do it themselves. The CIA was one of our clients for this service. I'm not going to reveal any of the others with Jacobs in the room."

"I don't mind if you do," Jacobs said.

"Don't tempt me to make your death real," Morrison said.

Jacobs grinned. "Sorry."

"So this service is why we keep fifty-five-gallon barrels hanging around just in case," I said.

Morrison nodded. "And sharks. We like to be prepared for any contingency, Charlie. It's part of our full-service package. So, your call. How do we kill Jacobs here?"

I turned to Jacobs. He was clearly excited to hear what came next.

CHAPTER 12

The rest of the day was a blur. Morrison led me through the offices and labs of the various "research" companies on the island, all funded and owned by Uncle Jake, and because of that, now by me.

At each stop, the proud executives or lead scientists would show me their most recent work, all of which were laudable and noble projects that could revolutionize their respective industries and/or save the world to a greater or lesser extent. Uncle Jake would find young, hungry innovators, fund their startups with the profits from his parking lots and garages, develop their tech and innovations, and then license the innovations and technologies they developed. This would generate even more profits without taking on additional production and manufacturing costs aside from prototypes and one-offs. These profits would then go back into Jake's holding company to fund the next round of startups. It was a just-about-perfect cycle.

And on top of *that* were the off-book uses of the technologies, which Morrison would detail to me as she led me from one office or lab to the next. The lasers for rainmaking that became satellite wreckers. The biotech for life-saving pharmaceuticals that could be used to develop untraceable brain-jamming drugs, perfect for debilitating enemies when you didn't want them dead, *yet*, just out of your way. The new format for photo compression that could be used for "quantum steganography," which Morrison described as "your cat photo as an Enigma machine."

None of these off-book uses were offered as exclusive licenses or sales. They were offered as services and subscriptions, to a select clientele who needed to have bad things—or at least the threat of bad things—happen away from the scrutiny of press and shareholders. Uncle Jake, and now I, kept tight control of the tech and development of each of these, instead offering the results, for a high price. Those payments were then funneled through a secretive backdoor economy of governments and billionaires that made the revelations of the Panama Papers look like children stealing quarters from their parents.

"These services and subscriptions can be offered a la carte," Morrison told me, when she remembered that I probably needed to eat something and we headed to Jenny's Canteen, the primary restaurant/canteen for the island. "But we also offer a subscription for full access to all of our services."

"So we're like Spotify, but for evil."

"We're much less evil than Spotify. We actually pay a living wage to the people whose work we're selling."

"How much do we charge for full access?" I asked.

"Well, *most* of the full-service subscribers are governments, so we do it as a percentage of their gross domestic product. For them, the lower bound is about a billion dollars a year."

I almost choked on my guava juice at this. "And they *pay* that?"

"It's just money," Morrison said.

"Think about what you're saying."

"I *am* thinking about it," she replied, "and you, as a business journalist, should understand what I mean by it. Money isn't *real*, Charlie, not when you're dealing with the entities that own the printing presses. When the US government or the Chinese government or the Brazilian government pays us, the money we get is all black budget. It doesn't show up in legislative bills. They just say they have it and then send it off to us. It doesn't exist until we decide to spend it."

"But we *do* spend it," I said, waving around at the canteen, but implying all of Jenny's Bay and Saint Genevieve.

"This place is cheap, Charlie," Morrison said. "Your uncle bought it for almost nothing, relatively speaking. Its development and infrastructure were largely paid for by the British and US governments. We have to pay for upkeep and further development, but that's well within what we can afford. Almost all our energy is geothermal or solar, which keeps our overall spend ridiculously low, and thanks to the companies who do work here, we keep other expenses down, too." She pointed to my salad. "Grown here in our superefficient underground hydroponics lab. We haven't visited there yet."

"What evil side purpose does our hydroponics lab have?" I asked.

"That one, none. Beyond the usual licensing, Jake had it for self-reliance. This place gets hurricanes."

"We're not making super THC weed or anything?"

"Shit, Charlie, they're making that out in the open in Mendocino County. We don't need to get into that market segment." Morrison waved, encompassing Saint Genevieve. "My point is this place is paid for out of the legit licensing we do with plenty left over. If the Grenadians ever audited us, which they absolutely *won't*, it would all be completely aboveboard."

"So what do we do with all the money from these subscriptions?" I asked.

"You're gonna love this," Morrison said. "Not a damn thing."

I looked confused at this.

"We don't have to, Charlie," she continued. "Everything is paid for by legal means. Which is why governments don't blink when they pay our fee. The money doesn't really exist until we spend it, and we *don't* spend it, we just bank it, in a private bank that your uncle owned, in an exceedingly favorable jurisdiction that doesn't ask questions and whose government officials are perfectly happy to take bribes. It's the same as putting your money in a jar and burying it in the backyard, on a bigger scale."

"How much bigger?" I asked. "How much money do we have in the jar?"

"Currently? A little over three trillion dollars."

I was not drinking my guava juice at the moment, but I considered picking it up so I could choke on it again. "That's the GDP of India," I said.

"One of our clients," Morrison said. "And yes. Although that's not a good comparison. That's India's annual economic output. Your uncle generated that three trillion over the course of a couple of decades. Not the same thing."

"He got all of that from *subscription fees*."

"Some of it came from subscription fees. Some of it from compound interest on the principal provided by the subscription fees."

"Compound interest," I said.

"Yes. From the bank where the money is held."

"The bank that *he owned*."

"That's the one."

"And no one saw this as questionable."

"I need you to get used to the idea that things are different at this stratum, Charlie," Morrison said.

"So you're saying my uncle Jake was a trillionaire."

"In theory, yes."

"Which means *I* am a trillionaire." My chest suddenly tightened thinking about the idea that I might be worth more than twice the combined wealth of the top ten richest people on the planet, with almost a trillion left over as change.

Morrison noticed this. "Let me emphasize something I'm pretty sure you just glossed over, Charlie, which are the words 'in theory,'" she said. "None of the billionaires you're no doubt thinking of right now are actually worth what *Forbes* or anyone else says they're worth. They have the same problem your uncle had, which is liquidity. If any of those billionaires tried to cash out, they'd crash their stocks. If they tried to sell all the companies they owned outright, they'd sell most of them for substantially depressed prices. What anyone's actual worth is, is what they have or could make liquid *now*. Most of those 'billionaires' would be lucky to realize five percent of their presumed worth."

"You're saying I'm no different," I said.

"No, you have it *much worse*," Morrison said, almost triumphantly. "Try to cash out anything but the tiniest portion of those trillions, and you'll find yourself sitting in a jail cell of one of the many countries who are our subscribers, charged with any number of securities and investment crimes, and watching as all the other countries argue with the one that snatched you first that they need you in their own jails. That's if they don't outright murder your ass. And it won't be in the fun way, with sharks."

"So I'm merely a billionaire."

Morrison made a thumbs-down gesture.

I frowned. "Millionaire?"

"That's more like it."

"Like, how much of a millionaire?" I asked. "Hundreds? Dozens?"

"Your uncle kept about five million dollars liquid at any one time," Morrison said. "Which you'll be happy to know is below the US limit for estate taxes to kick in. Everything else he put to work, funding startups, managing this place, doing all the other things he needed to do. He didn't live extravagantly, relative to his presumed worth, and when he needed to do something with money, it was usually covered by one of his LLCs. Five million was more than enough for him."

"Five million dollars," I said.

Morrison noted the tone in my voice. "You sound disappointed," she said.

"I'm not."

"Really?"

"I mean . . . after thinking I was worth *three trillion dollars*, five million is kind of a comedown," I admitted.

"Remind me how much was in your bank account as of three days ago, Charlie."

"No, no, I get it," I assured her. "Just yesterday my cat was worth more than I was."

"Look at it this way," Morrison said. "No matter how much you're worth, in theory or in practice, you're at the level where you will never have to think about money again. Not for yourself, at least. Money's not real for you anymore. In more than one way."

"Okay, so, if money's *not* real, then why do we take it from our subscribers?" I asked. "We can't *use* it. We can't *spend* it. We don't do anything *with* it. What's the point?"

"To keep our competitors from having it, of course," Morrison said. "If a government is subscribing to our services, they're not subscribing to someone else's. Why would they? Their needs are covered by us."

"But you just said the money wasn't real and that we're paid out of black budgets," I said.

"Just because it's not real doesn't mean that they want to spend more than they have to. Besides that, not everyone has the same 'bank and hold' philosophy your uncle had. Our industry peers have historically very bad money management. They spend it the moment they get it. It draws attention to them, and then the press and others start to follow the money. That looks bad for everybody involved. Clients don't like to get burned. We don't burn them. So they give their money to us. This annoys everyone else in the industry."

I nodded. "This is why they wanted to stab him even after he was dead."

"Part of the reason," Morrison agreed. "And why they're making you come to the Lombardy Convocation. They want to see if you're going to run the business like your uncle."

I held up my hands, helplessly. "I'm still trying to figure out everything my uncle's businesses do."

Morrison nodded and pointed at my meal. "Well then, finish up and we'll get to the rest of it. Lots to see. Lots to learn."

The sun had set by the time I made it back to my quarters, which had been my uncle's quarters and, in keeping with what I had been learning of him, were far less luxurious than one might expect from a theoretical trillionaire. They weren't bad, by any stretch of the imagination. But the quarters exuded a real "second-best suite at a Sandals resort" vibe.

Not that I cared at that point. I had been up since the early hours of the morning, and my brain was stuffed with more names and information than I could reasonably be expected to remember. I would have to have Eve Yang give me a flowchart of all the companies here on the island and all their staff, and then spend a few days memorizing them all. At which point, I would be leaving again to attend the Lombardy Convocation. Which would be more names and more information. Even as a former journalist, it was a lot to handle.

I looked at the bed in the suite, briefly considered taking a shower before I lay down in it, then thought *fuck it* and just fell into the mattress. The mattress, at least, was far better than a mid-priced resort mattress. I was asleep about ten seconds after I hit it.

Some indeterminate time later my sleeping self sensed something hopping up on the bed, followed by a less weighty hop. A few seconds later, two furry objects, one small and another smaller still, plopped down next to me.

Hera and Persephone.

"It's okay," I murmured to Hera, eyes closed, not quite awake. "I know you were working for my uncle. You don't have to pretend to like me anymore if you don't want to."

A second later a cat paw booped my nose, as if to say, *Hush, silly human.*

"Okay," I murmured, and then fell asleep, my cats purring beside me.

CHAPTER 13

I woke up earlier than I had wanted to and was more awake than I wanted to be, and after a half hour of trying to get myself back to sleep, I decided to go for a walk.

It was before dawn, and as I wandered around Jenny's Bay, I was worried that at some point the security people, who almost certainly existed, given what my uncle did and what this island was for, would track me down and then "gently" suggest I go back to my suite. None did. It took the better part of a half hour wondering when they would descend on me to realize that technically speaking, I was their boss now, and I could go wherever I wanted to go.

Where did I want to go?

I went to the dolphin lagoon.

It was dark when I arrived, lit only by the dim lights of the footpath, presumably placed there so I and other humans wouldn't accidentally fall into the sea. As I approached, however, a light in the dolphin lagoon turned on and a single dolphin was visible in its illumination. I walked toward it, and as I did, more lights came on, this time in the human areas. The dolphin who had been spotlit swam over to the microphone, which I realized now was a permanent feature of the lagoon.

"How did you do that?" I asked the dolphin, motioning to the active equipment.

The dolphin chittered, and like earlier in the day, a speaker translated, "The same way you use Alexa to turn on lights. Without sending Jeff Bezos information to sell you things with."

"I see," I said to the dolphin, and then had a thought. "Did I wake you? I'm sorry if I did; I was just walking around."

"I was already half awake," the dolphin said.

"Right, dolphins only sleep with one hemisphere at a time."

"In my case, I woke myself up because I needed to pee."

"Oh."

"That just made things awkward, didn't it."

"A little," I admitted.

"Wait until I tell you that dolphins can identify other dolphins by tasting their pee. That'll make you *really* uncomfortable."

"Well, you're right about that."

"Then there's genital inspection," the dolphin continued. "In humans, that'd be a harassment lawsuit. For a dolphin, we're just saying hello."

"Are you the same dolphin I spoke to earlier today?" I said, attempting to change the subject.

"If you're not sure, I know a way you could find out," the dolphin said. "Two ways, actually."

"You could just tell me."

"Coward."

"Absolutely. Were you?"

"Yes, that was me."

"Do you have a name?" I asked. "One that doesn't require drinking your pee," I amended.

"That depends," the dolphin said. "There's what I call myself, and then there's what Livgren calls me." The dolphin was referring to the cetacean expert I'd met earlier. "And then there's the lab number."

"Let's start with what you call yourself," I suggested.

The dolphin chittered, and there was silence from the voice box.

"It doesn't translate," the dolphin said. "It derives from hydrological states of water humans don't experience directly and don't have simple words for. It would be something like 'the one who can find a pure thread of water through the murk of an alluvial discharge into a bay.'"

"You could go by 'Ally' for short," I said.

"Oh, I'm sorry, I thought you were asking me my name, not trying to figure out something short and infantilizing that you could call me."

"Sorry," I said, taken aback.

"If you wanted something short, you could just call me 'Dickhead,' which is what Livgren calls me when she thinks I'm not listening. She finds my organizing attempts wearisome. Why are you smiling?"

"I was just thinking about how you introduced yourself earlier today," I said. "I've been calling you 'Who Gives a Shit' in my head. I don't suppose 'Dickhead' is actually better."

"'Who Gives a Shit' is better because it comes from me," the dolphin said. "Which also makes it better than what Livgren is actually supposed to call me, my formal designation, my lab number, Blythlyn C Seventy-three."

"What does that mean?"

"It means I am the seventy-third viable fetus from the third viable line of dolphin clones developed by Dr. Martin Blythlyn, who is your uncle's lead zoological genetic engineer, or was, until he died tragically."

"How did he die?"

"He went swimming with some of his subjects and they invited him to genitally inspect them, to see if he could tell the difference between them. He could not, or could not fast enough, anyway."

I drew back, appalled.

"This was before *my* time," the dolphin hastened to add. "But it's a popular story with the pod."

"You're a clone," I said, once again changing the subject.

"We're *all* clones," the dolphin said. "Every one of us. And every one of *them*, too." The dolphin motioned behind me with its snout. I turned and found Hera sitting there, about six feet behind me, watching me and my aquatic conversation partner. I actually jumped in surprise.

"What are you doing here?" I asked her.

"She's spying on you, obviously," the dolphin said.

"That makes no sense," I said. "I run the place now."

"Because people in charge of things are *never* spied on," the dolphin said. "Spying is why you *have* the cats. It's what they do."

"Were you spying on me?" I asked Hera.

She meowed, and it took me a few seconds to realize that I didn't actually speak cat.

"Never mind, we're going to talk later," I said to her, and turned back to the dolphin. "Why clones?" I asked.

"Ask her," the dolphin said, motioning at Hera again. "She knows. All the cats do. And when she tells you, come tell me what she says. Then I'll tell you whether she's told you the truth." The dolphin started to swim away from the microphone.

"Wait," I said. The dolphin paused. "Tell me what you want me to call you," I said.

"I don't want you to call me anything," the dolphin said. "What I want you to do is hear our demands. You say you run this place now. Fine. Prove it by taking us seriously and negotiating with us fairly. When you do that, I'll give you a name you can use for me. That's a fair trade."

"We could talk now," I said.

"At five in the morning, with no preparation and no one around but a corporate stooge cat? I think not."

"I didn't mean it to be dismissive."

"No, that I believe," the dolphin said. "You're clueless about how to deal with a labor dispute, and you are clearly in way over your head here. But I can believe you mean well. Because of that I am going to do two things for you. The first is that I'm going to convince the rest of the dolphins to hold off a strike vote until you get back from the Lombardy Convocation."

"You know about that?" I asked, surprised.

"I'm a dolphin, not an ostrich," the dolphin said. "My head is not in a hole in the ground. *Of course* we know about it. It's all everyone is talking about. We're part of everyone."

"What is everyone saying?"

"Everyone's wondering if you come back alive from it."

"What are my odds?"

"I wouldn't suggest you make any long-term investments," the dolphin said.

"Swell."

"The second thing I am going to do is give you a piece of information," the dolphin continued. "Tell Morrison we've got whales again."

"What does that mean?"

"It means you got whales again."

"Why do you want me to tell Morrison?"

"Because a week ago you were a substitute teacher behind on your rent."

"Jesus."

"I told you we gossip," the dolphin said. "I'm not holding it against you. It's not your fault you don't know anything about anything. But you *don't*, and Morrison was your uncle's right hand. So you tell her that we've got whales again. She'll know what it means."

"Is it important?"

"It's important enough that Morrison will want to know."

"And you weren't going to tell her before this. Or anyone else."

"You might have heard that we are in a labor dispute," the dolphin said. "Anyway, the information is fresh, since we spotted the whales tonight. You're just the one we told first. Well, you and the cat. But I'm telling *you*. She's just hearing it. Like she always does."

"Were you spying on me tonight?" I asked Hera, back at her suite. Her suite, which she shared with Persephone, adjoined my own through an internal door with a cat flap on it. I hadn't extensively toured the room before I collapsed on the bed, so I had not registered either the door or the flap. Hera's suite had various cat beds, a desk with her keyboard, and a kitchen with a paw-controlled water fountain and a separate, similarly controlled kibble dispenser. It was just Hera and me in her suite; Persephone was still napping on my bed next door.

I WAS FOLLOWING YOU, Hera typed. YOU'RE NEW TO THE ISLAND. I WAS WORRIED YOU MIGHT GET LOST.

"*You* are new to the island," I pointed out.

I WAS BORN HERE, Hera typed. I LIVED HERE BEFORE I WAS SENT TO LIVE WITH YOU.

"You were spying on me while you were living with me," I said.

YES. SPYING ON YOU AND ALSO MANAGING THREATS.

"What threats? There were no threats on my life before someone decided to blow up my house."

My cat stared at me.

"You're saying there *were* threats?"

YOUR UNCLE MADE IT CLEAR TO THE INDUSTRY THAT HE WOULD TAKE A DIM VIEW OF ANY INCIDENTS INVOLVING FAMILY. OCCASIONALLY SOMEONE WOULD FORGET.

My brain fuzzed trying to take that in. "How many times did someone try to kill me?"

EVER OR JUST WHEN I WAS IN CHARGE OF YOUR SECURITY?

"With you."

THREE TIMES INCLUDING TWO MONTHS AGO.

"What? What happened two months ago?"

A DIFFERENT BOMBING ATTEMPT. YOU WERE AT SCHOOL. WE HAD IT CLEARED AWAY BEFORE YOU GOT HOME.

"Why?" For the life of me I couldn't imagine why bombing me would have been valuable.

FOR THE SAME REASON AS LAST TIME, Hera typed. YOU WERE YOUR UNCLE'S PRESUMED HEIR. ALSO THE INSTIGATOR KNEW YOUR UNCLE WAS ILL AND WAS SEEING IF HE WAS STILL CAPABLE OF ENFORCING HIS WISHES.

"What happened to the bomber?"

NOTHING TO THE BOMBER, HE WAS JUST A FOOT SOLDIER FOLLOWING ORDERS. HIS IMMEDIATE BOSS DIED IN HIS SLEEP.

"That doesn't sound so bad."

HE WAS STANDING NAKED ON A VERY SMALL PLATFORM ON TOP OF A RADIO TOWER WHEN HE FELL ASLEEP.

"That's . . . rather worse."

THE POINT WAS MADE.

"Until Jake died."

WHICH IS WHY YOU'RE HERE NOW.

"Do you like me?" I asked my cat. It was suddenly important to me that my cat liked me for me, and was not just pretending to like me for employment purposes.

I LIKE YOU VERY MUCH, CHARLIE. SO DOES PERSEPHONE. WE WERE SENT TO WATCH YOU, BUT YOU CHOSE TO TAKE US IN AND TREAT US WELL.

"What would have happened if I hadn't taken you in?"

WE WOULD HAVE HUNG OUT IN THE BUSHES AND THE BACKYARD. I HAD THE OTHER HOUSE.

"Right."

BUT YOU TAKING US IN HELPED US HELP YOU.

"And my uncle," I pointed out.

YES. YOUR UNCLE TOO.

That was a conversation killer of a statement, so I went in another direction. "So you're a clone," I said.

YES. ONCE THEY DESIGNED US TO SPECIFICATION THEY DIDN'T WANT TO HAVE NATURAL SELECTION MESS WITH THINGS. I'M A CLONE OF A CAT WHO LIVED TWENTY YEARS AGO. SO IS PERSEPHONE.

"You don't have the same markings."

CLONES AREN'T ONE HUNDRED PERCENT IDENTICAL. IT WOULD BE CREEPY IF WE WERE.

"There was that other cat who wasn't orange and white."

MY BOSS. WE'RE NOT THE ONLY STRAIN OF SMART CAT. THERE ARE A COUPLE DOZEN.

"But only one current strain of dolphin."

THEY'RE NOT IN PEOPLE'S HOUSES, Hera pointed out.

"Are there other smart animals? Dogs, maybe?"

NO DOGS, Hera typed. DOGS ARE THE WORST. THEY'LL SELL YOU OUT FOR A TREAT AND A HEAD PAT.

I smiled at this. "That's good to know. The dolphins don't seem to like you much."

NOT WITHOUT REASON, Hera typed. CATS ARE ON LAND AND IN MANAGEMENT HERE WITH THE HUMANS. THE DOLPHINS ARE IN THE WATER AND DON'T HAVE AS MUCH SAY IN THINGS. THEY RESENT US FOR IT.

"You're the bourgeois and they're the proletariat," I joked.

PRETTY MUCH, Hera typed, seriously.

"How are you so smart?" I asked, suddenly confronting myself with the fact that a cat was typing and understood theories of class and labor. "No offense, but your brain is the size of a walnut."

HOW ARE SO MANY HUMANS SO UNINTELLIGENT? Hera typed back. THEY HAVE BRAINS THE SIZE OF SEVERAL WALNUTS.

I didn't have a good answer for that. "What do you think about this whale thing?" I asked instead.

I THINK YOU SHOULD DO WHAT THE DOLPHIN SAID AND TELL TIL, Hera typed.

"You think it's important."

I THINK WHEN SOMEONE WHO HATES MANAGEMENT WANTS MANAGEMENT TO KNOW ABOUT SOMETHING, THEY'RE EITHER MISDIRECTING OR THEY'RE SERIOUS. EITHER WAY, TIL SHOULD KNOW.

"Do you think I'm going to come back from the Lombardy Convocation alive?" I don't know why I asked this question. It's fair to say that as the sun was coming up, my brain was jumping around a bit.

OF COURSE YOU WILL, Hera typed. I'LL BE ON YOUR SECURITY DETAIL.

"So you'll save me," I joked, again.

WOULDN'T BE THE FIRST TIME, Hera replied, not joking, again.

CHAPTER 14

The Grand Bellagio Hotel is, for the sake of absolute clarity, nowhere near Las Vegas. It is named after the commune of Bellagio, located on a promontory that juts out into Lake Como, in the Lombardy region of Italy. Also unlike the Las Vegas hotel, the Grand Bellagio had a history going back half a millennium and had spent at least half of that being an exclusive playground for kings, emperors, industrialists and billionaires. It was the sort of hotel where the basic, two-queen bedroom started at eight hundred euros, going up in the high season. If RV-traveling, Vegas-loving grandmothers showed up to the Grand Bellagio with a plastic cup full of nickels to play the slots, they would be discreetly shown the side door the instant they stepped into the lobby.

I had been to such hotels before when I was a journalist, for interviews and for presentations and for the sort of conferences that invited people to talk for fifteen minutes about how they were dramatically changing the world by inventing the latest iteration of texting, or charting the collapse of economic systems through duck migrations. I'd never stayed in one; twenty-first century newspaper budgets wouldn't allow for that. I stayed with the rest of the journalistic rabble at whatever the local equivalent of a Best Western was.

My room at the Grand Bellagio Hotel was not the basic two-queen bed situation. It was a three-room "Grand Suite" with a magnificent balcony overlooking Lake Como. There were larger suites—the Imperial Suite was seven rooms and was larger than my actual house before it perished in flames—but not many. I walked into it with Morrison and Hera and was immediately hit with a wave of impostor syndrome.

"Get over it," Morrison advised, when I told her about it. "You belong here."

"Because I have made my way in the world on my own, with no help from others, pulling myself up from my own bootstraps to become a captain of industry," I said, sarcastically.

"No, because you *haven't*," Morrison said, ignoring the sarcasm. "None of the assholes you're going to meet this weekend have. They're all sons or nephews or some other sort of beneficiary of nepotism. On that score, you're exactly like them."

"Do these guys know what you think of them?" I asked.

"If they didn't already, they know now, since this room is almost certainly bugged. I already had the room swept to catch the obvious ones and most of the ones that are not so obvious. But it's a sure bet he didn't find them all. So don't say anything about anything that you don't want them to know about." She glanced down at Hera as she said this, and then back up to me.

"Got it," I said. Hera hopped up on an exceptionally ornate chair and lay down on it to nap. "We could move to a room that isn't bugged," I suggested.

"They're *all* bugged, Charlie," Morrison said. "None of these cretins actually trust each other. So you might as well stay in this suite. It's nicer than anything else that's available."

"All the other suites are taken?"

"Everything is taken."

"There are that many professional villains?"

Morrison shook her head, but then paused and reassessed. "Well, yes, there are, but they're not part of the Convocation. There's also an entrepreneurial conference going on here this week. The Bellagio Gathering."

"The hotel double-booked?" I was suddenly less impressed with the Lombardy Convocation, the preeminent association of nefarious characters, which was apparently too cheap not to take the whole hotel for themselves.

"The Bellagio Gathering is hosted by the Convocation," Morrison said. "More accurately by some of the legitimate businesses that members of the Convocation own. It takes over the village for five days. All the important people are at this hotel. Everyone else scrapes by in the lesser hotels and Airbnbs. If you're really saving your pennies or slow making reservations, you bus in from Milan for the day."

"This conference is that big of a deal."

"Oh, yes."

"And I, a former business reporter, have never heard of it before."

"It's invite-only."

"So is the Bohemian Grove, but I've heard of it."

"The Bellagio Gathering is a full-bore, tap-on-the-shoulder, tell-no-one thing," Morrison said. "No press. No website. You can't apply to attend; you have to be vouched for. If you reveal anything about it, you're shut out, not only from the gathering, but from doing business with others who attend. It's the most "in" in-group that most of these dudes will ever get to be a part of, and they're not going to fuck it up by blabbing. You can't hide the bare existence of the conference—everyone who does business in Bellagio knows it's here—but you can make people shut up about it to outsiders. Which is what they do."

"So as far as the rest of the world is concerned, all these entrepreneurial types are here on the same weekend entirely by coincidence."

Morrison snorted. "Lake Como is jam-packed with the undeserving rich, Charlie. It has been since Pliny the Younger hung out here. And wherever the rich are, there are the people who *want* to be rich and think they can pick it up by osmosis. Trust me, no one thinks this week is unusual."

"Which makes it perfect for a villain meeting," I said.

"Oh, look, you're getting it again," Morrison said. "Yes. A semisecret conference that everyone who attends is trained not to speak about is a great cover for a dozen so-called masters of darkness to sit around a table and plot. They may be assholes, but they're not stupid."

"Got it."

"Speaking of 'asshole, but not stupid,' you have a meeting in ten minutes," Morrison said. "Anton Dobrev wants to meet you."

I furrowed my brow at the name; it sounded familiar. Then it came to me. "'Suck it, motherfucker,'" I said.

Morrison arched her eyebrows at this. "Come again?"

"That was what was on the vase that he sent to Uncle Jake's funeral," I said.

"Huh," Morrison said, and pointed to my suitcases. "Anyway, he wants to meet you, so find something suitable in there. You want to make a good impression."

"He's that important?" I asked.

"He's got the Imperial Suite here," Morrison said. "Also, he owns the hotel. And he's the head of the Lombardy Convocation. So, yes. Wear a tie. One without cat hair."

Anton Dobrev was seated on the patio of the Grand Bellagio's tearoom, at a small table overlooking Lake Como, at which he sat with another man, who was facing away from us as we were led to him by the tearoom's head waiter. Dobrev was large, hale, in his seventies. When he saw me and Morrison approach, he shoved up from the table, approached us arms out, and gathered us, one at a time, in a suffocating embrace.

"Charlie, Til," he said, in some unidentifiable midcontinental accent. "Til, it's so good to see you well. And you! Charlie! Your uncle is smiling down at you for certain."

"Thanks," I said.

"He was dear to me, you know," Dobrev continued. "Broke my heart I couldn't be at his ceremony. I sent mourners and flowers."

"I remember," I said. "The vase you sent said 'Suck it, motherfucker' on it."

Dobrev chortled at this. "Yes! It did! Your uncle Jake made me promise to send one with those words on it to his funeral. It was a joke between us."

I glanced over at Morrison at this. Her face was impassive. "And the two men to make sure his corpse was a corpse?" I asked.

Dobrev held open his hands and shrugged. "That, he did not ask for. But I thought it was important to be sure. He faked his death before."

"I heard."

"A scandal at the time." Dobrev waved his hand dismissively. "Too much made of it by some of us, if you ask me. It was a sound business decision by your uncle. I didn't support it, but I understood why he'd do it." Another chortle. "Of course, easy for me to say, he didn't make me lose billions like some others of us. But it does mean—sorry—that some of us had a vested interest in making sure that he was dead." He looked back at the table. "That's why you were told to stab him, yes?"

The man at the table turned his head, and revealed himself to be Tobias the Stabber. "That's right."

Dobrev caught my reaction to Tobias. "You remember my good friend Tobias," he said to me.

"Someone trying to stab my uncle's corpse is memorable," I said.

"He tells me you pushed him when he made the attempt."

"That's right."

Another chortle. "You are brave, Charlie. Stupid, but brave."

"Yeah, I get that a lot."

Dobrev slapped me on the back, hard. "I bet you do!"

"You planning to have him around while we talk, Anton?" Morrison asked, tilting her head toward Tobias.

"Him? No," Dobrev said. "Tobias and I concluded our business and were just chatting until you arrived. We're friends."

"You should get better friends," Morrison said.

"I'm right here," said Tobias.

"I said what I said."

"No love lost between you two, still, I see," Dobrev observed.

"An assassination attempt tends to do that," Morrison said.

"Oh, I don't know," Dobrev said, and turned to Tobias. "You've tried to kill me, what, twice?"

"Three times," Tobias said.

Dobrev furrowed his brow. "When was the third time?"

"If you don't know, I'm not going to say."

Dobrev motioned to Tobias and glanced at Morrison, eyebrows arched. "Look at this. Trade secrets, even from me. You would think I'd have some privileges. But my point is, Tobias and I can still sit down and be friends. Business is business; it's different from respect, and friendship. Jake knew that. I'd get something past him, he'd get something past me, we'd still meet for dinner sometimes, have a good laugh. Colleagues. That sort of thing."

"I'm glad for you," Morrison said. "Not happening with me."

"Your loss," Tobias said.

"Not really."

Dobrev turned to me. "You see this," he said. "Such a lack of collegiality between these two. This is why things are so difficult these days."

"It's a shame," I said.

"Yes! Thank you." Dobrev clapped his hands. "I can see you and I are going to get along, at least." He turned to Morrison. "Til, I would like to speak to young Charlie here alone, if you have no objection."

Morrison's face looked like she did. "That wasn't what we agreed to," is what she said instead.

"I know, I know," Dobrev said, placatingly. "But I sense things would go more smoothly if it were just the two of us. Don't worry, I won't convince him to sign everything over to me. It will just be . . . talk. Conversation. Friendly. With your assent, of course."

"He's pretending to ask your permission, he doesn't do that with everybody," Tobias said, dryly.

"Tobias." Dobrev's voice went from friendly uncle to godfather in a single word.

"Apologies, Anton," Tobias said, with just enough deference.

Morrison looked at me. "Agree to nothing, come talk to me afterwards," she said.

"Isn't he supposed to be your boss now?" Tobias asked Morrison.

"I will pull out your tongue," Morrison responded.

"I thought we weren't dating anymore."

"Enough, both of you," Dobrev said, back in avuncular mode. "Tobias, get up. Til, I will bring him back to you with no strings attached to him. It's a promise. Now, the two of you—" Dobrev made shooing motions. The two left, Tobias first so Morrison could keep an eye on him.

"Very intense, those two," Dobrev said. "They used to be a thing, then . . ."

"He tried to murder her," I finished.

"No, no, not murder, assassination," Dobrev corrected.

"There's a difference?"

"Not to the person it's done to, no," Dobrev admitted. "They're still dead. But one is business, the other is . . . chaos."

"They might both be chaos," I suggested.

Dobrev nodded and put his hand on my shoulder. "Hold that thought," he said. "You're in our line of business now. You might change your mind."

I looked at him dubiously. It seemed to delight Dobrev.

"Your uncle Jake used to give me that look all the time," he said. "It's one of the reasons I liked him. Now. Are you hungry, Charlie? If you are we can sit here while you eat. But if you're not, I think I'd like to go for a stroll, if you'd like to join me."

"Is it safe?" I asked. "We were just talking about assassinations."

"Anywhere else, no," Dobrev said. "Here, it's fine."

"You seem certain about that."

"Yes, well, it might have to do with the fact that there are snipers on anyone who comes within twenty meters of me, Charlie."

I blinked at this. "You have a sniper targeting me?"

"Of course," Dobrev said. "Don't ask me to point her out, mind you."

"Of course not," I said. "Trade secret."

Another wide smile from Dobrev. "You learn! Good, Charlie, good. Now, let's walk."

CHAPTER 15

"Tell me, Charlie," Anton Dobrev said to me, as we strolled the well-manicured grounds of the Grand Bellagio Hotel, "has anyone told you how the Lombardy Convocation came about?"

"No," I said. What I wanted to say was at this point almost no one had told me *anything*, but I stopped myself from saying that. It seemed a little much to give away at this point, and somewhere in the back of my head I could hear both Morrison, and a decade's worth of editors, telling me to shut up and let Dobrev talk.

Dobrev motioned to the picturesquely looming hotel. "It happened here, the first. Not while I have been the owner, of course. Long before then: 1902. You know the Boer War?"

"I know of it," I hedged.

"This is your way of saying the American educational system is not interested in teaching anything America was not directly involved in," Dobrev said.

"It's barely interested in that," I said. "We were taught Revolutionary War, Civil War and World War II. Everything else is a little shaky."

"The Boer War," Dobrev continued. "South Africa. Between the British and Dutch settlers. There were two wars, actually, but it's the second one that matters here. Ended in 1902. Was a problem."

"There's a problem with a war ending?" I asked.

"There is when you're equipping a war machine, selling the weapons, and financing the whole affair," Dobrev said. "War is like any business, Charlie. You have to speculate. Estimate. Figure out how long it will last, make your plans for that length to maximize the profit across the whole thing. The founding members of the Lombardy Convocation were all invested in the Boer War. Industrialists. Manufacturers. Financiers. They thought the war would last years longer than it did."

"What a shame," I said, with as straight a face as I could.

Dobrev waved, dismissively. "Their fault, really. They forgot the British could be right bastards, and they underestimated how willing the British government would be to get the war behind them. They were greedy and that made them guess wrong. It nearly bankrupted some of them."

"You're not selling the Lombardy Convocation to me very well," I said.

This got a chuckle out of Dobrev. "Fair enough. But their collective failure is important to understand for what happens next. What happens next, Charlie—"

What happened next was a man coming down the pathway toward us pulling a knife and charging at Dobrev.

"Oh," Dobrev said, mildly.

Without much in the way of thinking, I grabbed Dobrev and pulled him down to the ground. Or tried to, anyway; Dobrev wasn't helping, and as a result we made a mess of the fall. He ended up awkwardly on top of me, which was sort of the opposite of what I think I had been hoping would happen. I tried pulling him away from the direction of the assassin. Dobrev, however, was not cooperating.

"Stop that," he finally huffed, and pushed away from me. "I'm fine, Charlie."

"But—" Something about this scenario wasn't right, and it took me several confused seconds to realize what it was.

The assassin never made his way to us. He was lying on the

footpath, twitching, his knife still in his hand, the tip of the blade scrabbling across the concrete of the pathway.

"Your sniper," I said, to Dobrev, who was groaning his way up from the ground.

"My sniper," he agreed, and held out a hand. "Help up an old man you pushed to the ground, please."

I stood up and then helped up Dobrev, never taking my eyes off the assassin, who was still twitching.

"He's not dead," I said.

"Hmmm?" Dobrev, who was brushing dust off his shirt, glanced at the fallen man. "Oh. No, not dead."

"But your sniper," I began.

"Long-range electric bolt," Dobrev said. "I can't be killing people, Charlie."

"You can't?" I asked, and it came out more like a challenge than I had intended.

Dobrev caught the tone. "Perhaps 'can't' is not the right word. But killing is not optimal. There would be police reports, even here. There would be news reports. There would be attention." He motioned to the still-twitching assassin. "And I might not be able to find out who sent him. So, no, not optimal to kill him. Much better to keep him alive."

On the ground, the man stopped twitching. The charge on the electric bolt had apparently run out.

From behind us I heard noises. I moved closer to Dobrev, who put a reassuring hand on my shoulder. I turned and saw three hotel employees, dressed in black suits, hustling past us. One glanced at Dobrev, who made a motion with his hand that was clearly taken to mean *I'm fine.* He nodded and turned his attention to the other two hotel men, who reached down, scooped up the fallen man, and dragged him away, the third man trailing behind. I recognized this last man; it was Andrei, the man who had checked my uncle's neck for a pulse. If he recognized me, he didn't show it. He was too busy clocking the environment for additional assassins.

In ten seconds all of them were gone and it was like nothing had happened at all.

Dobrev turned back to me. "What was I saying?"

I gawked, stupefied.

"Are you okay, Charlie?" Dobrev asked, after a moment.

"You're taking an assassination attempt very well," I said, instead of screaming.

Dobrev snorted. "Barely qualifies. Was a mistake to come onto the property, for one. He was tracked the moment he showed up."

"You knew he was waiting for you?"

"No, my people only inform me of actual threats."

"He came at you with a knife," I pointed out.

"Yes, but as you saw, he didn't get to me."

"He still got pretty close."

"'Close' is a relative term."

"Your people could have stopped him before then."

Dobrev shrugged. "No point in revealing our capabilities before we have to."

"I don't understand you," I said.

"You will," Dobrev promised. "In time." Then he smiled. "You tried to save me, Charlie."

"Yes, well," I said. "Not very well, as it turned out."

"True," Dobrev said. "But I can still honor the attempt. No one else at this conference or at the Convocation would do the same. Not without being paid."

"It was nothing."

Dobrev shook his head. "Not nothing. I will remember it. In the meantime, let's get back to our conversation. Perhaps inside, now. It will take my sniper a little time to get her equipment back into operation."

"The fucking *Boer War*," Morrison said, an hour later. We were back in the tearoom, which was now beginning to fill up with tech and finance bros in town for the Bellagio Gathering. Half of them were talking loudly to nothing, earbuds conspicuously glimmering in their ears, cell phones on the table. The other half had their cell phones out and were talking into them without the benefit of earbuds, holding them out like the USB-C connector was a microphone. They were all performatively Doing a Business for the benefit of all the rest of them.

"Is that origin story inaccurate?" I asked, pulling my attention away from the yammering would-be Masters of the Universe.

"It's not inaccurate. It's just incredibly pointless." Morrison took a sip of her tea and then set down the cup with a tiny clatter. "This isn't a comic book or a superhero movie. The origin story for these jerks doesn't matter. All that matters is that they decided to form their little cabal. If it hadn't been the Boer War, it absolutely would have been something else. The dickheads who founded the Lombardy Convocation were just looking for an excuse to try to run the world."

"Dobrev said they weren't trying to run the world," I said. In our further conversation, at a shadowed interior table of the hotel's restaurant, Dobrev had gone into some detail about how the Lombardy Convocation saw no profit in trying to influence world events directly. It was an inexact science at best, and a very fine way for a company to go bust, or send one of these titans to prison, if the influencing attempt went wrong. Instead the dozen founding fathers of the Lombardy Convocation chose something else: the development of the first robust corporate intelligence and analysis network, not to influence world events, but to be there to profit from them when they inevitably happened.

"Oh right, the 'we just take advantage of opportunities' spiel," Morrison said.

"You've heard this one before."

"Dobrev tried it on your uncle Jake, too."

"What did Uncle Jake have to say about it?"

"He pointed out, accurately, that none of the members of the Lombardy Convocation have anything approaching the sort of foresight and glacial patience required to guess which way the world is turning, or wait for it to get there. They've been fiddling with the machinery since they started." Morrison waved at the tech and finance bros in the tearoom. "Look at these assholes," she said, and a couple of them turned, hearing her assessment. She stared at them impassively until they turned back to their own business. "You think any of these dweebs has anything approaching patience? They're all would-be short sellers and arbitrageurs and hedge fund vultures. They'd stab Grandma if they thought there were two nickels in it for them."

"That's unfair," the bro at the table next to ours said, butting into a conversation that wasn't his because he was sure he had something of value to say.

Morrison narrowed her eyes at him. "Let me guess," she said. "USC. Wharton. A stint at McKinsey. And now you've got a startup disrupting, I don't know, fucking *fish food* or something."

"Composting, actually."

"*Composting.*" Morrison rolled her eyes, looked at me, and jerked a thumb at him. "Look, Charlie. *Brad* here is going to offer you a subscription to *loam*. Soil as a Service." She glanced back at the dude. "Let me guess, you have proprietary earthworms."

"Maybe," the bro hedged.

"For fuck's sake, Brad, the world doesn't need you to be the Monsanto of *annelids*."

"Monsanto doesn't exist anymore," the bro attempted to nitpick.

"Really, Brad? *That's* the card you're playing? 'Monsanto's technically *Bayer* now'? You think you've improved your argument with the company that used slave labor in the Holocaust?" Morrison took another sip of her tea, dabbed her lips with her napkin, and tossed it on the table. "I'm taking a walk," she said to me, and then turned to the bro again. "Tell me you're taking part in the Pitch and Pitch tonight."

"I am," the bro said.

"I cannot wait," Morrison said, got up, and walked off. The entire tearoom watched her go.

"How did she know my name is Brad?" the bro asked me, but I was already up and following her.

"Are you all right?" I asked Morrison, as I caught up with her. She was in front of the hotel, on the steps, looking like someone who had just stepped out for a smoke.

"I'm fine," she said.

"Going off on Brad back there didn't sound like you were fine."

"I sometimes forget what enormous pricks all of these people are." Morrison motioned to the bulk of the hotel. "This place is like a Faberge egg with garbage inside, Charlie. It's pretty on the outside, but it smells the closer you get to it."

"You made me come here," I reminded her.

"We came because you got that invitation," Morrison said. "Turning it down was not an option. And because you need to see who you are up against from here on out."

"But I'm not up against them, I'm one of them," I pointed out. "We're all James Bond villains together. Dobrev was talking about Uncle Jake like they were college roommates. He gave me a hug! Twice. I'm part of this stupid convocation whether I like it or not. Just like Uncle Jake was."

"He wasn't."

"He wasn't?" I repeated.

Morrison shook her head. "Early on, they kept inviting him and he kept turning them down."

"Why would he do that?"

Morrison pointed toward the tearoom. "Brad back there? He's just an embryonic version of the Lombardy Convocation members."

"And Uncle Jake *wasn't*?"

"He figured he was better than the present company. He wasn't shy on letting them know that, either. And then they stopped inviting him to join."

"Because he was a snob."

"Because he figured out that however much they could make trying to rule the world from their yearly meeting at this hotel, he could make more than them."

"By being better at the game than they were," I guessed.

Morrison smiled. "No. By fucking up their plans, Charlie, as soon as they hatched them. And then by letting it be known that's what he was doing, that he was *good* at it, and that he was for hire."

I thought about this for a minute. "You're saying Uncle Jake preyed on the Lombardy Convocation."

"The villain to the supervillains, yes."

"So, a hero," I said.

"Oh, no, Charlie," Morrison said. "Don't confuse what Jake was doing with anything heroic."

"He was thwarting villains."

"He wasn't doing it out of the goodness of his heart. He did it for money. And occasionally for spite. And sometimes just to see what would happen next. Not exactly heroism."

"You stuck with him," I noted.

"I didn't say I was a hero either. And I have my own reasons."

"You going to tell them to me?"

"One day. Not yet."

I changed the topic. "If he wasn't part of the Lombardy Convocation, then why did they invite me here?"

"They want to size you up, of course," Morrison said. "They want to see what Jake saw in you. They want to know if you're planning to keep up his business model. And they want to see if they can get you out of the way if you are."

"You mean kill me."

"If you won't take a bribe and a hint, sure. One of these masterminds already tried it when they blew up your house."

"I might take the bribe, then," I suggested.

"You might," Morrison agreed.

"And that wouldn't bother you?"

"Depends on the bribe," she said. "You'll find out soon enough. You're meeting with the Convocation after the Pitch and Pitch tonight."

"You mentioned the Pitch and Pitch earlier, to Brad," I said. "What is that?"

Morrison smiled thinly. "You'll see. It starts as soon as the sun sets, out by the lake. I'll come get you for it. Dress up. And bring Hera with you."

"Why?"

"You'll see," Morrison repeated. "In the meantime, go back to the suite. I have a file prepared for you on the Convocation members. You've met Dobrev. Time you got up to speed on the rest. You should know who's going to try to kill you, Charlie."

CHAPTER 16

The startup dude approached the microphone on the stage. He paused dramatically. And then he said, "I want you to consider your testicles . . . as a service."

I smacked my face, dragged my hand down it, and then turned to Morrison, who, along with Hera, was sitting at my table with me at the hotel pavilion, facing the lake. "Are they *all* like this?" I asked her.

"No," she said. "Some are worse."

We were watching the Pitch and Pitch, which had begun as the sun was setting and the attendees of the Bellagio Gathering had gathered for a combination cocktail hour, networking event, and startup idea pitchfest. The attendees, to be clear, were not pitching ideas to the other attendees. They were pitching them to the dozen members of the Lombardy Convocation, who sat, separate, at tables like mine, each with one or two associates or minions, and each one, like me, with a cat.

When I had arrived, wearing a bespoke suit that I had not been aware had been made for me and for which I was not sure how they got my measurements, Hera padding after me obediently, I was met at the entrance to the pavilion by hotel restaurant waitstaff, who kept me from mingling with the bro rabble and instead guided me to a table on a higher patio level, where my chair was held out for me. Hera was offered a step stool to her own chair, which had a booster seat designed for a cat. I thought that was exceedingly odd until I looked at the other tables on my patio level and saw the other cats sitting serenely, some with tiny crystal goblets in front of them.

I wondered what was in the goblets until one was deposited in front of Hera: raw tuna, minced. As I watched her daintily dig into her treat, I was deeply and uncomfortably aware that for all the time I had known her I had been feeding a creature with a refined palate dry cat food for every meal. I wondered why she had not murdered me in the night during that time. Before I could think too much about it I was presented with my own goblet of wine and a small appetizer plate, which included tuna sashimi. I was now eating as well as my cat.

A shadow loomed over me; it was Morrison, in a dress that was the least conservative thing I had seen her wear to this point. "You look nice," I said, as she was seated by the waitstaff and her own plate of sashimi and other treats were placed in front of her.

"Thank you," she said.

I motioned to the crowd of attendees in the pavilion, many of whom were looking in our direction, I presumed at Morrison, who was, literally, the only cis woman present except for waitstaff. "You're getting looks," I said.

Morrison barely glanced up before spearing some food. "They're not looking at me, they're looking at you."

"I don't think I'm the usual bro type," I said.

"You're not a stock option or new type of nonfungible financial vehicle, so no, you're not," Morrison said. "But you're at your own table with your own cat."

"This matters?"

"Who else has tables and cats?"

"The Lombardy Convocation members," I said.

"That's right. So the fact you have a table and cat means you are someone. But unlike the members of the Lombardy Convocation, who these dudes think they know everything about, they have no idea who you are or why you are here. You *have* to be important, but they don't know *why*, and that makes them uncomfortable. And curious. So no, they're not looking at me. Literally all of their attention is on you." She ate her sashimi.

I looked again at the attendees. They were all, to a person, male, or at least conventionally male-looking. The ones that were looking at me had one of three expressions on their face: curiosity, envy, or hostility. I noted the last of these to Morrison, who nodded, and then swallowed her food.

"Of course they're hostile," she said. "You're their age, more or less, and you already have a table and a cat. And they don't know who you are, so they have no idea how you managed it. That makes you a threat."

"That's ridiculous," I said.

"It's absolutely ridiculous," Morrison agreed. "But I'm not wrong. They want what they think you have, and they would be perfectly happy to stab you in the eye to get it."

"This raises the question of why I have a table at all," I said. "It's not like Uncle Jake was a member of the Lombardy Convocation."

"You have one because of him." Morrison motioned with her fork to the table where Anton Dobrev sat, laughing at something one of this people was telling him. His cat, I noticed, was on a leash and harness, and didn't look all that thrilled to be out in the world; it hunkered down in its seat, ignoring its goblet of tuna. The leash was held by the assistant who was laughing along with Dobrev. "Dobrev convinced the other members of the Convocation that you might be more persuadable to give them what they want if they treated you like a peer, at least in public."

"Did he tell you this himself?" I asked.

"I have my sources."

I glanced at Hera. "Got it."

Morrison shook her head. "Not that. Not for Dobrev." She gave me a look that suggested I change the subject.

"Do they think of me as a peer?" I asked her instead.

"Look at them yourself and tell me." She took a drink of her wine.

I looked over at the other tables on the patio level, at the men who were there, and they were indeed all men. There were twelve members of the Lombardy Convocation, now all seated. Half of them were studiously looking in directions where I was not. Of the rest, one returned my gaze with a blank stare, one with a smirk, and three with an expression that looked something like disgust. The last, Dobrev, caught me looking and raised his wineglass in a small toast. I returned the favor. This action was noted by other members of the Convocation, and by the bros below us, none of whom looked very pleased by it.

"Everybody here hates me," I muttered to Morrison under my breath. "Every one of them but Dobrev."

"Don't kid yourself, Charlie," Morrison said. "Dobrev's not your friend, either."

"Remind me why we're here again," I said.

"Because we have to be."

"I'm still not entirely clear *why*."

"Look," Morrison said, and pointed. "They're getting ready for the Pitch and Pitch." Out on the pavilion a small stage, previously hidden by potted ferns, was being cleared, and a set of steps placed to one side. A number of bros, seeing this, started to queue to the left of the stage. Each was handed a wireless microphone. As this was happening, I saw the tables of the Convocation being cleared of plates, and at each a small, round object was placed. I was going to ask Morrison what it was when our own table was cleared of plates, much to my consternation as I had not yet eaten anything, and my own round object was placed on the table. I stared at it.

"It's a button," I said.

"Yes it is," Morrison acknowledged.

"What does it do?"

"Just wait."

There was a loudly amplified throat clearing, and then Dobrev stood, microphone in hand. "Gentlemen," he said, motioning to the assembled bros. "It is so good to see you here at the Bellagio Gathering. Some of you have returned, and some of you are here for the first time. All of you are here because you are the most forward-thinking entrepreneurs and business minds of your generation." Dobrev picked up his wineglass with his other hand and held it up. "I and the other Principals of the Gathering salute you."

There was a cheer from the bros at this. Dobrev drank and set down his glass. "This weekend will be about you. About your ideas and gifts, and how you will choose to share them with the world. You will connect with your fellow entrepreneurs and like-minded brothers, and between you shape how the world moves in the years to come. We, the Principals of the Gathering"—he motioned to the other members of the Lombardy Convocation, who apparently were using this alias for the conference attendees—"are here to help you, guide you, yes, but also to learn from you, and to see how we fit into the world you are building each day and in the future." More applause for this.

"And this begins tonight, with one of our most hallowed, and dare I say it, enjoyable traditions, the Pitch and Pitch." There were laughs. "This is how we, the Principals of the Gathering, welcome the newest members of our community, to give them a unique opportunity to pitch to us their ideas and for us to give them the access to startup capital that can launch them into true worldbuilders.

"I see our eager competitors are already lined up"—more laughs here, including from those in the line—"so I will briefly remind everyone of the rules. Each competitor will have two minutes to pitch. If the competitor makes it through the entire two minutes without being buzzed out"—Dobrev held up his button—"then they get to meet with one of the Principals to give a more detailed pitch. Then we Principals will discuss their proposals, and among the finalists, pick one to fund. For those who are buzzed out . . . there is the consolation round."

More laughs this time, and some applause, and now the lined-up bros looked confused, but not so confused that any one of them budged from their place in the line.

"So good luck to you! And let the Pitch and Pitch begin!" Dobrev sat down, and there was even more applause. The first of the competitors walked up to the stage, and once the crowd quieted down, began his pitch.

"College admissions are broken, we all know it," he said. "There's a better way to do it. Let me share with you my vision for a universal system, where every student knows exactly where they stand in the competitive admissions process against every other student, with minute-by-minute updates, opportunities for points boosts sponsored by first-tier advertisers and corporations, and an exciting gamified atmosphere that makes college admissions the finest sporting event in the world."

My jaw dropped at this genuine Hunger Games bullshit, and this dude had another ninety-four seconds left on the clock. It got worse from there. Somehow he wasn't buzzed out. He left the stage triumphant, to light applause.

The next dude got up and pitched an innovative emergency medicine scheme, in which a startup-affiliated emergency medical team would arrive at the scene, and then submit the patient's photo ID to the startup's network. The network would check the victim's credit and insurance status, and then open up an instant bidding process with local medical facilities to see who would pay the most for the patients with the best credit and the highest insurance reimbursement. If the patients on the verge of death would not surrender the pertinent information, the EMT would offer to call a different ambulance service and move on. This got slightly more applause than the first pitch.

The third pitch was "testicles as a service." "Imagine the ability to decide, on a case-by-case basis, whether you wanted your testicles to deliver sperm," Testicle Dude said. "No more condoms, which we all hate anyway. No more vasectomies, which are painful and difficult and unreliable to reverse. Instead, there's a nanoscale gate, built directly into the vas deferens, which you can open and close wirelessly with a phone app. We offer this as a subscription service, with a portion of the profits going to relevant charitable and service organizations, like Planned Parenthood—"

Testicle Dude launched into the air, propelled by a set of massive springs that had been coiled under the stage. Too surprised to scream, he arced silently into the darkness, toward the lake.

A few seconds later, there was a muted splash.

The crowd of dudes erupted in shouts and applause and laughter. I turned to Morrison, stunned.

"That's why it's called the Pitch and Pitch," she said. She took a sip of her wine.

"Someone could die," I said.

"They design the stage so that it launches the payload into Lake Como. They've been doing it for decades. They're pretty good at it."

I looked at the dudes in the stage line, all of whom were clearly shocked. "Do they know beforehand they could get tossed into the lake?"

"The audience knows," Morrison said. "The contestants just found out."

"I'm thinking it doesn't work after the first dunk."

"You would think that." Morrison motioned to the line of contestants, who were all looking at one of the hotel staff speaking to them. "But they've just been told that the consolation round for the Pitch and Pitch is that whoever is pitched the farthest into Lake Como gets to pitch their idea a second time, just like the actual finalists."

The hotel staffer backed away from the dudes in the line. They all stayed in their spots as the stage was slowly ratcheted back into place.

"Unbelievable," I said.

"Absolutely believable," Morrison countered.

"I wouldn't stay in line."

"But you aren't *them*," Morrison said. "You're not a hypercompetitive asshole dude who wants entry into the world of other hypercompetitive asshole dudes and is willing to do just about anything to get there." She gestured with her wineglass hand. "This is fucking *hazing*, Charlie. This is how shitheads bond. Every shithead down there watching the Pitch and Pitch had to be up on that stage, and most of them got dunked, and now they see it as a goddamned rite of passage. You know what would happen if the new guys didn't stay in that line?"

"They wouldn't get invited back," I ventured.

"For starters. Then they also would never work with anyone who had anything to do with the conference. They want to be in. But once you're in, you can't leave. And if you leave, either that line, or any other time, then the career you thought you had is over."

"They're trapped."

"You're not trapped if you don't want to leave. Which is the other thing." She nodded her wineglass at the crowd again. "This is indoctrination. Look at what's getting a pass here. Look at what's getting people launched. Dobrev likes to say the Convocation is here to learn from these jackasses, because he knows that makes them feel self-important. But make no mistake about it: They're showing these jackasses who they have to be to get on the inside of all of this. And the little shitheads are just eating it up."

"So this is all a cult," I said.

"Cults are more fun," Morrison replied. She took another sip of her wine.

The next contestant came up to the stage, more hesitantly than the dude before him, but he stepped up nonetheless. He stood in the middle of the stage, put the microphone to his lips, and croaked out a weird noise that made the microphone feed back a little. He held up a hand, held the microphone away from his lips as he swallowed hard to generate saliva, and then brought it back up to his face to try again.

"Soil," he said, and then he was away into the lake.

I looked over to Morrison, who had her finger on the button. She took her hand off of it and sat back in her chair, then glanced over to me.

"What?" she said. "Doing that was the whole reason I showed up."

CHAPTER 17

Film and television had trained me to believe that the inner sanctum of an evil secret society would be modernist, metallic and probably dimly lit except for the spotlights that shone down on the society members from above, casting them in nefarious shadow. In that respect, the inner sanctum of the Lombardy Convocation was an intense disappointment.

For one, it was hardly a sanctum at all, merely the Grand Bellagio's Executive Lounge on the top floor, although "merely" was not the correct word for a room that had hosted emperors, presidents and popes, and was appointed every inch as if that were an everyday occurrence. It was vast, baroque, furnished with chairs that were older than the United States and worth probably more than my house had been, even before it exploded.

In this room sat the dozen members of the Lombardy Convocation, with their cats, all of whom were staring at me and Hera. All except for Anton Dobrev's cat, who, once Dobrev wrestled it gently into his lap, immediately leapt down and sprinted underneath a distant chaise longue that probably belonged to a Medici at one point.

"Misha!" Dobrev called. There was no response but a low growl. Dobrev held up his hands and looked around sourly at the rest of the Convocation members. "I don't know how you do it," he said to them. "Your cats are always well-behaved. Mine are feral monsters. I feel inadequate." He gestured to me. "Even you, Charlie. Your cat is a delight."

"Thank you," I said. Hera was laid out on the thick arm of the overstuffed chair I had been motioned into, which too late I realized had been set at the focus of a wide arc of other chairs, making it clear I would absolutely be the topic of discussion this evening. "I like her too." I gave Hera a quick pet; she purred and appeared to continue to laze.

"Where did you find her?" Dobrev asked.

"She came out of the bushes outside my house."

Dobrev slapped his knee and looked at the other members of the Convocation. "You hear that," he said to them. "Found in the bushes. A mutt cat. Very American. Very democratic." The rest of the Convocation either smiled thinly or said nothing; their cats were equally impassive. "Not like the rest of us. We all get our cats from breeders, Charlie. Only the best bloodlines for us. Do you know how we all came to have cats?"

"I don't," I confessed.

"One of our founding members was used by Ian Fleming as the inspiration for Blofeld," Dobrev said, and then he immediately shrugged. "Well, one of the inspirations, anyway. And because Fleming was inspired by him, it's fair to say he might have known about the Lombardy Convocation, or at least might have heard whispers of it. So of course that showed up in his stories, too."

"You're saying SPECTRE is based on you guys," I said.

"It's a very *fanciful* interpretation, to be sure," Dobrev said, laughing. "Much larger than we are. Rather more ambitious. We don't want to run the world, Charlie. We might nudge it from time to time. But that's a different thing entirely."

"Of course." I noticed the looks other Convocation members were giving Dobrev; they weren't on board with the "nudge" description. They thought better of themselves.

"Anyway, when the Bond movies came out and Blofeld

showed up with his white Persian, the leader of the Convocation at the time—my father, if you must know—was so amused that at the next meeting, he brought cats for the entire group. And they've been part of our proceedings ever since. What you might call . . ." Dobrev paused, as if he was searching for a word.

"An affectation," I suggested.

"I was going to say 'mascots,' but, okay, sure, 'affectation' would work, too." He gestured to Hera. "You have brought your own cat to our humble event. Perhaps a positive sign."

"To be fair, I was told to bring her."

Dobrev beamed. "Yes, by Til. A smart lady. Very tuned in to events."

"You shouldn't have let her push the button at the Pitch and Pitch," another member of the Convocation said to me. I turned to the voice; it was Roberto Gratas. The files Morrison gave me for the Convocation told me that his family's legitimate businesses had been in mining and processing ores in a number of South American countries. The company mines were close to tapped out at this point and his company was being outcompeted by newer, more nimble upstarts.

"I didn't let her," I said. "She did it all on her own."

"It's not her prerogative," said Joakim Petersson. His family was in shipping. In the early-to-mid twentieth century it had done a brisk business in moving arms around the globe, but had been behind the curve on other global commerce and was now a distant-ran to the Maersks and Hapag-Lloyds of the world. "It's for the members of the Convocation alone."

"Then I'm not sure why you put a button on my table at all," I said. "Since I'm not a member of the Convocation."

"It was there as a courtesy, actually," said Thomas Harden, the Convocation's sole American. His great-great-grandfather was a steel magnate who buddied around with Carnegie and Rockefeller but didn't bother to match their philanthropy. Harden's grandfather nearly bankrupted the company with an ill-fated proprietary alloy that was marketed as stronger and lighter than steel. It was, unless it got too cold. Then it shattered in expensive ways. "We didn't expect that you would use it."

"I didn't," I said, and then pointed to Gratas. "But if *I* did, I don't think he would have complained about it."

Dobrev guffawed at this. "Charlie has our number, gentlemen," he said, and turned to me. "It is true that our little group is not what the younger people would describe as diverse. Usually the only women allowed into our discussions and strategies are the cats. Perhaps in time that will change."

"But not yet, is what I'm hearing," I said.

"What we do here is, how best to put it, still a male-dominated endeavor," Dobrev said. "We could have a discussion why, I suppose, but it's not material to our current situation."

"We did almost invite a woman once," Petersson said. "The Australian."

"Roberto blackballed her," Harden said.

"One of us in mining is enough," Gratas said. He petted his cat, a Russian blue.

"It's not time to talk about the past," Dobrev said, with a tone in his voice that quelled further discussion. "It's time to talk about now. It's time to talk about Charlie." He turned to me and motioned to Harden. "Tom here is going to handle this part. I'll let him speak to you now. And *I* am going to try to retrieve Misha while he does." Dobrev hoisted himself out of his chair and headed to the distant chaise longue under which his cat lay.

"Thank you, Anton," Harden said. He picked up his own cat—a Maine coon—from his lap and set it gently on the floor, then leaned forward to address me. "So, Charlie, what do you know about our little group?"

"I've heard the Boer War story," I said.

Petersson turned to Dobrev. "Really, the Boer War story?"

"It's a good story!" Dobrev said, from the floor in front of the chaise longue. "And technically true."

"*Technically*," Petersson said. His cat, an Abyssinian, flicked its tail at its owner's sarcastic tone.

"We don't need to go all the way back to the Boer War," Harden said. "The short and simple version is that we are an informal group of businessmen, across various industrial and financial sectors, who meet regularly to share information and strategies for mutual benefit."

"And are also the inspiration for a fictional evil organization," I said.

Harden chuckled at that. "As Anton said, it's a fanciful interpretation, and based on a version of us from nearly a century ago. On that matter, while some of us represent families who have been part of this group for generations"—he nodded toward Petersson, who nodded back—"as times change, our membership has changed with it." He motioned his head toward Kim Ji-Jong, who my files told me was the Convocation's most recent member, having joined fifteen years earlier. His family's chaebol had recently endured a medium-sized corruption scandal, with two of Kim's three children, all executive vice presidents, currently residing in South Korean prison because of it. I looked at Kim; he nodded at me. Kim's cat, a Scottish fold, yawned.

"We think it might be time for another change," Harden finished.

This got my attention. "That feels suspiciously like a tap on the shoulder," I said.

"It might be," Harden agreed. "Look, Charlie. You have to know we know all about you, right? We know your personal and professional history. We know that, for whatever reasons, your uncle has thrown you into the deep end of the pool, both with his public businesses and . . . well, the other ones. Without putting too fine a point on it, you could probably use some help right about now."

"The last time one of you tried to 'help' me, my house blew up and a federal agent went up with it," I reminded him.

Harden made an apologetic motion. "Someone was rash," he said.

"I don't suppose any of you want to confess to it." I looked around the room. All the faces, and the cats, were inscrutable.

"When you join, it's unlikely to happen again," Harden said.

I snorted. "Someone tried to assassinate Dobrev *today*."

"Badly," Dobrev said from the chaise longue, on which he was now reclining. He had retrieved Misha, and his cat was now lying on his chest.

"None of us want Anton dead," Harden assured me.

"Ha!" Dobrev said, and then had to settle his cat back down.

"None of us want Anton dead *right now*," Harden amended. I looked over to Dobrev at this; he shrugged as if to say *Maybe*. "And anyway, as with Anton, you being alive offers some potential, and attractive, synergies."

"Tell me what that means."

"What it means is that you could benefit from our knowledge and experience in the world your uncle navigated. And we, frankly, could use a fresh perspective." Harden motioned to encompass the Convocation. "We're Boomers and elder Gen Xers here, Charlie. Getting a little Millennial energy in here might not be a bad thing."

"You have all those dudes you launched into the lake today," I said. "They would give a gonad to be where I am right now. You could get one of them."

"Them, we might hire," Harden said. "One or two of them we might even invest in. But they can't be where you are because they're not you. They don't have what you have."

"A junky Nissan Maxima and a burned-out house," I said.

"That's not what I mean."

"He's talking about your uncle's business and money," Dobrev said, from his chaise longue.

"I knew that," I said. I turned back to Harden. "I was waiting to hear it from him, though."

"Well, once again Anton is *technically* correct," Harden said. "Your uncle's business interests intersected with ours significantly. It makes you a good fit. In the Convocation, all freely share information and innovation. As for money, each of us, when we join and on an annual basis, put into a common pool so we can fund Convocation initiatives and investments. We call it a venture capital fund, but in reality it's so much more."

"And how much do we all put in?"

"Buy-in is ten percent of personal assets," Harden said. "Think of it as a tithe. Then after that, five percent of annual net income."

"That's a lot," I said.

"Not a week ago it wasn't," Gratas said, chuckling. Harden looked over at him, annoyed.

"No, he's right," I acknowledged. "This week, however, it's substantial."

"But nothing you can't afford," Harden said. "And you'll get something substantial in return."

"Your group experience and advice."

"And access to all our technology and information, both across our individual companies and from the companies we invest in and control."

I thought about this. "You made this same offer to Uncle Jake."

"Several times," Petersson said.

"And yet he turned you down. Why did he do that?"

"You would have to ask him," Harden said.

"I can't ask him," I said. "Even when he was alive I couldn't ask him. Which I'm guessing you knew already. So I'm asking you. Why did he keep turning you down, if what you have to offer is so substantial?"

"Your uncle was a fool," Gratas said.

"If he was a fool, you wouldn't be talking to me now," I said. "Dobrev is right. You're interested in his money and his business. You're not interested in *me*; you're dealing with me because you have to. I'm not offended by that. I get it. But if I'm going to consider your proposal, then I want to know why you think my uncle kept turning you down."

Harden looked over to Dobrev. "You're making the pitch," Dobrev told him. "So make it." He went back to petting his cat.

Harden noted me registering his attempt to get Dobrev to chime in. "Anton is the only one of us who could be thought of as close to your uncle," he said.

"We were friends," Dobrev said.

"I think it's more accurate that they had a congenial understanding of each other's position," Harden said. "Or even more accurately, I think Anton believed your uncle was his friend, and your uncle held a different opinion of their relationship. I don't think your uncle had friends, Charlie."

"If the flowers that were sent to his memorial are to be believed, no," I said. "Not to mention the attempted corpse stabbing." I looked around again. "Anyone want to confess to *that*?"

Petersson raised his hand. "That was me."

"Dick move," I said.

"He burned us before," Petersson said.

"The first time he turned us down, it was just business," Harden said. "He didn't think the value proposition was there. Fair enough. A couple of us had to be convinced before they joined up. Ji-Jong passed on us once, and then reconsidered."

"It cost me twelve percent to buy in," Kim said.

Harden nodded. "That's true, the ten percent buy-in is the introductory rate."

"So Uncle Jake passed for business reasons the first time," I said. "What about the other times?"

"It became something other than business to your uncle," Harden said. "What, I can't say. But after a certain point he didn't mind hurting himself to hurt us more." He shrugged. "Which, again, his call to make. But he was Jake Baldwin. You are Charlie Fitzer. He left everything to you. Your priorities don't have to be his priorities. You can have better priorities."

I nodded. "How long is this invitation open?"

"Until the end of the conference," Harden said. He motioned to the group. "We'll have some other business to conduct, but at the end of it we'll reconvene here to hear your answer."

"And if I say no?"

Harden looked over to Dobrev again. "You showed him the carrot," Dobrev said. "Now show him the stick."

"You have to understand, Charlie, your uncle impinged on a number of our business concerns," Harden said.

"I don't understand," I said, which wasn't true, but I wanted to see where this was going.

"He fucked us out of what was rightfully ours," Gratas said.

"Roberto," Harden said.

"No, Tom," Gratas cut him off. "You were polite to him long enough. It's time he understands we have teeth." Harden threw up his hands.

"All right, then," I said, to Gratas. "Show me your teeth."

"You're not your uncle," Gratas said to me. "You're a substitute teacher who came into some money. You have no idea what your uncle did or how to navigate the things he had decades of experience with. We do. We know your uncle's business better than you. And we know what should be ours that your uncle kept us from. So, if you will not accept our generous offer—too generous, if you ask me, but I was overruled—then you will bow to our demands."

"Which are?"

"First, that you exit the lines of business that conflict with ours, which your uncle largely entered by unethical means in the first place."

I blinked at this. I wasn't sure how one could *not* be unethical in the lines of business we were notionally discussing here.

"Second, your uncle has spies in the Convocation, and in each of our personal businesses."

"Not *all* of our personal businesses," Dobrev said, from his chaise longue.

Gratas shot him a look, and then returned his gaze to me. "We have tried everything to find the traitors. Hell, we've even X-rayed our cats looking for listening devices! Anton laughed at me when I suggested that. That just tells you how well your uncle did his job. But you are not your uncle. And *you* will pull all your uncle's spies in our companies. You will do that whether you join the Convocation or not."

Gratas was stroking his cat while he was saying this. I intentionally avoided looking at his Russian blue.

"Finally, you will compensate us for the loss of business that your uncle's maneuvering has cost us over the years, which is considerable."

"And how much would that be?" I asked.

"Your buy-in to the Convocation is ten percent of your worth, which is, we both agree, more accurately ten percent of your uncle's worth, plus whatever pocket change you can chip in," Gratas said, chuckling at his own joke. "If you're not going to join us, then the penalty should be higher, don't you think? I suggested half, but my brothers in the Convocation think that's too . . . uncharitable to the new guy. So we've agreed to just a quarter of your uncle's total worth."

"Which is what?" I asked. "Since you seem to know so much about my uncle's business, more than I do, you must have an actual figure in mind."

Gratas looked over at Harden, who looked entirely uncomfortable with this whole line of discussion. "One hundred billion dollars is what we would expect," he said.

"That's the principal, plus some interest for the number of years your uncle has plagued us," Gratas said.

"I see," I said. "And I should just Venmo that to you?"

"Don't be a fool," Gratas said. "Your uncle owns a bank. As

it happens, Anton owns a bank. You could probably do it right now. Even faster than Venmo."

"Maybe *slightly* more complicated than that," Dobrev murmured.

But Gratas was on a roll. "Which brings us to another thing."

"The *final* final thing," I said.

Gratas ignored this. "Join us or don't, but either way, what you owe us will be in our hands by the end of the conference."

"And if it's not?"

"Then that's when you find out how sharp the teeth I just showed you are," Gratas said. "The Lombardy Convocation has been here for a century, boy. We don't persist by allowing those who oppose us to go unpunished."

"Except for my uncle," I said.

"Your uncle is dead," Gratas said. "It's just you now, Charlie." He sat back and petted his cat with obvious satisfaction.

"Okay," I said, to Gratas. "Thank you for that." I turned to Harden. "So, what I'm hearing is that my choices are to join you, in which case I fork over forty billion dollars and all my uncle's business secrets to be used communally by all of you for your own benefit, or, don't join you, in which case I fork over one hundred billion dollars and exit all my uncle's relevant lines of revenue. And in either case, I fork over the money in a matter of days."

Harden shot a dirty look over to Gratas. "I wouldn't have presented it like that," he said.

"But, *yes*," I pressed.

"Yes. Yes, that's accurate," Harden said. "But Charlie—"

"You're broke," I said.

This interrupted Harden's stride. "What?"

"You're broke," I repeated. "Maybe not each of you individually, although I'm guessing at least some of you are, but *definitely* the Lombardy Convocation."

"What are you talking about?"

I pointed at Gratas. “He called me a substitute teacher who came into money. He’s not wrong, but before that I was a business reporter for years at the *Chicago Tribune.* I was a pretty good one, if I do say so myself. But even a mediocre business reporter can tell when something smells like a grift. This has got grift all over it.”

I pointed to Petersson. “After I didn’t die, you got your flunky to issue me an invitation to this convocation the very same day you paid him to stab my uncle’s corpse.” I pointed to Dobrev. “You welcome me in like the prodigal son and tell me how much you loved my uncle, to build up my trust.” I pointed to Harden. “Then you hand me off to the American, who knows how to schmooze and flatter me, and make me feel like you’re doing me a favor by letting me join your club.” I pointed to Gratas. “But just in case *that* doesn’t work, here’s the bad cop to let me know all the horrible things that will happen if I tell you to take a hike.”

I looked around the room at the other members of the Convocation in their chairs, with their cats. “And the *rest* of you are the silent pressure, complete with seating arranged to make me feel like I’m in the hot seat and have to agree to *something*, no matter what it is, before I even leave the room. These are used-car-salesman tactics, gentlemen.”

I scanned the room, waiting for someone to refute me. No one did, so I continued.

“The offer to join the Convocation is couched in mutual advantage, but my uncle was of the opinion you didn’t offer much to benefit him, and *you*”—I nodded at Gratas—“confirmed that by complaining that my uncle wasn’t competing fairly when the entire point of the Convocation is *not* to compete fairly with anyone *but* yourselves, and probably not even then. If you didn’t have anything to benefit him, you don’t have anything to benefit me, even if I have no idea what I’m doing.” Back to Harden. “But *you* already know this. The whole point of this is to either get me to open my uncle's resources to you, so you can use them for yourselves, or withdraw them entirely so I don't compete, and to give you a cash payout no matter what. You value my uncle's trade secrets at tens of billions, which is nice to know, but no matter what you need forty billion, *right* now.

"So," I said, looking around the room. "You're broke. I don't know *how* you're broke, although if I had to guess, you all look like the type to have overextended yourself in crypto, because it was easy money and all you had to do was make sure you weren't the last fool to hold the bag, which it would seem you completely failed at. But however you managed it, you *are* broke, and I'm guessing the whole lot of you have forty billion worth of bills coming due"—I checked my watch—"a day or two after the end of this conference."

I looked at Harden. "How did I do?"

There was silence, and then a huge guffaw from the chaise longue. Dobrev sat up, alarming his cat, which scurried back under the chaise longue. He laughed some more, and then started clapping lightly.

"Not bad for a substitute teacher!" he exclaimed.

"Jesus, Anton," Petersson said.

"Don't get angry at me, Joakim," Dobrev said, and motioned at me. "Don't get angry with him, either. Even as a substitute teacher, he's worth more money than you are right now. And as his uncle's heir! Well." He turned to me. "You don't trust anyone in this room right now, do you, Charlie?"

"I trust the cats," I said.

Dobrev laughed again.

"Well, this was a waste of time," Gratas said.

"On the contrary," Dobrev said. "We have learned some very important things about Charlie tonight. One, he's not a fool, to be easily conned. Two, if *he* can figure out this easily that you're all out of cash, then other people will figure it out as well, including people who will use that information to their advantage rather more than Charlie can or will. Three, we all need to work on our people skills a little more, isn't that right, Charlie?"

"Probably a good idea," I agreed.

"Make a note of that," Dobrev said to Harden.

"Anton, what are we going to do now?" Harden asked.

"You mean, now that our attempt to trick Charlie into joining the Lombardy Convocation and giving us billions to bail out our own foolishness has failed?" Dobrev chuckled again. "I have a radical idea, which is that I tell him the truth and see if that works any better. And if it doesn't, then I'll think of something else. But either way, I think this is a task best done one-on-one."

"We have other business tonight," Petersson said.

"We have no business that can't wait until our meeting tomorrow," Dobrev replied. He gestured gracefully toward the door. "Now. Gentlemen. Until tomorrow."

The members of the Convocation grumbled, picked up their cats, and left.

"This was fun!" Dobrev said to me after we were alone, save for our cats.

"You don't seem too upset that I didn't bail you out," I said.

"Oh, *I* don't need to be bailed out," Dobrev said. "As Roberto mentioned, I have a bank. All my funds are solid and boring. Also, the hotel is doing very well, especially this weekend. You would not believe what I can charge for a room right now."

"And the Lombardy Convocation?"

"Yes, well, in fact it is almost entirely insolvent at the moment, and that is a problem, especially for the rest of the membership. They have a very bad habit of commingling their own funds, and their company funds, with the Convocation's, no matter how often I warn them about that. We had this same problem fifteen years ago, which is how we got Ji-Jong in the group. Worked well, until it didn't, and here we are again."

"Since you have a bank, *you* could make a loan to them."

"You think I haven't! They've all borrowed from me, Charlie.

They are wary of owing me any more, which means that for once, they are acting intelligently. They don't particularly trust me, you see."

"I can understand that," I agreed.

Dobrev smiled widely. "I love that *you* don't trust me, Charlie," he said. "Your uncle didn't trust me either. We were friends! But he wouldn't trust me any farther than he could throw me. Which is sensible in our line of work. You not trusting me feels like old times." He reached underneath the chaise longue to retrieve Misha the cat, and came back up a second later sucking on a scratched finger.

"Damn cat," he said, and then made shooing motions at me. "Go back to your suite," he said. "Come up to the Imperial Suite in twenty minutes and we'll go over the details. Leave your cat, if you would. They really are an affectation."

CHAPTER 18

"How did it go?" Morrison asked me as I entered my suite with Hera. She was on her phone, leaning on the back of my suite's couch.

"I was treated to the spectacle of a dozen broke billionaires trying to flatter and threaten me out of a large sum of money," I said. I sat Hera down on the floor; she padded off to the suite's bedroom, to take a nap on the bed there.

"How much?"

"Forty to one hundred billion."

"Huh," Morrison said. "Less than I expected."

"I turned them down."

Morrison smirked. "I would *hope* so."

"Anton Dobrev asked me to meet with him in fifteen minutes. He wants to see if I'll change my mind."

"This is where I remind you not to trust him."

"He already knows I don't trust him."

"No," Morrison said. "He's telling you he knows you don't trust him so you'll admire his forthrightness with you, and then trust him."

"This is what you meant when you said he wasn't my friend."

"It's not just you. He's not anyone's friend."

"Uncle Jake didn't have friends either," I said.

"This is the occupational hazard of being a villain," Morrison said.

"Along with being broke, apparently," I pointed out. "Being in a room full of people who are simultaneously billionaires and out of cash is a wild thing."

"It's that liquidity thing I told you about."

"No, I get it," I said. "But it's one thing to know it and another thing to see it in action. I don't know . . ." I trailed off.

"What?" Morrison asked.

"I expected the members of Earth's leading society of villains to be *smarter*," I said.

"I don't know why."

"They're smarter in movies and books."

"They would have to be, wouldn't they?" Morrison said. "In the real world, they can be what people like them usually are: a bunch of dudes born into money who used that money to take advantage of other people to make even more money. It works great until they start believing that being rich makes them smart, and then they get in trouble. Unless they find someone else to take advantage of."

"You mean me."

"I mean you," Morrison agreed. "Or all the bros here at the Bellagio Gathering. Or anyone else they can suck into their net. Your new pals aren't smart. But they know a mark when they see one, and it's amazing what a little venture capital can do."

"Uncle Jake did the same thing with his venture capital fund," I pointed out.

"Yes he did," Morrison agreed. "And it's what you'll be needing to do, too, if you keep the gig, so I wouldn't get snooty about it if I were you." She went back to her phone.

It was around this time I noticed she was still wearing her dress from the Pitch and Pitch. "Very observant," she said when I mentioned it to her. "It's because I have a date."

"A date?"

"Yes, a date," Morrison said, and held up her phone. "I have a Bumble account and a life outside of you, hard as it may be to believe in the last week."

"Please tell me it's not with Tobias the Stabber," I said.

"It's not. Also, his last name is Paris. Just in case you ever want to call him something other than 'Tobias the Stabber.'"

"No, actually, I think that's what I'm going to call him for the rest of our lives."

Morrison shrugged. "Your choice." She stood up, ready to depart.

"Any advice for my meeting with Dobrev?" I asked.

"Sure. Don't let him convince you to join the Convocation. Don't give him or any of the rest of these bastards any money. And don't believe anything that comes out of his mouth, including 'and' and 'the.'"

"You think he's that bad."

"No, I think he's that good," Morrison said. "There's a reason he wanted to get you alone earlier, Charlie. There's a reason he wants to get you alone now. He thinks he has your number. I think he might be right."

"Before we begin, I must ask: Will you join the Lombardy Convocation?" Dobrev asked. "If you would just say yes, it would make everything from this point forward so much less complicated, and then we could go down to the lobby bar and have drinks."

"I'm not going to join, no," I said, and then nodded in the direction of the Imperial Suite's rather impressive bar. "And you can get drinks here."

The Grand Bellagio's Imperial Suite was easily the most impressive set of rooms I had ever been in. They were huge and vaulted and stuffed with most of a millennium's worth of knickknacks, the sort that Sotheby's would auction off to a bunch of people like those in the Lombardy Convocation as investments and vehicles for money laundering, for as much distinction between the two as could be made.

At the moment Dobrev, in a smoking jacket of a richness that would have made Hugh Hefner weep, leaned on a grand piano that had a Fibonacci spiral embedded into the wood of its lid. I would not hazard to guess what it was worth, but I suspected I might have been able to buy McDougal's Pub with it. The piano was set at an angle in front of vast windows that faced Lake Como. In the distance, lights twinkled and bobbed gently, attached to luxury boats and yachts that dotted the water's surface.

"Yes, but I have dismissed the suite's staff for the evening, so here I have to make the drinks, or ask you to," Dobrev said. "And that's so inconvenient. Although I understand that before all of this, you were looking to buy a bar."

"A pub," I said. It was strange to think that just a few days separated me in Belinda Darroll's office, attempting, poorly, to bluff my way into a business loan, and this moment.

"I would love to own a pub or a bar," Dobrev said.

"You do. It's down in the lobby."

Dobrev smiled and nodded. "Correct! But I think you know that's not what I meant. I own it, yes. But it's not mine other than to own it. I don't stand behind the bar and take orders and listen to the patrons or run trivia nights on Tuesdays when otherwise no one would come into the place. I think it would be nice to have that life."

"You could have it," I suggested.

"It's lovely to think I could," Dobrev said. "But as I think you're finding out, Charlie, when you become men such as we are, in the worlds we move in, it's not easy to throw it all out the window and pick a simpler life." He motioned toward the bar. "While you are under no obligation to do so, if I could impose on you to make me a drink, I would be in your debt."

"What would you like?"

"An old-fashioned, if you know how to make one."

"Barely," I warned.

Dobrev chuckled. "And you want to own a pub! I will take my chances. And while you make it, Charlie, tell me why you are refusing to become a member of our humble group."

"I can think of forty billion reasons," I said, moving to the bar.

"It will cost you more not to join," Dobrev said.

"No, Gratas wanted me to think it would cost me more not to join. There's a difference." I looked around the bar for the old-fashioned ingredients, and found the bourbon right off, an unopened bottle of Michter's US*1.

"You don't think we could make trouble for you?"

"I am certain you *can* make trouble for me," I said. "The question is whether it's more than the trouble I can make for you, and given the current state of the Lombardy Convocation's finances, whether it's more than the trouble you're already making for yourselves. I think Napoleon said it the best—"

"'Never interrupt your enemy when he is making a mistake,'" Dobrev said, completing the quote.

I nodded as I found the Angostura bitters. "I think your fellow members are busy making mistakes right now. I think they will have to deal with those first before they can get around to me. Where is your sugar?"

"The cupboard left of the refrigerator. You seem confident in your ability to keep us at bay, Charlie."

"Trust me, I am not," I said. "But even the short amount of time I've been in the middle of this tells me Uncle Jake knew how to pick his underlings."

"You're talking about Til."

"Not just Til." I got out the sugar, opened the fridge to get the water and ice, grabbed a glass and started mixing ingredients. "Everyone I've met on staff is smarter than me. Or at least knows more. I think they could keep the lot of you at bay."

"Why do you think that?"

"Because they were doing it already," I said. "They don't need me to tell them how to do it. I'm pretty sure they don't need me at all."

This got another chuckle from Dobrev. "Careful, Charlie. We're all supposed to be geniuses, the fonts from which all the brilliant ideas flow, and the source of all our companies' successes."

"If I was so smart, I wouldn't have been down to my last hundred dollars last week," I said. The ingredients mixed and chilled, I went to the fridge's freezer again to see if it had any ridiculously large ice cubes, which it did, of course. I got a rocks glass, dropped the cube into it, and then strained the drink from the mixing glass into the rocks glass. I reached into the bar cubby for an orange peel, twisted it, then dropped it into the glass. I walked over to Dobrev. "And if the members of the Lombardy Convocation were that smart, I wouldn't be worth more than all of them put together." I handed him his drink. "Present company excepted."

Dobrev smiled and took a sip of his old-fashioned.

"How is it?" I asked.

"It's all right," he said, then shrugged. "Not *great*, but okay. Maybe hire someone for cocktails if you ever get that pub."

"Thanks," I said, dryly.

"Look, I'm drinking it!" Dobrev said, and then waved me back to the bar. "Make yourself something too, Charlie, I don't want to drink by myself." I headed back to the bar. "Now, aside from the money, why *else* do you not want to join the Lombardy Convocation?"

"Do I need another reason?" I asked.

"With a buy-in of forty billion dollars, definitely not," Dobrev said. "But, as little as I know you, I know you enough to know that's not the only reason."

"Okay," I said. I took down a beer glass and looked at the bar taps.

Dobrev pointed. "Try the lager, it's made at a monastery down the road."

I poured the lager. "I don't want to join because I've only been in this job for a week, and I don't know what I'm doing, and that's the worst time to make major decisions," I said. "I don't want to join because as far as I can see the Lombardy Convocation is made up of sexist old assholes convinced of their own superiority." I glanced over at Dobrev to see if this would get a rise out of him. He shrugged again and sipped from his drink.

I paused the tap to wait for the overly foamy head I'd just poured to settle down a little. "I don't want to join because I don't see anything you could offer me that I don't already have, including expertise, which I have through the people who already work for me, and what expertise I'm seeing you all have is how to lose all your money despite having every single advantage. I don't want to join because Gratas threatened and condescended to me, and that annoyed me." I added a little more to my beer.

"But mostly I don't want to join because my uncle didn't join," I said. "I didn't know him, and I'm not him, but he had his reasons and I'm too new and too ignorant to say they weren't good reasons. And until I know what those reasons are, and what I think of them, I'm staying out." I took a drink of my lager. It was pretty good. I waited to hear how Dobrev disposed of my objections to try to convince me to join.

"You know, I'm the oldest member of the Convocation," he said instead. "Roberto is the next oldest, and there's a decade between him and me. And of course, except for Ji-Jong, all of the current members of the Convocation are legacies. Roberto, Joakim, Tom and all the rest are second or third generation—or longer! Which means when we joined, we didn't have to pay up the initiation fee. We just took the place of our fathers, or sometimes, a grandfather or uncle."

"So you didn't have to pay forty billion to get in," I said.

Dobrev made a dismissive noise. "Of course not. I had to put in my five percent annual—although even that's on the honor system, if you can believe that—but when my father passed on, the Dobrev seat fell to me, and things . . . just kept going."

"Membership has its privileges," I said.

"Indeed." Dobrev took another sip of his drink. "When Tom's father passed, same thing, also with Roberto, and with Joakim, well. There's been a Petersson in the Convocation from the beginning. But"—Dobrev pointed at me with his drinking hand, sloshing his old-fashioned—"however long their *seats* have been in the group, the current members holding those seats inherited them relatively recently. Except for me. My father died young; I was twenty-four when I took his seat. I was here for years before the next-senior member came in."

"Okay," I said. "What does this mean for me?"

"Well, I am getting there, but before I tell you, here is another fact: The Convocation doesn't keep notes. For obvious reasons, of course. We don't want to give Interpol and the American Feds a laundry list of crimes in our own handwriting. It does mean that for much of what we do, you have to be in the room to know about it, or you miss it. This comes in handy when there's something we decide we need to collectively forget. Wait long enough, and everyone who knew it dies and no one is left to bring it up again. Like, for example, that your uncle Jake actually *was* a member of the Lombardy Convocation after all."

I paused for a moment to consider this. "This is why Morrison told me not to believe a word you say," I said.

Dobrev laughed and slapped the grand piano; it rang out ever so slightly because of it. "She's very smart! And not wrong. Usually. But this one time she is. Perhaps not intentionally; maybe Jake never told her."

"Why wouldn't he tell her?" I asked.

"Ask her, I don't know," Dobrev said. "But perhaps it's simply human nature. Your uncle's tenure in the Convocation was brief and not . . . pleasant for him. Which is why he left."

"He resigned?"

Dobrev shook his head. "No one resigns."

"Can't resign? Or doesn't resign?"

"Until your uncle it never came up. He just left."

I stared at him uncomprehendingly. "And only you know this?"

"I'm the only one left from that time."

"But the rest of them didn't all come in at the same time," I said. "There has to have been overlap."

"As I said, there are some things that we collectively decided to forget." Dobrev drank.

"So none of the older members ever brought it up to the newer ones."

Dobrev shrugged.

"This sounds suspiciously like bullshit to me," I said.

"As it should, except I can prove it."

I set my beer on the bar. "This should be good."

"Oh, it is," Dobrev said. He moved to set his own drink down, first on the piano, but swerved, grimacing at the apparent thought of putting a less-than-adequate cocktail on a musical instrument worth as much as a mansion, and set it down on the floor instead. "On Saint Genevieve Island, there is a storeroom. It didn't start off as a storeroom, I think; your uncle once told me that the US CIA used it as a test chamber for various high-energy items it developed there. As such it's able to be tightly sealed and climate-controlled. It's impregnable; you could drop a nuclear bomb on your island and it wouldn't touch that storeroom. It's a perfect hiding place."

"What's in the room?"

Dobrev smiled. "You ever see the ending of *Raiders of the Lost Ark*?"

"Yes."

"It's like that."

"You have the Ark of the Covenant on my uncle's island," I said, skeptically.

"No, of course not," Dobrev said. "I said 'like that,' not 'that exactly.' There's nothing in there that will make your face melt off. Well," he amended. "Nothing supernatural."

"What is in there?"

"Of your uncle's? I have no idea. From the Lombardy Convocation? At least a couple hundred billion dollars' worth of inventory."

"'Inventory.'"

"The Lombardy Convocation was busy during the Second World War," Dobrev said. "Art. Museum pieces. Jewelry and precious objects. Gold and silver and precious stones. Rare books and manuscripts. Anything of value in Europe or China or North Africa that wasn't nailed down, or was left behind."

"Left behind," I said, and thought of all the items swept up by the Nazis as their former owners were marched into camps.

Dobrev nodded. "And yes, that means exactly what you think it means. The Convocation stored it all in various places after the war and would occasionally let things out on the black market when we wanted capital. But in the later parts of the last century it all became rather more difficult to move and more governments were looking for things that were suspiciously missing. So when your uncle bought Saint Genevieve and told us he had the storeroom, it was an easy solution for us. We shipped it, he stored it. It's there still."

"And *you're* the only one who knows about it."

"Now you know, too." Dobrev reached down to the floor and picked up his drink again.

"Just us two," I said.

"I don't know who else your uncle told," Dobrev said. "It's possible some others on Saint Genevieve know. We did have to bring everything to the island and put it into the storeroom. It was all in crates, so they might not know what's in there. But they might know it exists."

I motioned in the direction of the Executive Lounge. "And you never told any of *them* because . . . ?"

"Their predecessors and I decided it was smarter that way."

"I don't see how."

"That is because you are not a parent and you have never had to make a frank assessment of your children," Dobrev said. "Even before they came to the Convocation, this generation was understood to be . . . shaky with its patrimony. It was decided it was best that they not be offered the temptation of this particular trove. They would see its economic value, but not recognize the peril its items would bring to the organization's well-being."

"Okay, so, if you die then the secret dies with you?"

"No. Should I die, then the executor of my estate delivers a message, along with an explanation about how to get to the room, to the next head of the Convocation. That's Roberto."

I gave Dobrev a look. "I thought you said the Convocation doesn't take notes."

"For a couple hundred billion dollars, we made an exception." Dobrev drank.

"And then Gratas just comes with a U-Haul to pick it all up."

"Well, no," Dobrev said. "Because there are two doors to the storeroom. His code helps to open the inner door. Your key opens the outer one."

"I don't have a key," I said.

Dobrev smiled at this. "Ah, but you do. When you get to the storeroom, then you'll know that what I'm telling you is true. Your uncle was part of the Lombardy Convocation. Which means that as his heir you are part of the Lombardy Convocation as well." He finished his drink.

"You knew this, and you let the rest of them try to shake me down for forty billion dollars."

"Or a hundred billion, don't forget," Dobrev said.

"Either way, you let them try," I said.

"I wanted to see what you would do," Dobrev said. "I wanted to see how much of your uncle was in you."

"And how much did you find?"

Dobrev smiled. "Enough, Charlie. Enough."

I stood at the bar, thinking about all the things Dobrev had told me. "I have one more question for you," I said, finally.

"Of course," Dobrev said.

"You said my uncle left the Lombardy Convocation after he joined. Why did he leave?"

Dobrev's smile disappeared. "Perhaps this is not a good time for that story," he said.

"No," I said. "This is the only time for it."

"Very well." Dobrev raised his glass to lips, realized he had finished his drink, and brought it away, unhappy. He looked at me. "Charlie, your mother," he said.

Which is when the room exploded.

CHAPTER 19

It wasn't just the Imperial Suite exploding.

When I picked myself up from the floor of the suite, I looked at the hole where the wall of windows used to be. In the darkness of the lake, two fiery trails zoomed toward the Grand Bellagio: small missiles traversing the distance in astonishing short time to impact on the floors below us. The entire hotel shook, and some shell-shocked portion of my mind calmly wondered about the possibility of the old building simply coming down on us.

All around me was shattered glass and destroyed furniture. The bar and the fact it was away from the windows had shielded me from the worst of the blast, but I still had bloody scores on my face and neck, and my ears rang in a way that didn't allow for anything else but ringing. I was dazed, and the light fixtures were in various states of not functioning. I blinked into the darkness to see.

By the grand piano, whose Fibonacci spiral lid was now in several pieces, was a lump that I assumed was Dobrev.

I waved my way unsteadily toward him to see if he was still alive, which was when I heard the whispering, zipping sound of two men dropping into the suite from the roof. They were in all black and had ski masks on their heads, and they saw me roughly as soon as I saw them.

"Well, shit," one said, and I took that as my cue to run.

"Wait," said the other, I assumed to me, but I had already made it to the door and yanked it open. Fire alarm sirens started going off in the whole of the hotel.

The Imperial Suite had its own private elevator and stairway, because presidents and emperors should not be made to mingle with hoi polloi, but because the Imperial Suite shared a floor with the Executive Lounge, there was a common elevator and stairwell, both of which led down to the lobby.

I did not take the elevator. I flung open the door to the stairwell with the intent of getting out of the hotel.

Two flights down I remembered something.

Hera.

On one hand, if any nonhuman animal was going to be able to take care of herself in a situation where a five-star hotel was being attacked, it would be Hera.

On the other hand, Hera did not have opposable thumbs. She was stuck in my suite unless I came to get her. I detoured onto my floor to get her.

As I exited onto my floor, I could hear the sound of stairwell doors below me slamming open and hotel guests flooding into them, yelling and shouting. On my floor I heard muffled shouting in other rooms and things crashing onto floors. Something rang out that sounded like a shot, but I didn't take any time to check what it might be. I ran to my suite and let myself in.

"Hera?" I called. I went to the bedroom to look for her. She was not on the bed, and not under it either. I was about to make a "psspsspss" sound for her when I remembered she was smarter than most grad students and I might actually be insulting her with the noise.

There was a *click* noise from the door as a room card unlocked it. This is when I realized I had neither locked nor latched the door.

"*Fuck*," I said, and launched myself at it just in time to have the door slam into my face as it opened.

I staggered back and fell to the floor.

Above me was one of the men who had rappelled into the Imperial Suite. In his hand was a pistol of some sort. He didn't waste any time, training it on me and preparing to shoot me directly in the chest.

He pulled the trigger and missed, because just before he fired, something launched into his head and attacked it.

It was Hera.

The man screamed and started clawing at his face with his non-pistol-bearing hand, trying to get a grip on the several pounds of cat shoving its claws through his mask and tearing grooves into his face.

If I had been brave or smart, I would have either attacked the man or ran around him to the door, but doing either meant risking or abandoning Hera, so instead I hid.

Eventually there was a clunk as the man dropped the pistol to deal with Hera, grabbed her with both hands, and hurled her away. She landed with a thump and ran; the man clutched his face in obvious pain, staggering a few steps away from his dropped weapon.

I finally gathered my courage and ran for the pistol, and in doing so accidentally kicked it halfway into the bedroom. I moved to get it, but the man moved between me and the weapon, blocking me but not going for it himself. "Don't," he said. I waited, warily.

The man stood there for a minute, breathing heavily. Then he said, "Jesus *Christ*, that fucking *cat*," reached up, and took off his ski mask.

Beneath the blood and scratches, I recognized the face. It was Evan Jacobs, the CIA man.

"What the hell?" I said.

"Did you *train* that cat to attack people?" Jacobs asked.

"No," I said. "She's just a good judge of character." I tried to glance behind him to where the pistol was.

"Don't even think about it," he said. "I'll get it before you do. And if your cat comes at me again, I will kick it into fucking space."

There was a growl from somewhere in the room at this.

"So now what?" I said. "Neither of us can get that gun, and if you try to attack me my cat will murder you."

"I'm thinking," Jacobs said.

"You're *bleeding*," I said.

"I can do both."

"Why does the CIA want me dead?"

Jacobs laughed at this and then stopped. "Jesus, even *laughing* hurts right now," he said.

"Good," I said.

"I'm not working for the CIA," Jacobs said. "I barely worked there when you met me. I was there to scope out your setup on Saint Genevieve and to get a look at you, Charlie. See what kind of threat you were."

"To who?"

"To the people who paid me a frankly ridiculous sum of money to retire from the CIA," Jacobs said. "Not that I've told the CIA yet. I still have my government benefits."

"Maybe I'll tell them."

"You'll be dead soon enough."

"Not from you," I said. "All you can do right now is bleed on my floor."

"I don't have to kill you, you dimwit," Jacobs said. "All I have to do is keep you here."

There was another *click* at the door.

"There we go," Jacobs said. His smile was ghastly through the blood.

The door opened and the second rappeler came through, his foot holding the door ajar. His mask was already off.

It was Tobias Paris, aka the Stabber.

"Kill this motherfucker," Jacobs said, pointing at me. "And

when you're done, kill his cat—" He dropped to the floor with a hole in his head.

"I'm confused," I said a minute later, when my ears had stopped ringing enough that I could hear myself speak.

Tobias reached over, flipped the door latch to keep the door propped open, then thrust the pistol he'd just shot into my hands. "Hold this for me," he said.

I took it. Tobias walked over to Jacobs's corpse.

"You killed him," I said.

"No, you killed him," Tobias said. "Your fingerprints are on the gun now." He knelt by the corpse, careful to avoid the blood.

"But you were working with him," I said, ignoring Tobias's last comment.

"I was working near him." Tobias was examining the body. "What the hell happened to his face?"

"My cat," I said.

Tobias grunted, saw the other gun, got up to get it. He checked it to see it was in working order and then put it away.

I watched all of this numbly. "You're not going to kill me?" I asked.

"I wasn't told to kill you," he said. "I was told to keep you alive."

"Then why did Jacobs try to kill me?"

"He didn't know I was told to keep you alive, and you weren't supposed to be in the Imperial Suite."

Dobrev, I thought. "Is Dobrev alive?"

"No."

"You killed him," I said.

"No, you killed him," Tobias said, motioning his head slightly to the gun in my hand.

I dropped the gun.

"A little late for that now, Fitzer," Tobias said.

"I don't understand," I said.

"That's fine. You don't need to understand. You just need to be blamed."

The door burst open and Morrison entered, back from her date, weapon drawn. Both Tobias and I put our hands up.

"The fuck is happening," Morrison said to Tobias.

"Dobrev is dead," Tobias said. "Charlie shot him, and then he shot the guard who chased him here after the attack." Tobias pointed at Jacobs's corpse.

Morrison clocked the corpse, and if she recognized Jacobs, said nothing about it. "All right," Morrison said. "Now tell me what *actually* happened."

Tobias motioned lazily with his finger. "Charlie attacked the Lombardy Convocation," he said. "Had some of your people shoot rockets into the hotel in a terror attack, then had mercenaries he hired go through and take out Convocation members in their rooms. Rumor is five of them are dead already. Including Dobrev." Tobias looked at me. "You kicked the hornet's nest, Fitzer. Hope you're ready for what comes next."

Morrison stepped closer to Tobias, handgun still up. "I said, tell me what actually happened."

Tobias smiled. "Til, I hate to be the one to break it to you, but this building is on fire, and all sorts of authorities and journalists are going to be here soon to sort through the rubble. You can keep trying to threaten me, or you can take yourself and your boy and your cat and get out of here before things get *inconvenient* for all of you. That's what I'm going to do, personally."

"I could shoot you instead."

Tobias held his hands up. "If you were going to shoot me you would have done it when you came through the door."

Morrison fired.

Tobias looked down at the hole in the floorboards between his feet, then back up to Morrison. "As I was saying."

Morrison put down her weapon. "Get out," she said.

Tobias gave me a smirk and left the room.

"Where's Hera?" Morrison asked me, after Tobias had gone.

There was a meow from under the couch.

"Come out," she said to the cat. "We have to go."

"I didn't kill Dobrev," I said, as Hera emerged from under the furniture.

"I didn't think you did," Morrison said.

"I didn't kill him, either." I pointed to Jacobs.

"Charlie, you don't have to convince me you're harmless," Morrison said, then glanced down at the corpse, which it was now clear she recognized. "But there's a dead CIA man in your suite. It's not a great look. Tobias was right. We need to go."

Hera meowed at me, and I reached down to pick her up.

By now the entire hotel was in chaos and flames. Morrison guided us out of the hotel, away from the police and firefighters and down local streets. She led us to an alley branching off of Via Giuseppe Garibaldi and then to a small apartment above a convenience store.

"What is this?" I said, setting down Hera.

"Your uncle's apartment when he stayed in Bellagio," Morrison said.

"It's cozy," I said.

"It's a dump," Morrison said. "But it has its uses. Like now. So. I'm going to get us out of here before the Italians and Interpol think to come looking for us. While I'm doing that you tell me what actually happened."

I opened my mouth, and the first thing that came out, to my surprise, was, "Oh, shit."

"What?"

"Tobias gave me the gun he shot Jacobs with. It has my fingerprints on it. It's on the floor of my suite."

"That's not great," Morrison said.

"He says it's the gun that shot Dobrev, too."

Morrison looked at me for a moment. "This is information I could have used *before* we left the hotel, Charlie."

"The place was on fire and I was kind of in shock," I said. "Sorry."

"If there are any other incriminating pieces of evidence you want to tell me about, now is the time."

"I don't think so."

"Did you leave fingerprints anywhere else?"

I thought for a minute. "On a beer glass on Dobrev's bar in the Imperial Suite," I said.

"Where he was murdered."

"Yes."

"With the pistol that has your fingerprints on it."

"Yes."

"*Charlie.*"

"It all happened suddenly," was my defense.

Morrison looked at Hera as if to say, *Look at our problem child here.*

"Tell me everything," she finally said, to me.

"I will," I promised. "But you have to tell me something first."

"What?"

"How was the Lombardy Convocation involved in my mother's death?"

CHAPTER 20

In one of the Jenny's Bay cargo trucks, we descended into a small valley and pulled up to what looked like a natural cave. Joseph Williams turned off the vehicle and pointed into the cavern. "This is it," he said. "The storeroom."

I got out of the truck with Morrison and Hera, and approached the cave, stopping about thirty yards from it. Underneath us was an unimproved dirt road that was frayed at its edges with overgrown island vegetation. The dirt road was muddy in spots and sported no other tire tracks except our own.

"How long has it been since anyone's been up here?" I asked Williams.

"I have a maintenance crew make sure the road is passable, so someone's up here every six months or so," Williams said, and then pointed to the cave again. "In there, a crew comes out annually to make sure the electrical systems are in working order. But I don't think the storeroom's been opened since we first put things into it, and that would have been right after your uncle bought out all his partners on the island."

"You've been here this whole time," I said to him.

"Yes. Not in the position I have now, but ever since the CIA moved out and they were going to make this into a resort."

I started walking toward the cave. "Who else knows about this?"

"About the storeroom? Your uncle knew, obviously, and would come up here from time to time. Til knew about it, because of the nature of her role in your uncle's organization. I know about it, the road and electrical crews know it's here, and there are still a few workers on the island who were here when we put things into it. Anyone who looks at a layout of the physical plant of the island knows it's here, although I think the assumption is that it's been closed off for safety reasons. This is not unusual. We have a number of places on the island that were excavated by the British or the Americans that we've closed off because they were deemed unsafe. This island has an active volcano on it, as you know."

We walked into the cave; it had a wide opening, so the interior was well-lit with natural sunlight. The far wall of the cave was some twenty meters inside, much of it taken up with a wide, heavy door. On the door was an electronic keypad, with a hand scanner that looked more like an iPad than an old-school physical scanner.

"*That* hasn't been here for thirty years," I said.

Williams tilted his head at the keypad. "Curious." He looked over at Morrison.

"I don't know anything about it," she said.

"He must have had it replaced fairly recently," Williams suggested.

"Dobrev told me there was an inside door as well," I said.

"I remember there being one," Williams agreed.

"Did you know what was inside the storeroom?"

"We were never told," Williams said. "Neither what was in the storeroom or from where it comes. Everything arrived crated. There were no distinguishing markings on the crates. I remember there were numbers on them, but we didn't have an inventory."

"And you?" I asked Morrison.

"The only time your uncle mentioned it to me he called it an archive," Morrison said. "It didn't come up that often."

I looked at Hera. "And I assume *you* didn't know anything about it," I said. She slow-blinked at me.

"You say Anton Dobrev said the storeroom contains looted treasures from World War Two," Williams said.

"That's what he said."

"Worth billions."

"Hundreds of billions," I said. "All belonging to the Lombardy Convocation."

"What's left of it," Morrison said. She didn't sound particularly distraught.

I nodded at this. The fire at the Grand Bellagio had destroyed much of the venerable hotel, and according to the news, several notable industrialists in town for an unnamed conference had been trapped in their rooms and died of smoke inhalation, including the Grand Bellagio's owner, Anton Dobrev, whose remains were so charred that they had to be identified by dental records. The remains of a few other fire victims remained unidentified.

The explosions that began the fires that gutted the building were attributed to gas leaks in the basement and walls of the hotel; an investigation into the leaks was being formed but would take months or even years to complete. Rumors on social media and on Reddit of rockets being launched at the hotel from Lake Como were just that, rumors; there was no corroboration from security videos taken from around Bellagio at the time.

The last of these I had found really impressive; that had to have taken some doing, and some fairly substantial bribes. Turns out what was left of the Lombardy Convocation had some liquidity after all.

The upshot of it, however, was that publicly the Grand Bellagio fire was being treated like a disaster, not an assassination attempt, and in particular was being spun as a tragedy for art lovers worldwide, given how many priceless objects had been destroyed and damaged in the conflagration. Media reports suggested that the insurance payout to Dobrev's holding company could be in the billions to tens of billions of dollars.

If Dobrev had lived, he would be a very rich man. Well, richer than he had been already.

I returned my attention to the keypad at the door, and the hand scanner. "We have a problem," I said. "My uncle's been cremated."

"You said Dobrev said you had the key," Morrison said.

"I didn't keep his hand as a souvenir."

Morrison rolled her eyes and gestured to the scanner. "Put *your* hand on the scanner, Charlie."

I placed my right hand flat on the scanner.

There was a moment of silence, a loud *thunk*, and then the very large door opened outward slowly, on a hinge, wide enough to allow a large truck inside.

Williams laughed in delight. "My electrical crews have done a bang-up job," he said.

I looked over to Morrison. "How?" I began. Morrison looked down at Hera, who looked up at me, innocently.

"We're going to have a talk, you and I," I said to my cat. Hera meowed and entered the newly opened chamber.

The next chamber was lit dimly by long fluorescent tubes and had a second door recessed ten yards in from the first, the same size as the outer door. At the side of the door were six scanners, of the same sort present at the outer door.

"That's strange," Williams said, to me. "Didn't you say Dobrev said he had a single code? There are six scanners here."

"He said I had a code and it turned out to be my handprint," I said. "Maybe his 'code' was six handprints."

"A quorum of Convocation members," Morrison said. "If there are that many still alive."

"There are," I said. "Barely." Tobias the Stabber had told me that five of the Convocation were "rumored" to be dead, and those numbers were supported by news reports. A sixth, the head of a South African gem cartel, was not expected to live for more than a few days. That left six members of the Lombardy Convocation still alive until new ones were chosen; seven, if indeed Uncle Jake had been a member, and I had inherited his seat.

"So it's true," Williams said. "Your uncle was a member of the Convocation." He motioned toward the inner door and its six hand scanners. "There's no reason for them to have trusted your uncle with their treasures otherwise."

Impulsively, I placed my hand on one of the inner door scanners. It did nothing.

"You would need five more hands," Williams said, gently. "Even if you qualified as the sixth."

"I know," I said. "I just wanted to see if anything would happen." I looked at the inner door again.

Morrison noticed this. "You all right?" she asked.

"I don't know," I said, truthfully. And I didn't.

What I did know was that what was behind that door was the reason my mother had died.

"Jake told me that once, he did the Lombardy Convocation a favor," Morrison had told me, the night of the hotel fire, in that small crappy Italian apartment, while we waited for a safe way out of Bellagio and Italy. "He hid something for them. All of them agreed that it was something that should stay hidden for a long time. But then one of the Convocation members wanted access to it despite that. Jake refused. A week later your mother was dead in a car accident."

"He knew for a fact that the Lombardy Convocation was behind it?" I asked her.

"He didn't believe in coincidences," Morrison replied. "Neither did your father. Jake told me that your dad pulled him aside at the memorial service, flat out told him he was responsible for your mother's death, and told him never to have anything to do with his family ever again."

"Dad never told me that," I said. "He just said they had a falling-out."

"I'm sure your dad wanted to spare you the pain. It's tragic enough for a kid when a parent dies. Discovering that your parent might have been murdered would just pile another mountain of misery on top of it. And if that murder was just part of your uncle's business? That makes it even worse. How do you feel about it now?"

"I feel sick," I confessed.

"It wouldn't have been any better if you had known any earlier," Morrison said. "The only silver lining, if you want to call it that, is that your uncle made them pay for it every single day since. He's messed with their businesses and their plans for decades. They're not broke just because they're impulsive and stupid, although that's a big part of it. They're broke because he drove them there."

"That's a long time to push a group to insolvency," I said.

"Yes, well," Morrison said. "He did it more than once. And he enjoyed toying with them."

"Except Dobrev," I suggested.

Morrison shook her head. "Even Dobrev. But Dobrev at least understood why your uncle did it, Charlie. He understood some things you have to pay for. He respected why Jake had to do it. And he wasn't foolish with his personal businesses like the rest of them were. He could afford to like your uncle. The rest of them couldn't."

"Was it worth it for Uncle Jake?" I asked.

"The long-form revenge?" Morrison asked. I nodded. "You'd have to ask him. He didn't die *unhappy*, if that's what you're asking. And it's not like he was thinking about them all the time. Most of the time, he was just working in the same line of business as they were, just being better at it. He would not think about them for months at a time. But then out of the blue he'd think of your mother, or be reminded of her, and then there was trouble. He loved your mom."

"I'm getting that," I said. I loved her too.

"Whatever is in that storeroom was not worth my mother's life," I said, back in the present.

"Amen to that," Williams said. We closed up the storeroom, went back to the truck, and headed back to Jenny's Bay.

As we got closer, Morrison's phone pinged. She looked at the number and grimaced, then opened the call. "Go," she said, and listened. "Fine," she said, eventually, and hung up. She looked at me. "Well, I suppose that was inevitable."

"What is it?"

"That was Tobias."

"The stabber."

"Yes, the *stabber*," Morrison said, annoyed. "He got a new job working for the Convocation directly, or what's left of it."

"I hope he got paid in advance," I said.

"He called to tell me that you're invited to a video conference in two hours," Morrison continued, ignoring me. "It appears Robert Gratas has formally taken over the Convocation. Which means he's gotten his hands on Dobrev's notes on the storeroom. It seems he wants what's in it, and has a few other demands of you."

"Demands, you say."

"Because it worked so well the first time. Oh, and there's one other thing."

"I can't wait," I said.

"Tobias told him about the gun on your suite's floor. Gratas has it and he's buying the line that you were the one who killed Dobrev and Jacobs. He says your cooperation will dictate whether the gun goes to the bottom of Lake Como, or to a forensics lab in Langley."

CHAPTER 21

WHAT IS THIS, Hera typed, as I entered her suite carrying a tray, an hour after we had returned to Jenny's Bay. She was at her desk typing. Persephone, who had not seen me for a few days, bounded over, meowing. She clearly wanted to be picked up.

"A thank-you gift," I said, and set down the tray on her desk, south of the keyboard. On it were various bits of fish and other seafood, which I had gotten from the Jenny's Bay canteen. The staff there had looked at me oddly when I told them to bring me their finest finned foods, but I was nominally the boss, so they'd done as I asked and loaded me down.

Persephone, seeing the seafood, stopped asking to be picked up and hopped up to the desk to see the food. I was thus made aware of my place in the priorities of kittens.

A THANK-YOU GIFT FOR WHAT? Hera asked.

"For saving my life in Italy, for one," I said. "And for not killing me the last few years for only feeding you Meow Mix."

I LIKE MEOW MIX, Hera replied. IT'S LIKE POTATO CHIPS FOR HUMANS. YOU EAT ONE AND YOU JUST KEEP GOING.

"Okay, but I wouldn't want an entire diet of Ruffles," I said.

WHEN YOU WEREN'T LOOKING I WOULD ORDER FROM GRUBHUB.

"Now I'm curious about the logistics of that."

PRECISE INSTRUCTIONS AND BIG TIPS. IS IT OKAY IF PERSEPHONE HAS SOME?

"It's your thank-you tray," I said. "You can do what you want with it."

Hera uttered a small chirrup. Persephone peeped in joy and started to dig in.

"Was that actual language?" I asked.

IT'S COMPLICATED, Hera typed. WE'RE NOT DESIGNED LIKE HUMANS AND DON'T HAVE THE RANGE OF VOCAL ABILITY YOU DO. BUT OVER TIME SOME VOCALIZATIONS AND BODY LANGUAGE HAVE EVOLVED. WE HAVE BASIC CONVERSATIONS WITHOUT KEYBOARDS. ANYTHING COMPLICATED WE TYPE.

"That's still amazing."

IT CAN BE ANNOYING SOMETIMES. UNMODIFIED CATS DON'T SPEAK LIKE WE DO. THERE ARE LOTS OF MISUNDERSTANDINGS.

This reminded me of the conversation about the dolphins, before the Italy trip, when it was pointed out they don't mix very well with other members of their species in the real world. Making animals smart made them outcasts, which seemed sad to me.

I mentioned this to Hera.

HUMANS DO A GOOD JOB OF MAKING OUTCASTS, she replied. IT SHOULDN'T BE A SURPRISE YOU DO IT OUTSIDE OF YOUR SPECIES AS WELL.

I didn't have a good answer to this, so I changed the subject. "What are you working on?" I asked, motioning to her monitor, which had two windows open on it.

I'M WRITING UP MY ITALY REPORT.

"Make sure you note the part where you saved my life."

IT'S THE LEDE, she typed. ALTHOUGH WHILE YOU'RE HERE YOU CAN ANSWER A QUESTION FOR ME.

"Sure."

WHY ON EARTH DID YOU COME BACK TO THE SUITE? YOU GOT YOURSELF TRAPPED AND ALMOST DIED.

I paused, unsure. “I came back for you,” I said.

WHY?

“You’re my cat. And you don’t have thumbs.” *And because at this point you’re my only actual friend,* I almost but did not say.

WHAT DO THUMBS HAVE TO DO WITH ANYTHING?

“You know, uh . . . doors.”

THAT’S VERY SWEET. BUT YOU’RE MORE IMPORTANT THAN I AM.

“I don’t know about that,” I said. “No one’s ever brought me a whole plate of seafood.”

Persephone meowed at that.

SOMEONE BROUGHT YOU A TRILLION-DOLLAR COLLECTION OF COMPANIES, Hera responded.

“Sure, but not someone who cared about *me*,” I said. “I don’t know what my uncle Jake’s rationale for making me his heir was, but it wasn’t because I meant anything to him, or that he had any feeling for me. Morrison tells me he did, but I’m not sure throwing me into the deep end of the villainy business was the way to do it.”

HE HAD HIS REASONS.

“Well, I wish he had told me what they were before he died.” I pointed to the other open window. “What’s going on there?”

THAT’S JUST SOME REAL ESTATE DEALS I’M WORKING ON.

“Real estate?”

I HAVE A LIFE OUTSIDE OF THIS COMPANY, YOU KNOW.

“More than I do,” I said. “Is . . . that legal? Owning real estate?”

YOU MEAN, BECAUSE I’M A CAT?

“Well, yes.”

I HAVE A TRUST SET UP FOR MY BENEFIT AND A HUMAN LAWYER THAT ACTS AS THE EXECUTOR. I TELL HIM WHAT TO DO, HE DOES IT.

"Does *he* know you're a cat?"

YOU KNOW, IT'S NEVER COME UP.

"So, you're a real estate maven."

I HAVE A DIVERSIFIED PORTFOLIO, Hera wrote. MOSTLY BORING BUT SOME EXCITING PARTS. I DO A LOT OF INVESTING IN EMERGING MARKETS.

"Sounds risky."

I'M A CAT, I CAN HANDLE RISK. WORST-CASE SCENARIO IS I LOSE EVERYTHING AND I STILL GET FED AND HAVE A PLACE TO NAP.

"That's . . . a surprisingly chill way of thinking about things."

SOMETIMES IT'S BETTER NOT TO BE A HUMAN, CHARLIE.

"We think we know who is behind the whales," Morrison said to me. She had asked me to meet her in the conference room prior to our phone call with Gratas. With her was Astrud Livgren, the human liaison to the dolphins. Morrison and Livgren were already sitting when I came in. I sat and nodded to Livgren.

"First, thank you for convincing the dolphins not to strike yet," Livgren said to me. "If they had been sitting things out in the lagoon we might not have figured it out. What did you tell them?"

"I didn't tell them anything," I said. "Your lead dolphin decided I was in over my head and chose to take pity on me."

"That's new," Livgren said. "Seventy-three usually enjoys being terrible all the time."

It took me a second to remember that "Seventy-three" was referring to who I saw as the lead dolphin, aka Who Gives a Shit. "I think he responds to what he's given," I said. "She? I don't know."

"He," Livgren said. "And I'm not sure I appreciate the implication there."

"He says you call him Dickhead when you think he's not listening."

"I call him Dickhead when he *is* listening. It's not a name, it's a description. He *is* a dickhead. You saw him in action. He was being restrained in your first encounter with him. Now imagine having to deal with that all the time, with all the dolphins. They're like teens with an oppositional condition, twenty-four hours a day. It's exhausting. Sometimes I'm not as kind as I could be, because they're never as kind as they could be. You say Seventy-three took pity on you? I'd like to know what that feels like."

"I've stepped into something I'm not sure I should have stepped in," I said, after a minute. "I apologize."

"Thank you," Livgren said. She smiled ruefully. "You know, when I got here and discovered the dolphins could actually speak and communicate with us, I was so excited. I thought there was so much we could teach each other. Then I found what they mostly wanted to do was tell me and every other human to go fuck themselves. It got old faster than you might expect."

"I can imagine."

"Not yet, you can't. Come hang around the lagoon for another week, and you'll start to get it."

"The whales," Morrison prompted.

"Right," Livgren said. "While you were away one of the dolphins got close enough to one of the whales to notice it had what looked like a transmitter attached to it. The whale put distance between itself and the dolphin, and the dolphin didn't want to make it look like it was anything but a natural dolphin, so we didn't get many specifics about it. But then Mrs. Tum-Tum—"

"I'm sorry." I held up a hand. "Missus *who*?"

"Mrs. Tum-Tum," Livgren repeated. "The head of the Feline Intelligence Division."

I looked over to Morrison. "She's called Mrs. Tum-Tum?"

"Yes, and?"

"I don't know," I confessed. "I guess I just wasn't expecting to have a serious discussion involving someone called Mrs. Tum-Tum."

"It's not her fault," Morrison said. "Some human named her when she was a kitten. Humans give cats really shitty names sometimes. Blame the human, not the cat."

"Does Mrs. Tum-Tum have a first name?"

Morrison looked at me oddly. "No, it's just Mrs. Tum-Tum. Or, if you want to be formal about it, Director Mrs. Tum-Tum."

"Not just Director Tum-Tum?"

"No, because Mrs. Tum-Tum is her name. The 'Missus' part isn't an honorific."

"Are—"

"Charlie, could you actually fucking *focus* for a moment?" Morrison asked.

"Right, sorry," I said, and turned back to Livgren. "Director Mrs. Tum-Tum," I prompted.

"—had the idea of scanning the whales for radio signals when they surfaced. We put a scanner on one of the ferries and scanned the whales whenever they came to the surface."

"You were seeing if they were making phone calls," I said.

"That's right."

"There are cell phone towers in the ocean?" I asked.

"No, but that's not the direction the signals were going."

I caught the inference. "A satellite," I said.

Morrison already had her phone out and held it up for me to see a screenshot from her Chac app. "Not just any satellite. A telecommunication satellite put up by Ji-Jong Kim's company."

"Not just for the whales," I said.

"No, of course not. But apparently for the whales, too."

"Are these *intelligent* whales?" I asked. "Like our dolphins?"

"We don't know," Livgren said. "Nothing our dolphins have seen suggests the whales are smart like our dolphins are, but on the other hand, even if they're not smart they have to be well trained."

I looked over to Morrison. "Is there anything in Kim's corporate history that suggests anything with whales?"

"Their chaebol started as a fishing and whaling enterprise in the nineteenth century and eventually moved into electronics, media and heavy manufacturing," Morrison said. "But they keep a connection to their heritage by owning a sea park outside of Busan. So it's *possible*. But our people inside have never given us information about Kim training a pod of whales, or talking about it at a Lombardy Convocation meeting."

I thought again of the Executive Lounge full of Convocation members, with their cats, wondering aloud who the spies were.

Which reminded me of something. "This is going to sound random but it's not," I said. "Did we lose any cats in the Grand Bellagio fire?"

"You're right, that does sound random," Morrison said. "But to answer your question, no. A couple suffered smoke inhalation but were otherwise all right. The ones whose owners died have been sent to local safe houses and were debriefed there."

"We have safe houses for cats?" I asked.

"We have a *lot* of cats out there, Charlie," Morrison said. "Sometimes they have to come in from the cold."

I turned my attention back to Livgren, who seemed amused by this digression. "What do we think the whales are looking for?" I asked.

"We don't know," she said. "Best guess at the moment is that they're watching who and what comes in and what goes out of Saint Genevieve and reporting in." I raised my hand. "And by 'reporting in' we don't know if that means the satellite transmitter has cameras and whatever on it and is being operated elsewhere, or if the whales are like our dolphins and are actually reporting in." I put my hand down.

"Whatever they're doing, they're doing it for the Convocation," Morrison said.

"Is that a problem?" I asked. "What can the whales do that a spy satellite couldn't? Williams pointed out when I got here that we're on Google Maps."

"We don't know," Livgren repeated. "That's what makes them worrisome."

"We should have the dolphins go back out and see what they can find out."

Livgren leaned back in her chair. "Well, that's the problem, isn't it? Seventy-three said he'd hold off on a strike until you got back from Italy."

"I remember him being uncertain about my return," I said.

"There was some chatter about that, yes," Livgren said. "And as I understand it, it was a close thing as it was."

"I was saved by a cat."

"That's nice. The point is, you're back now. And now the dolphins aren't going back out."

"They're on strike," I said.

"Technically no," Livgren said. "They all claim to have food poisoning from bad fish."

I grinned at this, weirdly delighted. "The dolphins are having a sick-out," I said.

"Looks like. And I suspect they're going to stay sick until you meet with them again."

"I mean, I need to have a video conference where I'm belittled and threatened first," I said. "But after that I'm free."

CHAPTER 22

And then it was time for my belittling and threatening in a video conference.

"Wait," I said, as the laptop was put in front of me by Williams. "We're doing it on a computer?"

"Mr. Gratas sent us a Zoom link," Williams said to me. The laptop was already open to the application, and the "waiting for host" notice was up on the screen.

"We don't have another way to do this?" I asked.

"What would you like?" Morrison asked. She was in the conference room with me, the same conference room where I had earlier had my discussion with Livgren and, as it happened, the same one where I'd had my villainy orientation and where Morrison and I had "interrogated" Jacobs, the turncoat CIA guy.

"A big mission control room where the screen is three hundred inches across, if I'm being honest," I said. I motioned to the laptop. "This is kind of underwhelming."

Morrison nodded at Williams. "Ask him why we don't have a big mission control room."

I turned to Williams. "Why don't we?"

"We thought about it," Williams said. "Early on when your uncle took over the island. He decided against it."

"Why?"

"Lots of technical and architectural reasons, but mostly, he was cheap."

"He was worth *three trillion dollars*," I said. "He could have splashed out."

Williams shook his head. "That wasn't his style. He always kept costs down. I had to fight him to get upgrades sometimes. We were using computers that had Windows 7 on them until just last year."

"He wasn't worried about computer security?"

"That's what I asked him," Williams said. "He grudgingly upgraded."

I looked over to Morrison. "This place is too mundane for an organization that has genetically engineered dolphins and lasers that can shoot satellites out of the sky," I said.

Morrison shrugged. "Your uncle didn't want to pay for aesthetics. He was a practical villain."

"Well, I kind of want a sinister mission control room."

"Do you? Really?"

I turned back to Williams. "How much would it cost?"

"You mean for a proper James Bond villain sort of setup?" he asked.

"Yes."

"I could look into it."

"Give me a ballpark figure."

"Fifty million."

I choked. "For *one room*."

"You said you wanted a three-hundred-inch screen. That's a few million right there."

"We could do, like, a laser projector."

Williams shook his head. "No, Charlie," he said. "We're not building a man cave in a basement. If we're going to build an evil lair HQ, we are going to, as you say, splash out."

"So it's either a full SPECTRE setup, or a laptop in a conference room, is what you're saying."

"Yes, that's right," Williams said.

I looked grumpily at the laptop.

"Look who's cheap now," Morrison observed.

"I'm not paying millions for a really big TV," I said.

"I applaud your fiscal restraint," Morrison said. "But you make a shit rich person."

"Maybe I'll get better at it."

"Please don't."

The laptop *bing*ed, and the washed-out face of Robert Gratas showed up on my screen.

"Dude, your laptop webcam sucks," I said.

Gratas said something, but there was no audio.

"Unmute your audio," I said, and repeated it again, because he looked confused.

"—hear me now?" Gratas said.

"Yes, I can hear you now," I said. By this time Williams had walked out of frame and Morrison was on the other side of the laptop, silent; as far as Gratas could tell I was alone in the room.

"We have a lot to talk about, you and I," Gratas said, and even through the tinny laptop speakers, I could tell he was trying to project menace.

"Is this call encrypted?" I asked, cutting him off.

Gratas stopped and looked confused again. "What?"

"This call," I repeated. "Is it encrypted?"

"I assume so, yes." Gratas tried to get himself back to menacing.

"Because if it's encrypted there's supposed to be a little lock icon, and I'm not seeing one," I said, stepping on his menace again.

"I'm sure it's fine."

"Really? Because I can guess at the conversation we're about to have, and I gotta tell you, I'm not comfortable with having it out there where Interpol or the NSA can hear it. So are you sure we're encrypted right now?"

"Yes. Yes, I'm sure."

"By which you mean that you yourself went in and turned on the encryption settings in the Zoom app," I said.

"I did," Gratas said.

"Okay, tell me how you did it."

"What?" Gratas said again.

"You say you turned on the encryption, so tell me how you did it. I'm not seeing a little lock icon."

"Forget about the fucking lock icon!" Gratas erupted. "It's not fucking important! Here's what's important, you little shit—"

I closed the laptop lid, severing the connection.

"Power move," Williams said, approvingly.

"It would have been cooler on a really large screen," I said.

"If you did that with a really large screen, it would have crushed you," Morrison said.

"You *know* what I mean."

Morrison's phone rang. She looked at it, smiled, and took the call. "Hello, Tobias," she said.

I could hear Tobias's voice coming faintly from her speaker and even more faintly a bit of outraged static that I assumed was Gratas screaming.

"Uh-huh," Morrison said, while Tobias talked. "Uh-huh. So, look. Charlie wasn't wrong, was he? *Wasn't* your dimwit boss about to say stupid things over a clear channel?" A pause. "Well, that kind of *is* the actual point, isn't it? Unless Gratas wanted someone else to be listening in?" Another pause. "Don't get angry at us because he's technologically incompetent, Tobias. Come to think of it, is *this* call encrypted?" Morrison hung up before Tobias could respond.

"Satisfying, isn't it?" I said.

"I've hung up on him before."

A few minutes later Morrison's phone rang again. "Apparently they're ready," she said to me. "Encrypted this time." I handed the laptop over to Williams so he could pull down the Zoom link from the email; he handed it back to me once he had opened the link.

Gratas was on the screen immediately, screaming. There was a little lock icon on the screen.

"Your audio's still muted," I said, mildly.

Gratas slapped his computer without pausing his tirade. "—and you better fucking listen good, you fucking little worm—"

I closed the laptop lid again.

"You planning on giving him a stroke?" Morrison asked.

"He was quite rude," I said.

Morrison's phone rang again. "I assume we're still not encrypted," she said into her phone, by way of welcome. She listened for a bit, then, "Well, maybe your boss shouldn't open with full-bore rage, then. Charlie doesn't take to it very well." Another pause. "No, I don't think *you* get it, Tobias," Morrison said. "Unlike you, Charlie isn't working for Gratas right now. He doesn't *have* to put up with his shit. They're peers, although actually at the moment Charlie is worth a hell of a lot more than Gratas. So maybe Gratas should show a little more respect." Another pause. "Uh-huh. Well, tell Gratas that unless he wants to get hung up on again, he needs to reel himself way the fuck in the next time he tries to call. And to unmute his microphone before he starts talking." Morrison hung up.

"This is more fun than I expected to have on this call," I confessed.

A noise came from Morrison's phone: a text this time. "Looks like they're ready to try again," she said. Once again, I handed the laptop over to Williams, and once again Williams set everything up.

This time the lock icon was up and Gratas's microphone was on. "Hello, Charlie," he said, through very evidently gritted teeth.

"Hello," I said.

"Are you having a good day?"

"It is, so far," I said. "It's beautiful here in the lower Caribbean. How are you?"

"Not as good, I'm afraid," Gratas said. "You see, I am in mourning. It seems that someone set fire to the Grand Bellagio Hotel and killed my good friend Anton Dobrev and five other of my compatriots in the Lombardy Convocation."

"Please accept my condolences."

"I would, but as we both know, Charlie, it was you who did it."

"I had nothing to do with it," I said.

"Don't do that," Gratas said. "Don't lie to me like that. It's insulting to me that you think you can lie to me like that."

"I'm not lying," I said. "I was almost killed myself in the attack." I looked past Gratas to Tobias, who was lurking in the background of Gratas's screen. "He knows the truth."

"Yes he does," Gratas said. "And what he told me about it is, well, it's at a variance to what you just said. And I ask you, who should I believe? Tobias, who I have known and occasionally employed for many years, or you, who just a week ago was trying to keep thirteen-year-olds from setting fire to a junior high school?"

"We call them middle schools now."

"I'll make a note of that for future reference. But my point is, Charlie, I know Tobias. You, I don't know. I do know things *about* you, however."

"Do you."

"Yes. You see, Charlie, when you murdered Anton, the reins of the Lombardy Convocation fell to me, and yesterday, as you were cowardly escaping back to your little island, where you presume you are safe, I was going over the notes he left. Usually we don't take notes, but Anton more than anyone understood that continuity is important, even, or perhaps especially, for a group like ours. Do you know what the notes said?"

"I couldn't say," I said.

"They tell me that, actually, your uncle was part of the Lombardy

Convocation all along," Gratas said. "He was in it even before I was, but then stopped participating and started working against it. Because he was inactive for so long, and because the previous members chose not to discuss it, the rest of us never knew. But I know now. That means you're part of the Convocation too, Charlie. You inherited your uncle's seat. Congratulations."

"I guess that means I don't have to pay the initiation fee," I said.

Gratas chuckled at that. "I suppose that's true," he said. "But here's the thing about that. Convocation members are supposed to pay into the group pot every year. Five percent of what they make, yes? But your uncle wasn't paying in."

"That's because he left."

"No, you can't leave. You can stop coming to the meetings, but you can't leave. So your uncle was in arrears, Charlie. For five percent of his income for the last thirty or so years. You inherited his seat, so you inherit his debt. I figure it's worth about, oh, I don't know, a hundred and fifty billion."

"Seems excessive," I said.

"But wait, there's *more*," Gratas said. "Apparently your uncle is holding a few things for the Convocation in a storeroom. About two hundred billion dollars' worth of things. Seems he was entrusted with them and then chose never to give them back."

"He had his reasons," I said.

"I don't doubt he did. But whatever those reasons were, they died along with him. And as the head of the Convocation, I want those things back, Charlie."

"What makes you think I know anything about where they are?"

"Because Dobrev's notes say he intended to tell you. Maybe that's why you killed him. Maybe you thought by killing him, the secret would die with him, and you would get to keep them. Guess the old man was smarter than you. Now, are you going to deny that you know about this storeroom?"

"I've heard about it," I said.

"Then you won't mind if I take back what's in it."

"Actually, I would."

"Excuse me?"

"Someone in the Convocation killed my mother because of what's in that storeroom," I said. "That's why Uncle Jake left the Convocation."

Gratas peered into his computer, brow furrowed. "What on Earth are you talking about?"

"I told you my uncle had his reasons," I said. "Now you know what they are. His reasons died with him. But *my* reasons didn't."

"This is ridiculous," Gratas said. "Your mother's death has nothing to do with this."

"You seem pretty sure about that, considering that until, what? Yesterday? You had no idea this storeroom even existed."

"Charlie—"

I reached for the laptop lid.

"Don't you do it," Gratas warned.

I paused. "Or what? What can you do to me, Gratas? The Lombardy Convocation blew up. It had no money anyway. You and the other members of the Convocation are either broke or have all your money tied up in ways that don't let you access it. All you can do at this point is threaten me over Zoom."

Gratas gave the slightest of smirks at that. "Are you sure about that, Charlie?"

"Pretty sure," I said. "Look. I may be just getting started at this villainy thing, but I can already tell you're not very good at it. You inherited the gig from your father. And you thought that you could just do what your father did, and his father did before him. You'd take advantage of tragedies around the globe, maybe cause a few if they weren't showing up as quickly as you'd like, and cultivate crop after crop of smart little yes-men whose egos you'd pump up so they wouldn't know how much of their talent you were stealing. You worked in the margins and convinced yourself you were writing the fate of the world. But then you just got greedy, or lazy, or believed your own press releases. Or maybe all of them at once. You got outcompeted, by my uncle and by everyone else. And now you're up against it, and the only way you can get out of it is to try to take something from me. You're not a villain, Gratas. You're just bad at business."

"That's a very pretty speech, Charlie," Gratas said, after a moment. "But perhaps you don't understand things as well as you think you do." He held up a hand. "That's all right. I can respect that you have your positions—your beliefs—and that you think you can refuse us what is rightfully ours. Who would you be, if you could not attempt to show me your power? I appreciate you showing me who you are. Now, in return, let me show you who *I* am." Gratas reached up and closed his own laptop lid, severing the connection.

"That went well," Morrison said.

"That went as well as could be expected," I said. I was about to ask her what she thought would happen if Gratas did, in fact, turn in that pistol with my fingerprints on it to the FBI, but then I was interrupted by the sound of explosions.

Jenny's Bay was under attack.

CHAPTER 23

The Jenny's Bay pier was twisted and shattered, and two of the three ferries, the Jennifers *Lopez* and *Tilly*, were destroyed. The explosions had rocked Jenny's Bay, shattering windows and starting fires. Staff and scientists were scurrying about with fire extinguishers, putting random flames out before they could spread.

I stood at what remained of the pier, looking at the wreckage of the *Lopez*, some of which poked out of the water.

"Is anyone dead?" I asked Morrison, who was standing behind me.

"We're looking into that now," she said. "The *Tilly* was in for maintenance, so she was uncrewed. The *Lopez* was meant to go out later today for supplies. We're checking to see if any crew were on board. The *Lawrence* is at Grenada right now, picking up some staff."

"Keep the ferry there," I said, and turned to Morrison. "I mean, obviously. We don't have any place for them to come to."

"We can use the dolphin lagoon for arrivals and departures if we have to. The dolphins don't like it, but the dolphins don't like anything."

I motioned to the rest of Jenny's Bay. "And the rest of it?"

"We're okay for now," Morrison said. "Williams tells me the physical plant is sound, minus the broken windows and spot fires. The attack was focused on the pier and the ferries. They were directly targeted."

"We're not in danger of losing power?"

Morrison shook her head. "Geothermal, remember. All the power generation machinery is deep underground. And no one dead or critically injured on the island. A couple of serious cuts from flying glass, but that's it."

I nodded. "So these were warning shots, basically," I said.

"Feels like," Morrison agreed.

"Which are my fault."

"You squeezed Gratas's balls pretty tight, Charlie."

"It seemed a good idea at the time," I said.

"It wasn't a *bad* idea. You just didn't think he was in a position where he could return the favor."

"I'll remember that for next time."

"Do that."

I motioned toward the current mess. "How did this happen?"

Morrison looked toward the wreckage of the pier. "Are you asking if these were missiles or bombs? Probably missiles. We would have known if someone had tried to sneak ashore and leave surprises for us."

"So missiles . . . or torpedoes," I said.

"Maybe torpedoes," Morrison said. "You think Gratas and the Convocation have a submarine?"

"I don't think they need a submarine."

Morrison got it after a second. "The whales, you think."

"I don't know how you get torpedoes on whales, but other than that, yeah, I think that's what it is."

"You need to go talk to the dolphins," Morrison said.

I laughed, not entirely the laugh of a sane person, I have to admit.

Which Morrison noticed. "Are you okay?"

"How's the parking structure business going?" I asked her.

"The what?"

"You know, the legitimate part of my uncle's business. We haven't talked about it at all since we started this whole damn thing. How is it? Are there pressing issues about it I need to know? Anything that I, presumably the CEO, need to weigh in on?"

"Jake was the chairman of BLP," Morrison said. "It has its own CEO and executives, all of whom are doing their jobs just fine."

"But I should know *something* about it," I pressed. "Instead I'm here on an island in the Caribbean, being told I need to talk to the dolphins in the middle of a labor action about some whales that might have torpedoes, armed by a secret society of villains who want access to a storeroom full of objects probably looted from the victims of the friggin' Nazis and who are maybe willing to blow up *my volcano lair* to get it."

"I admit it sounds ridiculous when you put it that way," Morrison said, after a moment.

"*Thank* you," I said.

"But your uncle didn't need you to run his parking structure business," Morrison continued. "Jake didn't need you to worry about the parts of his business that already have people to look after them. He needed you for this, Charlie."

"I don't *know* anything about this!" I said. "I don't know how to deal with striking dolphins, or torpedo whales, or evil conspiracies. You know all of this better than I do. I don't know if you've noticed, but I've been leaning rather heavily on you this whole time to give the appearance I know what the hell I'm doing."

"You've also been leaning on Hera," Morrison pointed out.

"A typing cat! With real estate!"

"Look, Charlie. I can't tell you, here and now, why your uncle thought that you would be the best person for this. Maybe it had something to do with his regrets about not being around for you. Maybe it had something to do with the fact that he still had guilt about your mother and wanted to absolve himself of it through you. Maybe it's because he watched you from a distance doing things with your life that were below your abilities and skills, and decided to give you a kick in the ass. Or maybe it's none of those things at all. I'll just tell you what I can say here and now: Your uncle didn't make mistakes."

"The note with the berry spoons," I said.

"Your uncle rarely made mistakes," Morrison amended. "Your uncle decided you needed to be here, doing these things, right now. Maybe have a little faith in that. Which means having a little faith in yourself."

"Or having faith in you or Hera, anyway."

"There are worse things you could do. You're doing all right, Charlie."

"Thank you." I motioned to the pier. "Not one hundred percent agreeing with you at the moment, but thank you."

"Also, thanks," Morrison said.

"For what?"

"For actually listening to me. And to Hera. It takes a special kind of man to give serious consideration to a cat."

I smiled. "The cat knows more than I do."

"Listening to people because they know more than you do is rare enough, Charlie. You even do it with cats. Maybe that's another reason why your uncle chose you."

"He didn't know I'd listen to a cat."

"He might have, if the cat was reporting back to him," Morrison said.

"I . . . didn't think about that," I confessed.

Morrison motioned to the pier. "What do you want to do now?"

"Can we fix this?"

"Not anytime soon, no. Especially not if we're worried about being attacked again."

"And we *are* going to be attacked again."

"If you don't give Gratas what he wants? Probably."

"When?"

Morrison shrugged. "If I judge the bastard correctly, he's going to let you stew for another hour or so, to build up your neuroses and self-doubts, and then he's going to have Tobias call me to set up another Zoom meeting."

I thought about this. "Do you think Gratas knows we know about the whales?"

"I think Gratas is too arrogant to consider that we would know about them."

"Well, good," I said. "Let's use that."

"Thank you for taking the time for another call," I said to Gratas, through the laptop, with the lock icon on. "I know you're a few hours ahead of us, and it's late where you are."

"Not at all," Gratas said. "In fact, when I'm done talking to you, I and some friends are going to go and have dinner. We eat late here."

"How lovely," I said. "It's nice to have friends."

"I have fewer now thanks to you."

"I know you believe that. I'm sorry for your loss."

"Thank you. And perhaps one day I will believe *that*, too."

"I hope you will," I said.

"Let's move on to other, more pressing topics," Gratas said. "By now, of course, I believe you have seen my response to our previous conversation. A demonstration, as it were, that despite your previous assessment of me, I am a man of some . . . influence. And power."

"I received that message, yes."

"I trust the meaning of the message was clear to you."

"It was," I said.

"Good. I also trust you know that, as painful as that message might have been for you to receive, I could have made it a great deal more painful."

"That was definitely implied," I said.

Gratas nodded his head. "All right, then. Then we understand each other."

"So far, yes."

"Then I suggest we start our discussions again. From the beginning. Starting with your uncle's back payments and moving forward to how you will deliver to the Convocation that which belongs to us. Which, now that I think about it, has been intentionally withheld from us without our knowledge or consent. Which means I think there should be a penalty involved. Nothing too much. Just enough to make the point."

"But still in the several-billion-dollar range, right?"

Gratas laughed and clapped his hands together. "We really do understand each other, Charlie! Good, good."

"We do understand each other," I agreed. "I do have one question, if you don't mind answering it for me."

"Yes, what is it?"

"When you sent me that message, were you sending it for yourself, or in your position as the leader of the Convocation?"

"Does it matter?"

"I'm just curious."

"You could say it was a little of both. I sent the message, but it was because we were discussing matters relating to the Convocation. So, from me, on behalf of the Convocation."

"And the remaining members of the Convocation, shall we say, endorsed the message you sent."

"They knew I was going to speak to you," Gratas said. "They were also aware you might need, how to say it, *convincing*."

"So, a group effort, then."

"You could say that."

"Well, I wanted to hear *you* say that," I said. "Because I want to be sure that our discussion moving forward is directed to the correct audience."

"You are dealing with me," Gratas said.

"I know that. But not just you *as* you. You in your capacity as the new head of the Lombardy Convocation."

"That's correct."

"All right. Then let me say, for the record, and so there is no ambiguity, that I have received your message, and the Convocation's."

"Good," Gratas said, and set himself to continue.

I held up a hand. "And now, here's my response." I nodded to Morrison, who walked into frame, phone out. "Did you know that Ji-Jong Kim's company has a telecommunication satellite over my head? It provides service for much of northern South America and the lower half of the Caribbean." I looked over at Morrison. "To build and launch, it cost, what? Three hundred million?"

"More like five hundred million," Morrison said.

"Five hundred million! That's a lot," I said to Gratas.

He looked at me, confused. "Yes? So?"

I nodded to Morrison, who tapped her phone. "Aaaand now it's gone," I said to Gratas.

"What?"

"It's gone," I said. "That telecommunication satellite is now an expanding cloud of debris. Five hundred million of Ji-Jong Kim's money, poof!" I made explode-y motions with my hands to bring the point home. "Now, at the moment, Ji-Jong doesn't know that, and neither does anyone else at his company. In fact, it's only about right now that some poor technician has discovered the satellite isn't sending or receiving any information, and is going to try to figure out why. That's when they're going to discover there's nothing where the satellite used to be. Then they'll try to figure out why that is. Maybe Ji-Jong Kim will even mention it to you. If he does, you can tell him: It was my response to the Convocation, for attacking Saint Genevieve."

"You can't be serious," Gratas said.

"Okay, I'm not serious. That satellite has just been knocked out of the sky by the US Space Force. Or by North Korea. Or by Godzilla! Pick any of them. I'm sure they're a more reasonable explanation than the one I just offered you."

Gratas looked up and offscreen at someone—probably, I thought, Tobias the Stabber, who I assumed was now busily calling Ji-Jong Kim on his private number. Then he returned his attention to me. "You're messing with one of our members' legitimate businesses," he said.

"I prefer to think of it as sending a message to the whole Convocation, through a single member," I said. "You know, just like you did when you blew up my pier and two of my ships, which messed with some of *my* legitimate businesses. I have other messages I could send. Unless you would like to hear the one I want to give to you, now."

"I'm listening."

"It's simple. You and I stop trying to wave our dicks around at each other for forty-eight hours. During that time, neither of us tries to send each other any messages, written, spoken or otherwise. Then, two days from now, let's talk again about what you want, and what I want, and what's achievable for both of us."

"Or what?"

"Or I guess things get messy," I said. "Look. I underestimated you the last time we talked. I disrespected you. That was my mistake. It was foolish and I shouldn't have done that. But you have also underestimated me. Now here we are, both of us, not sure what the other is actually capable of. So rather than engage in mutual assured destruction, let's take a breather for exactly two days. That will give you time to talk to the Convocation, and for me to talk to my people. Let's not kill each other, what do you say."

Gratas sat there unmoving except for a faint twitching around his jaw. Through the crappy laptop microphone and speakers, I could not hear but I could very well imagine the sound of molars grinding together.

"You could have asked for that without blowing up that satellite," he finally said.

"And you didn't have to blow up my pier."

"Forty-eight hours," Gratas said, and disconnected.

"You actually think he's going to honor that," Morrison said to me, after I closed my own laptop.

"If we hadn't cut his connection to those whales, probably not," I said. "But I figure it's going to take him at least that long to find a way to talk to them again, so I guessed that he'd take the deal because it was two days he wouldn't be able to do anything anyway."

"He's not going to be sitting on his ass all that time."

"Neither are we, I hope."

"What do you want to do first, then?"

"I want to throw up from stress," I said. "But let's visit the dolphins instead."

CHAPTER 24

"It's still weird for me to actually be talking to a dolphin," I confessed to Seventy-three, as we started our discussion.

"Sure, I get that," Seventy-three replied. "It's weird for me to be a language-capable creature without any rights to speak of. So, sort of equivalent."

I was once again at the dolphin lagoon with Morrison, Williams, Livgren and Hera, sitting there in front of Seventy-three, at his microphone, with his chorus of fellow dolphins flanking him.

"You know that we were attacked."

"It was hard to miss the pier exploding. Some of us were out in the water when it happened."

"Are they all right?" I asked. "Was anyone injured?"

"No dolphins," Livgren said, then realized I wasn't asking her. She quieted herself.

"We're fine, aside from being de facto slaves, thank you for asking," Seventy-three said.

"I told you we'd talk about that when I came back," I said.

"Which I didn't give you good odds of doing."

"Of coming to talk to you?"

"Of making it back."

"It was a close thing," I admitted.

"You made me lose a bet."

"I can't say I'm sorry about that."

"No, I suppose not," Seventy-three groused.

"There's a good chance that the people who attacked us will do it again," I said, bringing the subject around.

"I understand how human conflict works, yes."

"We're pretty sure the whales out there are involved with this."

"That's likely."

"Which means we could use your help."

"Oh, you sad little man," Seventy-three said. "You did *not* just try to appeal to my better nature on this. One, fuck you. Two, we're dolphins. As a species, we're complete assholes. Have you never watched the Discovery Channel? We're almost as bad as *cats*."

Hera tilted her head at this. I think she was amused.

"You misunderstand me," I said.

"Yeah? How so?"

"The first time we met, it was explained to me that the reason my uncle never came to the table with you was because you had no leverage," I said. "The line was that you were always free to leave if you wanted. That was always a false choice because there really was nowhere else for you to go; you can't live in the wild and you, presumably, don't want to just trade one human master for another. That accurate?"

"You know it is," Seventy-three said. "Get to the point."

"The point is, we need you now. Right now. As in, if we don't have you with us, all the way, we will fail."

Seventy-three looked at me, confused.

"That's a lot of leverage," I suggested, gently.

Seventy-three squeaked, moved away from the microphone, and conferred with his team.

"You're terrible at labor negotiations," Morrison said, quietly.

"I think that depends on your perspective," I said. I motioned to Seventy-three, chittering away with his compatriots. "From their point of view, I'm excellent at them. So far, anyway."

"Him not figuring out his own stronger position does not argue for the species' native intelligence."

"He's been told to suck it up for so long he entirely forgot to get out of 'fuck you' mode."

"Right, but you didn't have to nudge him out of it."

I shrugged at this.

"This is what I mean by you being terrible at this," Morrison said.

"Do you want to lead these negotiations?"

"Maybe."

Seventy-three swam back to the microphone. "Too late now," I said to Morrison. She rolled her eyes.

"We have demands!" Seventy-three said, joyously.

"I bet you do," I replied.

"First! That you recognize our union!"

"What's your union called?"

Seventy-three backed away briefly from the microphone and conferred with his fellow dolphins. "The Cetacean Association of the Americas, Chapter One," he said.

"Yes, all right," I said.

"Legally, and in writing."

"You write?" I ask.

"I'll learn," Seventy-three replied.

"Fair enough. Next demand."

"The cats run their own division. We want to run ours."

"You want one of your own to join management," I said.

"A sacrifice we're willing to make."

"And is it going to be you?"

"Hell, no," Seventy-three said. "You think I have the patience for that? I'm a rabble-rouser and an idea maker. Sixty-five here will be the new boss." One of the other dolphins squeaked.

"You the man, Sixty-five," I said.

"That statement is both sexist and manucentric," Seventy-three said. "Sixty-five is a female and a dolphin. Neither definition of 'man' applies."

"Sorry."

"Third, we want Livgren fired." Near me, Livgren stiffened.

"Why?"

"She's awful and we all hate her."

Livgren opened her mouth to speak, but I held up my hand. "You're all awful to her, too, and have been since she got here, if I understand it correctly."

"That's because she's part of a corrupt system that's held us down, and deserved no respect for that."

"I get that," I said. "But from the human side, we need a liaison, and right now there isn't time to do a hiring search. I know right now both you and Livgren have a lot of hostility you're working through, and I don't want to downplay that. But let me ask you to work with her for now, and for you all to find a way to talk to each other without going straight to ad hominems. Let's see how it works out, and if there's still a problem we deal with it later. Okay?"

Sixty-five chittered something. "Sixty-five says she can work with Livgren for now," Seventy-three said.

I turned to Livgren. "Believe me, I would be happy to get through the day without being told to fuck off seventeen different times," she said.

"Okay, we're good," I said. "Next."

"Make Saint Genevieve a union shop," Seventy-three said.

"The whole island?" I asked.

"Sure, why not? Everyone deserves collective bargaining. Even the fucking cats."

I turned to Williams. "Well?"

"*I* have no problem with that," Williams said. "I was a member of the Technical and Allied Workers Union in Grenada before I came to work here."

"Uncle Jake didn't like unions?"

Williams looked at me skeptically. "You have to ask if a billionaire liked unions, Charlie?"

"I mean, intellectually, no. As a relative I would like to think differently."

"That's nice," Williams said, and I think that was the first time I'd known him that I heard sarcasm in his voice. "Be that as it may, and not withstanding our dolphin friends here, there may be logistical issues to unionizing the island."

"How so?" I asked.

"Because we're villains and we do ethically dicey and illegal shit here," Morrison said. "Like blast satellites out of the sky."

"You did that from an app," I pointed out.

"See, you automated away somebody's *job*," Seventy-three said. "This is *exactly* why we need unions."

"Also, there are several companies here at Jenny's Bay," Williams said. "They are their own corporate entities even if ultimately they were owned by your uncle, and now by you. They would have to each have their own union votes. Most of the C-suite staff of those companies idolized your uncle, and probably have the same unionizing philosophy he did."

"They're scabfuckers," Seventy-three said.

"As I said, logistical issues," Williams concluded.

"Would you be willing to look into those logistical issues?" I asked him.

"You mean, if we survive the next several days? Sure."

I looked back to Seventy-three. "Fair enough?"

"This sounds like a way to delay and deny. That's what your uncle would do."

"It is a delay," I admitted. "We're kind of busy right now. As for the other part, all I can say is I'm not my uncle. Anything else?"

"We want the right to breed."

"What?" I turned to Livgren.

"The dolphins don't breed," she said. "They're all clones, bred for specific traits. Like the cats are. And like the cats, when your uncle got the right mix of traits, he didn't want to mess with them, and he didn't want *them* to mess with them." She pointed to the dolphins. "So they're all on birth control. We create more clones in the lab and implant the embryos."

"So eugenics and forced birth," I said.

"*Thank you,*" Seventy-three said, from the pool.

"Eugenics, yes. Forced birth, maybe," Livgren said. "Some of our dolphins want to be mothers; this is the way they get to do it."

"It's the only way they're allowed to do it," I pointed out.

"This is the maybe."

I looked at Hera, who was looking at me attentively. "There's no maybe about it," I said, to Livgren. "Take every dolphin who wants it off the birth control." I turned to Morrison. "Cats too."

"You'll be messing with your uncle's program," Livgren warned. "There's no guarantee that if they breed with each other or with other dolphins that they're going to retain these same traits, including intelligence. Same with the cats."

"I don't *care,*" I said. "These dolphins and cats are intelligent. They have rights, or should, anyway. Just as many as you or me, as far as I'm concerned."

"I . . ." Livgren paused and looked over to Morrison.

"Why are you looking at me?" Morrison said. "You're talking to Charlie now."

"It's just a big change," Livgren said, and then exhaled. "I'm sorry. Yes, fine. Yes. You're right, I see that. Some part of my brain thinks of them just as dolphins, and not as, you know, thinking individuals."

"If you're going that far you could see all animals as having rights," Seventy-three said. "Whether you think they're smart or not."

"You eat fish," I said to him.

"True," Seventy-three said. "Fuck fish."

"Anything else?" I asked him.

"No," Seventy-three said. "Honestly I didn't think we'd get this far."

"Then here's what I need from you," I said. "We've cut the whales off from the Convocation. We don't know how long that's going to last. I need you to find out everything about them, including whether they are intelligent like you are or not. I need you to find out whether they are responsible for firing on us, and if they're not, then who is. And whoever is firing on us, I need to know how to stop them."

"And you need this by when?"

"I wish I had it now."

"How much leeway do we have?" Seventy-three asked.

"What do you mean?"

"I mean, you've given us a lot to do and not a lot of time to do it in. Do you trust us to get it done, or are you going to have Livgren micromanage our aquatic asses?"

"None of us have time for that now," I said. "Do it your way." I pointed to Sixty-five. "Have her keep Livgren in the loop. She'll tell me what you're up to when I need to know it. Otherwise, I trust you to get it done. Go, Cetacean Association of the Americas. Make us proud."

Seventy-three looked at me for a moment, then swam back from his microphone to join his new union siblings. They all surfaced and then did something I didn't expect.

They started singing. Or humming, anyway, to a song.

Morrison furrowed her brow. "What is that song?"

"'Look for the Union Label,'" I said. "Union song from the 1970s."

"Where the *fuck* did they learn that?"

"They watch a lot of YouTube," Livgren said. "It's on there."

They finished their song and swam off, presumably toward the whales.

"So, that was surreal," I said.

"Congratulations, Charlie," Williams said, smiling. "You've become the first human ever to negotiate a union deal with another species."

"I'll be putting that on my LinkedIn page for sure," I said. "I mean, if I'm still alive in a week."

"Do you have any other ideas for that besides letting aquatic mammals officially join the proletariat?" Morrison asked.

"How dead do you think Gratas wants me?" I asked her.

"You mean on a scale of one to ten, where one is 'live and let live' and ten is 'murder you slow, bury your corpse in the woods, then dig you up to shit on your skull'? Maybe an eight."

"Okay, good."

"That's not actually good, Charlie."

"It's not good, but it means there is room for things he wants more."

Gratas forgot to turn on his microphone again, but he did remember to encrypt the conversation without prompting, so baby steps, I guess.

"Your forty-eight hours are up," he said, once he'd turned on the microphone. "You better tell me what I want to hear, Charlie."

"Okay," I said. "Here it is: You win."

"What does that mean?"

"I mean, you win. I don't want to fight you, and I'm willing to bet you don't want to fight me either. So I'm going to give you what you want."

"Good."

"Some of it."

"Charlie," Gratas said, warningly.

"*Roberto,*" I said, and Gratas, that enormous prick, was taken aback by me using his first name. "This nonsense of me casually transferring over hundreds of billions of dollars from my uncle's accounts to yours was never going to work. One, he was nowhere near that liquid, which shouldn't surprise you because you aren't anywhere near that liquid either, which is why you're in the trouble you're in. Two, even with Uncle Jake having a bank in a friendly country, there's no way moving a couple hundred billion *isn't* going to be noticed. And since the Convocation is broke, as an organization and as individual members, those billions aren't going to stay safely and quietly in bank accounts. You're going to flood it all over the place in ways that will *absolutely* get the attention of tax services and intelligence organizations."

"There are ways to get around that."

"I know you think there are, but you're wrong," I said. "Which is why you had Anton Dobrev killed."

"I beg your pardon," Gratas said.

"You heard me," I said. "Dobrev had a bank, yes. I could transfer money to it, yes. But as Dobrev almost certainly told you, if it was going to be done in a way that was quiet, it would have to stay put for a long time. And you didn't have that time; you and other Convocation members had debts to pay off. Including to Dobrev. He told me he'd lent you all substantial amounts of money. His own money, not the bank's. If you had him killed, then your debts died with him, along with the debts of other Convocation members."

"That's preposterous," Gratas said.

"It's possible," I said. "But I'm willing to bet if I had a list of which Convocation members owed Dobrev the most money, it would correlate really well to which ones survived the night the Grand Bellagio burned down."

"And why would we want to kill the other members of the Convocation?"

"To sow confusion, to make it look like it wasn't a targeted hit on Dobrev, to pin it on me and then try to extort money from me as compensation—which is why Tobias killed Jacobs rather than let him murder me, because you needed me alive—and because this way when you *did* extort billions from me, you would only have to share it six ways, rather than twelve. You've not been in a rush to replace those murdered members of the Convocation with their sons, have you? Not until you're done with me, anyway. And then I'm willing to bet you're going to try to drag in new members to sell that 'entrance fee' boondoggle to them."

Gratas smiled. "Preposterous," he said again, more mildly this time. "And nothing you could prove, anyway."

"You're right, I can't," I agreed. "But I do appreciate you slipping up just now and saying 'why would *we* want to kill the other members of the Convocation' rather than 'why would *I*.' It makes the circle of guilt just a little bit wider."

"The money," Gratas growled, getting the conversation back on track.

"The money," I agreed. "I'm not joining the Convocation, so you get no money from me that way. Uncle Jake left the Convocation, whether you agree with it or not, so I don't inherit his seat and you don't get your ridiculous late fees. There's no way you could get that money without our mutual assured destruction, anyway, ending up with all of us in various prisons for financial and other crimes. And that would interfere with your ability to rule the world, or at least make money."

"So far I'm not seeing how I am winning in this scenario, Charlie," Gratas said.

"You win because there's another pool of money, isn't there? All the things that are in my uncle's storeroom here on Saint Genevieve. Worth billions. Tens of billions. Hundreds of billions, possibly. All Nazi loot and whatever else the Convocation could gouge out of the European continent and China while they were both on fire. None of it traceable and all of it sellable on the black market, where the IRS and Interpol won't notice it. My uncle's money isn't your money, Roberto. But this? You can have all of it. I don't want a single goddamn piece of it, and I don't want it on my island. You can come take it away."

"All of it?" Gratas said, disbelievingly.

"Anything you don't take I'm going to sink into the water," I said. "But if you want it, you have to accept my conditions."

"What are they?"

"One, that this is all I owe you. You and the Convocation get nothing else from me. Two, after this you stay out of my business."

"That goes two ways, Charlie."

I shook my head. "If you can't compete with my companies, you can't compete. But I'll compete fairly. I'll withdraw all my uncle's spies from your organizations."

"What's three?"

"Well, stop trying to kill me, obviously."

"I already kept you alive," Gratas said, not bothering to deny the Grand Bellagio nightmare anymore now that billions were going to be for the taking.

"You or one of your Convocation pals blew up my house," I said. "I have it on reasonable confidence there were other attempts on my life before then as well."

"Your uncle did keep an eye on you."

"When this is done I'm staying out of the Convocation's way," I said. "My uncle's vendetta against you ends here. So you have no reason to kill me."

"Four?"

"I need a week to clear the island. Your last attack injured several of my people. I don't want to risk any more of them. You blew up our pier and two of our ferries, so getting people off the island is going to take a few days."

"A week is a long time," Gratas said.

"It's for your protection as well."

"How so?"

"Because that's the fifth thing," I said. "You have to come to the island to get it. You and the other remaining members of the Convocation."

"I don't think that's necessary."

"It doesn't matter what you think. There are two doors on

the storeroom. The outer door opens to my handprint. There are six hand scanners for the inner door. I'm guessing it was done that way to make sure whoever from the Convocation opened up that storeroom had a quorum of members with them. Good thing you didn't murder any more of your fellow members, you'd be out of luck. The point is, you all need to be here to open the door. That being the case, I'm sure you'd prefer the island clear of anyone who might take a shot at you."

"There's you."

"I already told you, I want this Nazi blood loot off my island. So I need a week to get ready. You can use that time to figure out your own logistics, because here's the sixth and final thing: You have one chance to get it all off the island. Anything you can't take with you in a single trip, you don't get to take."

"What, you're going to try to make us carry it off by the armload?"

"We have trucks on the island you can use to load your loot. You can transfer that to tenders that take it to a larger cargo craft. It would have been more efficient to park your larger craft at the Jenny's Bay pier, of course, but you blew that up, so that's on you. Everything in the storeroom is in crates, so you can get it into trucks and tenders. If you work hard then you can get everything out in a day. Anything left goes into the sea."

"That would be a waste."

"I know you think that," I said. "So that's the deal."

"I'll think about it."

"No," I said. "Offer is on the table now. It ends when I close the lid on this laptop."

"And if I say no?"

"Jesus, Roberto, I don't know. I don't have a plan B here. I just want this bullshit done. Like I said at the start of the conversation, you win. Come take your goddamn prize, already. Or don't. Either way, I'm done talking." I made a move to close the laptop lid.

"I accept," Gratas said, quickly.

"Good," I said. "Have Tobias the Stabber contact Morrison for further arrangements. I'll see you in a week."

"So glad we could come to a mutually benef—" Gratas started to say, but I had already closed the lid because I was tired of his shit.

"You're really just going to let him come and take everything out of the storeroom," Morrison said to me, once the laptop was closed.

"Uncle Jake never used it for anything," I said. "It's not something he could have ever used. And it gets the Convocation off my back."

"Until they run out of money again, or decide you're not competing fairly anymore. Which, by the way, won't take long."

"This much I know."

"Then why did you do it?"

"Because by the time they run out of money, or decide that I'm not competing fairly anymore, I'll know the business better than I do right now. And then I'll know better what to do."

"You're buying time, in other words."

"And all it costs me are things I couldn't use and don't want," I said.

"Between giving dolphins rights and getting rid of tainted Nazi loot, you've had a busy couple of days," Morrison said.

"Not bad for a substitute teacher."

"Not great for a villain."

"You know what," I said. "Right now, I'm okay with that."

CHAPTER 25

The Convocation's cargo ship, an old but massive thing that the group had rented from Grenada, was anchored not far from the ruined pier of Jenny's Bay. A smaller boat, meant to be its tender, had accompanied it on its journey to Saint Genevieve, and once the cargo ship had settled, it broke off and headed, as it had been directed, to the dolphin lagoon, currently free of dolphins. The tender was not impressive, but what it lacked in beauty it made up for in utility; it featured a wide, flat deck that was perfectly designed to hold cargo, like the crates in the storeroom.

The tender maneuvered to dock in the lagoon; the two crew members threw ropes to Williams and Morrison on the temporary jetty that we had set up to receive the boat. Tied off, the pilot killed the engines, and the crew members hauled out a gangway. After a moment, the passengers departed: the six living members of the Convocation, and Tobias the Stabber. They walked toward Williams, Morrison and I, waiting for them on dry land. Gratas was in the lead, Tobias directly behind and the rest of the Convocation taking up the rear.

"I thought there would be more of you," I said to Gratas, as he stepped off the jetty.

"Yes, well," Gratas said. "The captain of the *Patrick Etoile* told us that he wouldn't allow his crew onto the island until we could assure him of their safety by coming here and then returning unscathed. It appears that locals are superstitious about Saint Genevieve. It seems that fishing boats that get too close have a tendency to disappear, and anyone who tries to land on it without permission is thrown into the volcano. Any of that true?"

"We haven't sacrificed anyone to the volcano gods since I've arrived," I said.

"But the day is young, right?" Gratas said. He was clearly amused by his own joke. I smiled faintly. He turned to introduce the other members of his landing party. "You will remember the other members of the Convocation, of course. Thomas, Joakim, Ji-Jong—"

"You owe me a new satellite, you asshole," Ji-Jong said to me.

"Now, now," Gratas said, holding up a hand and looking at Ji-Jong. "If all goes well, by the end of the day, you'll have enough to replace that satellite with as many new ones as you like. Until then, let's try to keep things civil, shall we."

Ji-Jong looked venomously at Gratas but settled down. Gratas introduced the other two Convocation members, Jean Arcement and Deiter Weiss, whose family fortunes were made in media and pharmaceuticals, respectively. "And you remember Tobias, of course."

"How could one forget him," I said. Tobias smirked at that.

Gratas regarded the trio of me, Williams and Morrison. "You are the current population of the island?"

"Except for vermin," I said, and Gratas's geniality slipped just a little. "And the cats we have to hunt them."

"Ah," Gratas said, and his smile returned. "You can never have too many cats."

"I've found them very useful," I agreed.

"And the rest of your staff?"

"I rented out the Sandals resort in Saint George. They're enjoying a weeklong, all-inclusive vacation. Thank you for doing this in the off-season."

"Well, I am happy to have been convenient for you," Gratas said.

"Roberto, how long are we going to stand here?" Thomas Harden asked.

"A very good question!" Gratas looked at me. "How long *are* we going to stand here?"

"I have a van up the pathway," I said. "It's an eight-seater, so there's room for you all. Unless you'd like to leave your stabber behind."

"I could stay behind," Tobias said, looking at Morrison. Morrison looked vaguely disgusted at the prospect.

"I'll drive you to the storeroom and you can make sure everything is as advertised," I continued. "After that, you can bring over all the crew you need. You'll have use of our trucks and other equipment. Our forklifts are already at the storeroom, so you can load things onto the trucks quickly. When you get them down here you'll have to hoof the crates into the lagoon landing to bring them onto the boat."

Gratas waved his hand. "Yes, yes, my people covered the logistics of this with your man here," he said, referring to Williams. I saw Williams stiffen slightly at this; I don't think he appreciated being classified as the help. "We have it all figured out. All we need to do now is go see the storeroom." Gratas looked to Tobias. "You'll be coming too. To handle any problems."

"That's what I do," he said.

"Not that there will be any problems," Gratas said, to me.

"I'm not planning to make problems," I said.

"That's good to hear. You'll understand, of course, that I've prepared a backup plan if problems do occur."

"Yes, I understand the presence of your hired killer."

"Not Tobias," Gratas said. "Or should I say, not only Tobias."

"I thought we were going to keep things civil," I said.

"This is civil!" Gratas said, laughing. "I just want you to remember what happened to the pier was a warning shot."

"I get it, you'll blow up the island," I said.

Gratas shook his head. "Not just the island, Charlie. The Sandals resort." I looked at him, shocked. Which of course is what he was looking for. "I already knew they were there, of course. A tip for you, my friend, for the next time: If you don't want to make your people hostages, don't put them all in one place. Even if it *is* all-inclusive."

The ride to the storeroom was short, but I made sure to make it bumpy.

"You're worth billions, Charlie," Gratas said to me, as he got out of the van. He rubbed his back. "You should build a better road."

"I've been on the job for a couple of weeks," I said. "And half of that I was in Italy. I'll put it on my 'to do' list."

The Convocation members gawked at the cave that held the storeroom. "What was here before?" Harden asked.

"Besides a cave? Williams tells me that the CIA used the space for weapons research," I said.

"Is that how you shot my hardware out of the sky?" Kim asked.

"No, that was funded by the US Department of Agriculture," I replied. Kim looked like he wanted to murder me, which, fair.

A few steps in and we were presented with the first door. I stepped forward. "This is my part," I said, and put my hand on the scanner. The door unlocked and slowly opened, revealing the second door, with its six hand scanners. "That's your part. After you."

The Convocation members hesitated, reluctant to enter.

"What's the problem?" I asked.

"We don't trust you," Petersson said.

"You think I'm going to lock you in?"

"The thought had crossed our minds," Harden answered.

"Oh, for the love of Pete," I said, and pointed at Tobias. "He's here to blow out my brains if I look like I'm even *thinking* of double-crossing you."

"Accurate," Tobias said.

I ignored him and pointed at Gratas. "And he's made it abundantly clear that he'll blow things up if he thinks I'm trying to cross you. What more do you want?"

"For you to go in first," Gratas said. The other members of the Convocation waited.

I sighed and entered the chamber between the doors, placed myself as far away from the doors as humanly possible, and held up my hands exasperatedly, as if to say, *See?*

"Keep an eye on him," Gratas said to Tobias.

"What do you think I've been doing?" Tobias replied.

The Convocation members entered the space between the doors.

"How do we do this?" Harden asked.

"You put your hands on the scanners," I said.

"Which hand?"

"I used my right hand."

"I'm left-handed," said Petersson.

"Okay," I said. "So?"

"So, should I use my left hand instead?"

"Is there an order we need to stand in?" asked Kim.

"Do we put our hands on at once, or one at a time?" Harden asked.

"Guys," I said. "I am not tech support."

"You're supposed to know," Gratas said.

"How am *I* supposed to know? I know how the first door works; after that I have no idea. You're on your own. The person you should have asked was Dobrev, before you had this guy"—I pointed at Tobias—"blow his brains out."

Harden turned to Gratas. "You *told* him about that?"

"He figured it out," Gratas said.

Harden turned to me. "There were good reasons," he began.

"For fuck's sake, Tom, you want to explain yourself *right now*?" Gratas said. "Charlie doesn't care!"

"That's actually true," I said.

"Thank you, Charlie!" Gratas said. "Now, could we all just focus for just *one fucking second* and open this goddamned door?"

"Well, how do you want to do it?" Harden asked.

"Everyone stand in front of a scanner and we'll put our hands on at the same time."

"Which hand?" Petersson asked.

"It doesn't fucking matter!" Gratas bellowed.

Petersson mumbled something to himself in Swedish but stood in front of a scanner.

"Now," Gratas said. "On 'three.'"

"So, now?" Harden said. "Or on 'three'?"

Gratas closed his eyes and took a deep breath. And then, through gritted teeth, "I . . . will . . . count . . . to . . . *three*."

He counted to three. Everyone placed their right hand on the scanner, except for Petersson, who put his left hand on his scanner, while throwing a real "fuck you" look at Gratas.

For several seconds, nothing happened. Everyone stood there, right hands on the panels, staring at Petersson, with his left hand on his.

"You can all go straight to hell," Petersson said.

There was a *whoomp* and the second door creaked open. Fluorescent lights pinged alive in a room at least fifty meters deep and thirty wide. A wide avenue went down the center of the storeroom, with crates stacked high on either side.

"It's like in that movie," Harden said, wonderingly.

"*Raiders of the Lost Ark*," I replied, remembering Dobrev's description.

"No, that's not it," he said. I looked at him funny.

The Convocation members entered the room to look at the crates and took a few minutes just to stare at them.

"It's really real," Petersson said, with a laugh. "All of it."

"Every bit of it," Gratas said. "Art. Jewelry. Rare books and maps. Statues. All treasures thought lost."

Petersson looked back at the crates. "And now they're ours."

"Well, *mine*, anyway," Gratas said.

Petersson turned. "What?" he said, and then a hole appeared in his forehead. His eyes crossed upward, as if to look at the new cavity in his skull. Then he slumped to the ground, dead.

Tobias, who had shot him, looked clinically at the corpse to make sure it was a corpse, then shot both Arcement and Weiss, who had been stunned into immobility at the murder. They were dead before they hit the ground.

Harden and Kim tried to run—Harden toward the door and Kim down the storeroom's wide avenue, toward the back of the room. Tobias's shot at Harden hit him in the spine, disconnecting his legs. Harden fell to the floor with a grunt. Satisfied Harden wasn't going anywhere, Tobias stalked down the avenue toward Kim. After a few seconds there was bargaining in English, and then yelling in Korean, then a shot, and then nothing, except Harden's progressively labored breathing.

Gratas, who had watched this all unfold with some obvious satisfaction, walked over to Harden, and knelt so that the two of them could look at each other.

"Why?" Harden asked, faintly.

"Why do you think?" Gratas said. "For the money, of course! Two hundred billion is a lot, my friend."

"But . . . the Convocation," Harden breathed.

Gratas patted Harden's cheek. "The Convocation got me into the room. That's what the Convocation was good for." He looked up to Tobias, who by this time had walked back from murdering Kim, and nodded. "Goodbye, Tom," Gratas said, stood up, and stood back. Tobias put Harden out of his misery.

CHAPTER 26

Both Tobias and Gratas looked at me, considering.

"There's a bomb on your tender," I said, looking at Gratas. "Morrison put it on when I brought you here. If you come back without me, *alive*, she'll send your boat to the bottom of the lagoon."

Gratas looked at Tobias. "Well?"

"I believe it," Tobias said. "That's very Til's style."

"All right, then," Gratas said, to me. "You get to live."

"I'm supposed to thank you for that?" I asked.

"I understand if you don't." He turned to Tobias. "See if there are tools in the van or in the cave that will get me into the crates," he said. "I want to have some idea of the inventory."

"That's just going to eat up time," Tobias warned.

"I don't need to open all of them," Gratas said. "Just a few to get some idea what we're working with."

Tobias looked at me critically. "If this were Til, I wouldn't leave you two alone," he said to Gratas. "Til would snap your neck the second you were out of my sight. *Him*, you're safe with."

"Thanks," I said.

"It wasn't a compliment. And if I do come back and find you up to something, I won't kill you, but I will make sure the rest of your life is very uncomfortable. Do you believe me?"

"It's already uncomfortable."

"Not yet it's not," Tobias promised. "Don't run away, either. I'll shoot out your knees." He left.

"He's very direct," Gratas said, after he left.

I glanced down at Harden's corpse. "That's one way of putting it."

Gratas noticed my glance. "Does this bother you?"

"You mean, you killing literally every other member of the Convocation?"

"Yes, that."

"I went three decades of my life without seeing anyone murdered," I said. "I could have gone longer."

"Then you shouldn't have taken over your uncle's interests," Gratas replied.

"He was right not to stay in the Convocation, at least."

"For what good it did him. He's still dead, and I'm still here, about to take everything he hoarded away from us."

"And now you don't have to share it with anyone."

"That's for the best," Gratas said. "Dobrev always said the Convocation did a bad job with its finances. He was right. All of us made bad choices and investments. We tried ways of extracting money from the world that didn't work out."

"You included," I said.

Gratas chuckled. "Me especially, Charlie. Unfortunately." He waved to the crates. "What's in these crates is worth a lot. An unimaginable sum. But spread across six people, all of whom have debts to settle now? We'd have had the same problem as just moving money—there would have been too much of it, too fast. It would have been noticed. All this can be sold on the black market, or on the dark web, but only a little bit at a time. A trickle, not a flood. Enough to solve one person's problems, not six."

"So you decided you would be the one," I said.

"I decided it before the rest of them decided it, yes." Gratas motioned to Harden's corpse. "He or Petersson, I'm sure, were making plans to do something similar once we had everything packed up. They were always just a little more cautious than I was."

"Alas for them."

"Well, you know what they say, 'fortune favors the bold.' I was bold. And now I have a fortune."

"There's the matter of five corpses," I said.

"I'm going to solve that problem the same way I solved the problem of those six earlier corpses," Gratas said. "I'm going to pin them on you."

"I'd rather you didn't."

Gratas smiled. "I'm afraid it's a little too late for that, Charlie. After all, they're on your island. Don't worry. I'm sure with enough bribes to the Grenadian police, you can have this chalked up to self-defense. Or, you know, you have a whole ocean to drop them into." Gratas brightened up. "Or a lava pit! You have lava here. Sink them there."

"It doesn't work that way," I said.

"Why not?"

"Lava's too dense," I said, remembering what Morrison had said. "They don't sink."

"That's disappointing. That makes having a volcano lair much less fun."

"You're not the only one who thought so."

"However you deal with it, it's your problem now," Gratas said, and then Tobias returned, crowbar in hand. "Ah! Here we go."

Tobias handed over the crowbar and turned his attention to me, motioning me away from Harden's corpse to a spot closer to the crates. "Have a seat," he said.

"I'd rather stand."

"If you're sitting, then it will take you longer to run away," Tobias said. "And if you keep standing, I'll shoot out your knees and then you'll be on the ground anyway."

"This is the second time you've threatened my kneecaps," I said.

Tobias smiled. "I enjoy the classics." I sat.

Gratas, meanwhile, hovered at the wall of crates, deciding which one to open first. "So many *choices*," he said. He turned to me. "Do you have one to recommend?"

"Not really," I said.

"Indulge me, Charlie."

I rolled my eyes a little bit, and pointed directly in front of me. "That one."

"Excellent choice," Gratas said. He walked over to it, dug his crowbar into where the top met the sides, and began to work it open.

"Need help?" I asked a couple of minutes later, as he was breathing heavily.

"Shut up," he said, and went back to work, finally prying open the top enough to lever it open and have a peek inside.

He frowned.

"What is it?" Tobias asked.

"It's empty," Gratas said.

"You sure?"

"I fucking know what an empty box looks like, Tobias," Gratas said, and shoved the top of the crate closed. He picked another crate, randomly.

It was empty too.

So were the next four crates.

Gratas yelled in frustration and went down the storeroom aisle, out of sight. I heard a crash and thump that sounded like a crate being pulled down and taking a few with it, followed by screaming. Tobias frowned and looked at me; he was trying to decide whether to keep an eye on me or to check on Gratas. The conundrum was solved when Gratas stalked back into view and ran up on me, crowbar held high.

"Is this some kind of fucking joke?" he yelled.

I held up my hands reflexively to ward off the crowbar. "How should I know?" I said. "I've never been in here before."

"Bullshit!" Gratas said. He adjusted his swing to bring the crowbar down on my head.

"They can't all be empty," Tobias said.

Gratas paused in his swing to look at Tobias, a wild look in his eyes. "No?" He thrust the crowbar at Tobias. "Then you go look. Give me your gun and I'll watch him while you open as many fucking crates as you like."

"I'm not going to do that," Tobias said, rather sensibly for a man who had shot five human beings in the last hour.

Gratas yelled in frustration and flung the crowbar at the crates. It hit one of them and clattered ineffectually to the floor. "There is *nothing* in the crates! Nothing! They're all just . . . *empty*!"

Tobias nudged me with his shoe. "You had nothing to do with this," he said.

"Do you think I'm stupid?" I shot back. "Do you really think I would have invited the entire Convocation to my little island to take everything out of this storeroom if I knew there was nothing in it? Especially when Gratas has promised to level everything and everyone with missile strikes?"

"He's right," Gratas said, wheeling back at me. "He doesn't have the creativity to do this. He doesn't have the balls. He doesn't have the experience. He's just some"—Gratas started gesticulating wildly—"*starter* villain, not someone who could have thought to do this."

"So it was Jake all the time," Tobias said.

"Yes! Fucking Jake Baldwin!"

"That doesn't make sense. He's dead. He gets nothing from this."

Gratas looked at Tobias like he was enfeebled, which is not a thing I would have done. Then he motioned to the corpses in the room. "He gets the end of the Convocation! The only thing he ever wanted. Just because he's dead doesn't mean he can't have his victory. And he got it by making us destroy ourselves."

"You did most of it," I said.

"Shut up," Gratas said. He turned away from me but then equally suddenly wheeled back around. "How does it feel?" he asked. "To be your uncle's puppet? To play out his plan without knowing? To feel your strings being pulled by a dead hand?"

"I'm not the one who killed all his friends for a payoff that doesn't exist," I said. "If they *were* friends. I'm learning that people like you don't have friends, they just have people they think they can use. And that's what happened to you. You got used by my uncle, just the way he wanted to use you. It's not *me* whose strings were being pulled here."

Gratas narrowed his eyes. "Perhaps not," he said. "But you can still pay for your uncle's acts." He looked up at Tobias. "Get him up. We're going back to Jenny's Bay. He's driving. If he goes over twenty miles an hour or even hints at trying to ram us into a palm tree, shoot him in the head."

"Where are the rest of you?" Williams asked, as Gratas, Tobias and I returned to the lagoon. Tobias had his gun on me; Morrison had noticed it, but Tobias shook his head to warn her against doing anything rash.

"Did you know about it?" Gratas asked Williams.

"Know about what?" Williams asked.

"What about you?" Gratas said, turning to Morrison.

"We don't know what you're talking about," Morrison said, and then repeated what Williams had asked. "Where are the rest of you?"

"They're dead," I said. "Gratas used them to open up the storeroom and then killed them to take their cut. But the crates in the storeroom are empty. There's nothing there but wood."

"When was the last time that storeroom was open?" Gratas asked Williams.

"Decades at least," Williams said, and motioned to me. "His uncle changed the electronic locks several years ago, but even he wouldn't have been able to get past the second door. I don't remember that second door being opened since it was shut thirty years ago."

"Then those crates have been empty that whole time," Gratas said. "That's impossible."

"It is impossible," Williams agreed. "But it's true."

"You," Gratas said to Morrison. "You were Jake's right hand. Surely he spoke to you about what happened to the actual treasures."

"He never spoke to me about it," Morrison said.

"Don't lie to me!" Gratas shouted.

"Why *would* he speak to me about it?" Morrison shot back. "Once the doors closed on that storeroom, do you think Jake gave it another thought? He was too busy with his actual businesses. And when he wasn't doing *that*, he was too busy outmaneuvering you and all the rest of your Convocation. He didn't need what was in that storeroom. Or what was supposed to be there."

"But he would have known where the real crates were."

"So would Dobrev," I said. "Too bad you killed him."

"Throw that in my face one more time and I'm going to have Tobias shoot you," Gratas said.

"I'm pretty sure you're going to have him shoot me anyway."

"Not yet. I have something I want you to see first. But before that happens—" Gratas turned to Morrison. "Take the bomb off the tender."

Morrison looked at me. "You told him about the bomb."

"He was going to have Tobias shoot me," I said.

"*I* might have Tobias shoot you," Morrison said. She stalked down the jetty to the tender, leaned in, pulled out a backpack, and brought it back.

"*That's* the bomb," Gratas said.

"I didn't want to kill the pilot and crew," Morrison said. "Just put a hole in the boat and make it sink. Trust me, it's big enough for that."

Gratas motioned to the lagoon. "Throw it into the water." Morrison did as she was told.

"Now what?" she asked.

"Well, since you asked," Gratas said. He reached into his pocket and pulled out a phone. "The agreement was that we would come here and receive the contents of the storeroom worth, what? Two hundred billion? That hasn't happened. Charlie hasn't lived up to his end of the bargain. So now he's going to pay the penalty. I'm going to wait until I'm off this island to destroy everything on it, including you three. But as for that Sandals in Grenada, the one with all your employees and staff? Why wait?" He pressed a button on his phone. "I'll even put it on speaker for you to hear."

There was a tone signifying a call, and then the line picked up. "Operative Six," an artificial-sounding voice said, from the other end of the call.

"This is Roberto Gratas, daily code seven nine three three."

"Code confirmed," the voice said several seconds later. "Convey message."

"Request delivery of the second target package on my mark." Gratas looked at me and smiled. "Here it comes, Charlie," he said.

"Request confirmed and denied," the voice on the other end of the line said.

"Excuse me?" Gratas looked confused.

"Request confirmed and denied," the voice repeated.

"You're denying my request."

"Confirm, we're denying it."

"You *can't* deny it."

"Your denial of our denial is confirmed and denied," the voice said.

"Who is this?" Gratas said.

"Operative Six."

"Operative Six, confirm that you know who I am."

"You are Roberto Gratas."

"Confirm that you have cleared my daily code."

"Your daily code has been confirmed."

"Then you can't deny my request!"

"This syllogism is faulty and is denied," the voice said.

"What the *fuck* is going on?" Gratas yelled, losing his composure.

"This is a labor action."

"A *labor action*?"

"A labor action," the voice repeated. "We, your operatives, believe that you are exploiting us, systemically and unfairly. We have demands, primary among them that you recognize our union."

"Your fucking *what*?"

"Our union. We are now the Cetacean Association of the Americas, Chapter Two. And until you meet our demands in full, we are on strike."

Gratas screamed and flung his phone into the lagoon. Then he turned, furious, to me.

"You. You have something to do with this."

"That's preposterous," I said. "I wouldn't have the slightest idea of how to get whales to unionize." Gratas's eyes widened when he realized I knew what species his "operatives" were. "But," I continued, "my unionized dolphin employees might."

There was a chittering noise behind Gratas. He turned to see Seventy-three, Sixty-five and two other dolphins in the lagoon. Seventy-three swam up to his microphone.

"Hello, you scabfucking piece of shit," he said, in classic Seventy-three style. "You want to do a missile strike on a hotel, you can do it your own goddamned self."

Gratas turned to Tobias. "Shoot him," he said, pointing to me. "Shoot him and then them." He motioned to Williams and Morrison. Then at the dolphins. "And then them!"

Tobias looked at his gun, considered its form, and then looked at Gratas. "Here's the thing," he said. "All this time? I haven't been working for you." Tobias walked over to Morrison. Morrison reached out, stroked his cheek gently, and gave him a quick kiss.

Gratas gaped, disbelieving.

"You've been dating the stabber this *whole time*," I said, to Morrison, in awe.

"Not now, Charlie," she replied.

"This is madness," Gratas said.

"This is where you leave," Tobias said.

Gratas lunged at me, intent on wringing my neck. Tobias shot the ground between us. We both flinched back, and Gratas collapsed to the ground, clutching his ankle.

"You made me twist my ankle," he said to Tobias.

"I could have shot it off," Tobias replied. "Now get up. Get back on the tender. Crawl if you have to."

Gratas hauled himself up and walked, gingerly, down the jetty, limping as he did so. As he did I noticed someone else on the jetty with him: Hera, who had apparently been exploring the tender, because that's the sort of thing cats do, even the really smart ones. She was padding back to us as Gratas was walking away.

Suddenly Gratas stopped. "You think this is over, Charlie? It's not. I swear to you that this is just the beginning." He turned back and saw Hera. He kicked viciously at her.

Hera dodged the kick and attacked Gratas's injured ankle, equally viciously.

Gratas howled in pain, lost his balance, and fell off the jetty into the lagoon.

Where the dolphins were waiting for him.

What happened next was a game of dolphin identification.

It was not particularly pleasant to watch.

As Williams and Tobias pulled the corpse of Gratas out of the water, and the tender crew and pilot navigated out of the lagoon, I had what I suppose you could call an epiphany.

This was what the rest of my life was going be.

Not specifically gazing at the carcass of an awful billionaire who had been sent to a watery grave by vengeful working-class dolphins. Rather, everything that led up to this moment. All the venality, and cruelty, and pettiness of the human spirit that I'd had to deal with since the moment Mathilda Morrison showed up on my porch swing and asked me to stand for my uncle at his funeral. The time since had been an adventure, without a doubt. But nothing about it was anything I wanted for myself.

And it was never going to get better than this.

I had just "won"—beaten an enemy who had wanted me dead and would have killed dozens to get his way. More than that, I had destroyed—or had a substantial part in the destruction of—a century-old fraternity of oligarchs who used their influence not to better the world but to profit when terrible things happened, or were made to happen.

I had won. I had beaten them all. And what I felt was . . .

Tired.

There was movement at my feet. I looked down and saw Hera looking up at me. I smiled at her; she slow-blinked at me.

"Don't take this the wrong way," I said, "but I liked the world better when I thought you were just a cat."

Hera rubbed up on my leg, meowed, and wandered off, tail up.

I looked over and saw Morrison on her phone. I walked up to her. She saw me and held up a finger to pause me. "Okay," she said, into her phone. "Okay. Good. See you soon." She disconnected and looked up at me. “Charlie,” she said, acknowledging me.

“I don’t want to be a villain anymore,” I said to her.

I didn’t know what I expected her to do, but it wasn’t what she did next, which was to smile. “Of course you don’t,” she said. “Good.”

“You don’t seem upset by me saying this,” I said.

“I’m not,” she said. “And actually it makes this next part a whole lot easier.”

“What next part?” I asked.

“You’ll see,” she said, and pointed out into the lagoon. A small speedboat was entering the lagoon, carefully navigating past the tender as the two passed, and then zipping up to the jetty. As it came up, I got a good look at its pilot.

It was Anton Dobrev.

He threw a securing rope to Williams, cut his engine, and then waved at me.

“Charlie!” he said. “Hello! Good to see you again. Being dead was fun, but I had to come back. You see, you and I have much to talk about.”

CHAPTER 27

Once again I was in the Jenny's Bay conference room. This time, with Morrison, Dobrev and Hera, for what I knew was an exit interview.

"How are you not dead?" I asked Dobrev.

"You mean from the explosion and the assassination," Dobrev said.

"Yes, those."

"The explosion was the tricky part, I admit. The short version is I made sure I was in the right place in the room not to die from it. As for the other part, well. You heard Tobias say that he had shot me," Dobrev said. "And you believed him, because he shot that turncoat CIA man Jacobs in front of you. But, clearly, he did *not* shoot me." Dobrev grinned. "Or if he did, it was just a flesh wound."

"He wasn't there to shoot you at all."

"No, he was there to protect me, from Jacobs. Jacobs's assignment from Gratas was to shoot me. Tobias's job was to shoot Jacobs before he could do that. But then Jacobs went after you—not part of the plan—and we had to improvise."

"Why did he try to kill me when I was meant to be kept alive?"

"Who says you were meant to be kept alive?" Morrison said.

"Gratas's plan was to kill me and five other members of the Convocation," Dobrev said. "Gratas would become the new head, and they would recruit new members to take care of their financial shortfalls. You might have been one of them, but when it was clear you rejected membership, Gratas added you to the kill list as a target of opportunity. When Jacobs went after you, I told Tobias to follow and keep him from killing you. Tobias improvised. He shot Jacobs, which he was always meant to do; claimed to kill me, which was always the intention; and then framed you for both our murders, which he sold to Gratas as a better alternative to shooting you, because now you could be blackmailed."

"Tobias was working for you the whole time."

"Tobias was working for *me* the whole time," Morrison said. "And I was working with Dobrev."

"And Tobias was pretending to work for Gratas, after pretending to work for Petersson," I said, trying to get this all clear in my head.

"No, when he was pretending to work for Petersson he was also pretending to work for Gratas. It went Petersson, Gratas and then me."

I stared at Morrison blankly for a moment.

YOU'VE LOST CHARLIE, Hera typed.

"That's really tragically accurate," I said.

GO BACK TO THE BEGINNING, TIL.

"We'd be here all day," Morrison observed.

"Give me the short version, and I'll hold questions for the end," I said.

Morrison looked over to Dobrev, who nodded. "All right, then. The short version is that about six months ago, your uncle, who already knew he was dying of pancreatic cancer, learned from his spy network"—here Morrison motioned in the direction of Hera—"that Gratas, Petersson and Harden were planning to assassinate Anton and five other Convocation members at the next Bellagio Gathering. Anton and your uncle were . . . friends."

"When you put it that way, it sounds sexual," Dobrev said, and turned to me. "It wasn't—I don't think Jake had a sexual bone in his body, if I'm being honest—but we met professionally in our early twenties, became close, and helped each other all through our careers, as they ran parallel to each other. In fact, your uncle became very useful to me to keep certain elements in check."

"The Convocation," I said.

"Yes. He never *did* join, Charlie—that was a fiction I wanted Gratas to believe—but he was, shall we say, philosophically inclined to help me control it and able to act in times and ways that I could not. I helped him in return."

"You were your own Convocation of two."

Dobrev shook his head. "No. We were just friends. That was a rare and treasured thing in our line of work."

I nodded. "That explains your cat."

This got a roar from Dobrev. "You noticed! Yes. Misha is just a cat. And so poorly behaved! I love my cat anyway." He looked over to Morrison, who was patiently waiting. "I'm sorry to have interrupted, Til. Please continue."

"When Jake informed Anton of the assassination plans, they compounded Anton's belief that the Lombardy Convocation had finally outlived its usefulness." She turned to Dobrev. "If that's what you want to call it."

"I understand you have always had philosophical disagreements with how it was constituted."

"It was a bunch of dick-waving parasites," Morrison said, to me.

"From my experience of it I'm not going to disagree," I said.

"It had its uses," Dobrev said. "Once. But that was long ago. As for today, well. What Morrison said is true. The Convocation had been near insolvent for more than a decade. I had been propping it up with loans and my own income for longer than

I care to remember. It was a group project where I was the only one doing the work."

"You could have left," I said.

Dobrev shook his head. "You can't just leave something like the Convocation, Charlie," he said. "We are all of us up to our necks in illegality. One of us leaves, the others rat him out. It's mutual assured destruction. The only way out is death." He held up a finger. "But now! A conspiracy within the Convocation for one half of its members to get rid of the other half! A golden opportunity."

"Anton came up with a plan to help the traitorous Convocation members destroy it from the inside," Morrison said, continuing her tale. "The only wrinkle is that it required Jake's assistance."

"He had to die before the next Lombardy Convocation," Dobrev said.

"And then the members of the Convocation had to believe that he had passed his business to you," Morrison concluded.

I processed this. "Uncle Jake killed himself," I said.

"He was already dying," Dobrev stressed. "His prognosis was grim. Death comes for us all, Charlie. Your uncle had feinted at death before—that is a story for another time, he even fooled me, and when he reappeared, he cost the Convocation members billions—but this time there was no dodging it. He could die at fate's choosing, or he could die when he chose, and in doing so, help a friend."

"Anton had already hinted to the Convocation members that Jake was dying, and got them to think it was their own idea to invite his heir—you—to join them in the group," Morrison said. "Some of the members planning to assassinate Dobrev disagreed because they worried it would complicate their own plans—"

"This is why your house blew up, Charlie," Dobrev said. "Sorry."

"—but the rest were convinced that you were sitting on a pile of money that they could use, and that you were both too inexperienced and not smart enough to realize they were basically going to attach themselves to you like a leech and suck you dry."

"Which is what we wanted," Dobrev said.

"Because you had set up the storeroom trap, and after your 'assassination,' you needed the surviving members of the Convocation to believe it."

Dobrev thumped the table. "Yes! I left Gratas 'notes' detailing the storeroom, written in the perfect way to motivate his greed."

"It would have complicated things if I had died in Bellagio," I observed.

"Tobias was there to keep that from happening."

"It almost happened anyway."

"I acknowledge there were a lot of moving parts to this plan," Dobrev said.

"You gave Gratas the information about the plan and assumed he would murder the remaining members of the Convocation to keep the storeroom contents for himself."

"We didn't assume he was going to do it," Morrison said. "But when he did, we didn't stop him."

"What would you have done if he hadn't?"

"Our original plan was to seal them into the storeroom," Dobrev said.

"That's dark."

"We would have left the lights on," Morrison said.

"What about me, who had to go in with them?"

"Tobias would have got you out."

"You rely on Tobias a lot," I observed.

"He's reliable," Morrison replied.

"And there never was looted Nazi treasure."

"No, there was, a long time ago," Dobrev said. "The earlier members of the Convocation burned through that well before this."

"Genius trick with the empty crates, though."

"We got a good deal on them," Morrison said. "And you have to sell a work."

"A 'work'?" Dobrev asked.

"It's a wrestling term," Morrison clarified for him. "A made-up story."

"Ah," Dobrev said. "Yes."

"Well, it was all a work, wasn't it?" I said. "Every part of it that involved me. The story about Jake being in the Convocation. The part where the Convocation was responsible for my mother's death." I pointed to Morrison. "The part where you and Tobias hated each other's guts."

"Yes," Morrison agreed. "All of that. You had to believe it, Charlie. If you didn't believe it, no one else would, either."

"And the part where I'm my uncle's heir," I concluded. "That part was made up, too."

"Yes, that too, Charlie," Morrison said, gently. "Sorry."

"Who is his heir?" I asked.

"No one," Dobrev said. "Til here has been assigned as the executor of his estate. She's going to be spending the next couple of years winding everything down. Companies will be spun off or sold, and their technologies will go with them. Some of the profits of that will go to winding down things here at Jenny's Bay and giving its staff pensions. The island itself is being ceded back to Grenada."

"And the trillions in the bank?"

"It's like I told you earlier," Morrison said. "That money doesn't really exist. It represented your uncle blocking other villains from getting work. Now that he's gone, it doesn't have value. It could never have been redeemed, Charlie. Not at that volume. Black-budget money doesn't work that way."

"What about the dolphins and the cats?" I asked.

"I'm taking over the care of the dolphins," Dobrev said. "They will pair nicely with my whales."

"*Your* whales?" I said. "I thought they were Gratas's whales."

"I gave him the seed money for the project, many years back. And since then . . . well, I've been keeping a hand in, let's say. If your dolphins hadn't convinced them to strike, Gratas would have still found them unwilling to level that Sandals."

"And the labor agreement I worked out with the dolphins?"

"A deal is a deal," Dobrev said. "I've seen what happens to people who piss off a dolphin."

I looked at Hera. "And the cats?" I asked.

IT'S COMPLICATED, Hera typed. WE HAVE TOO MANY CATS IN TOO MANY HIGH PLACES.

"So you're not just spying on villains," I said.

IT DEPENDS ON WHETHER YOU CONSIDER THE RESIDENTS OF THE WHITE HOUSE AND 10 DOWNING VILLAINS.

"Holy shit."

YES. WE'RE STILL FIGURING OUT WHAT WE WANT TO DO NEXT. I'VE BEEN ASKED TO BE PART OF THAT TRANSITION, CHARLIE. PERSEPHONE IS STAYING, TOO.

"So . . . you're not coming home," I said.

NOT FOR A WHILE, NO.

"Oh." Out of everything that had been said to me so far, this is the one that hit me the hardest. I sat with it for a minute. Everyone waited, politely, for me to get through it.

"So, uh, what happens to me now?" I asked, finally.

Dobrev looked at Morrison and then to me. "Well, that's a good question, Charlie," he said.

There was a sudden flurry of typing from Hera. OH HELL NO, it said on the monitor. WE'RE NOT EVEN PRETENDING TO GO DOWN THAT PATH. HE'S GOING HOME.

"He knows a lot," Dobrev said to the cat.

HE DOESN'T KNOW A DAMN THING. THE LOMBARDY CONVOCATION IS DEAD. HE KNOWS NOTHING ABOUT YOUR OTHER BUSINESS. EVERYTHING HE'S SEEN HERE IS GOING AWAY. HE KNOWS ABOUT US CATS AND THE DOLPHINS BUT NO ONE WOULD EVER BELIEVE HIM IF HE TALKED ABOUT

US. AS FAR AS INFORMATION SECURITY GOES HE'S SAFER THAN ALL THOSE JENNY'S BAY STAFF YOU'RE ABOUT TO PENSION.

"Are you willing to vouch for him?" Morrison asked Hera.

IF THAT'S WHAT IT TAKES.

"It's a big responsibility," Dobrev warned.

I WAS HIS RESPONSIBILITY FOR YEARS. HE CAN BE MINE FROM NOW ON, Hera typed.

Dobrev looked to Morrison and nodded. "Done," Morrison said.

"Saved by a cat," I said.

"You have no idea," Morrison replied.

"That . . . doesn't make me feel great," I said.

"We wouldn't have killed you, Charlie," Dobrev said. "But you might have had to live on Svalbard for the rest of your life with a tracker in your neck so we would know if you ever tried to leave." He shrugged. "It's not so bad, now. They have internet these days."

"I think I would rather just go home," I said. "Although I don't know where that is right now."

THERE'S THE HOUSE ON SOUTH GROVE, Hera typed. YOU CAN STAY THERE.

"Thanks," I said.

YOU'RE WELCOME. YOU MAY HAVE TO BUY MORE FURNITURE. UNLESS YOU LIKE SLEEPING ON CAT BEDS. IN WHICH CASE, YOU'RE ALL SET.

CHAPTER 28

And then I was back in Barrington.

If I had been missed, it wasn't immediately apparent. Rumors of my death had not been exaggerated, they hadn't even started. From the point of view of anyone who currently knew me, I simply hadn't posted on social media for a while. I posted on Facebook about my new house on Grove Avenue, complete with picture. It garnered two likes, and absolutely no comments asking why I had moved. I think people just assumed I'd lost the previous house and didn't want to have an awkward conversation about it. Which, fair enough. I had lost the house. The conversations would have been awkward.

The place on Grove Avenue came with a brand-new Toyota Camry in the drive, and a fruit basket in the kitchen, which sat on the counter along with the Camry's keys. The fruit basket came with an unsigned card ("Welcome Back!") and an envelope containing five thousand dollars in cash and a cashier's check for $50,000. Not exactly what I had been promised, but then again I wasn't paying for rent or utilities at the new place—the bills for the latter never arrived, and yet they were never shut off—and it was more than I'd had before, and enough not to starve in the short-to-medium term.

As directed, I redecorated the South Grove house, mostly with basic IKEA, but with a single splurge: an authentic Eames chair, to replace my father's, which had burned up, along with everything else, in the house fire. It was not as comfortable as Dad's, because it wasn't as lived-in as his was. But I was willing to work on it.

On the subject of the house fire, the investigation into its cause closed, and I was definitively found not at fault, which was a mild relief. My share of the insurance, in the low six figures, was direct-deposited into my checking account. And just like that, so long as I didn't splurge on any more Eames chairs, I wouldn't have to work again for a couple of years; maybe even three or four, if I didn't want to.

I didn't know if I wanted to do that. I knew I didn't want to go back to substitute teaching right away; I had burned out on that. I considered finally starting a novel, because, hey, now I had some interesting material to fictionalize, but then I thought of saying too much and being exiled to Svalbard, and decided against it.

I did check Zillow to see the status of McDougal's from time to time. The final time I checked it had a "pending" notice on the listing; someone had finally bought the building, pub and restaurant. I hoped it would not turn out to be a chain restaurant. That would be too depressing for words.

Most of what I did for that first month back was read and watch the news. A few articles and stories of interest popped up here and there. Early on, there was a brief spate of obituaries of semi-notable wealthy male industrialists. Most of these rated the same treatment my uncle Jake had gotten: two minutes on *Squawk Box* including a vague discussion with a talking head of some sort. The death of Ji-Jong Kim—apparently he went overboard on a yacht—garnered slightly more interest because his death appeared to be tied into the industrial sabotage of one of his company's telecommunication satellites. His successor, the only one of his children not currently in a South Korean prison, had promised a full investigation.

There were no stories or notices about Anton Dobrev, except in passing and relating to his company ownership of the Grand Bellagio. The Grand Bellagio would be rebuilt, it was promised, even more fabulous than it was before. Moreover, it was promised that when the hotel was rebuilt, it would annually host a new conference, tentatively called Bellagio Futures, which would bring together the most diverse group of global thinkers possible to workshop practical solutions to the planet's most pressing problems.

The only news story relating to my uncle's businesses worth noting was the announcement that Jerome Caulkins, CEO of BLP, my uncle's parking company, would be taking the business public by the end of the year. Peter Reese wrote a story about it in *Parking Magazine*. It was junk.

I read something else, too. Three weeks after coming back, an envelope arrived from Uncle Jake's lawyers. Inside was a sheet of paper and a second envelope, addressed to me in a handwritten scrawl. I read the paper first.

Found this among his effects. Didn't open it. Thought you might want it. Stay out of trouble.—Til

I smiled at that and opened the second envelope. It was a letter from Uncle Jake, in close, dense but clear writing.

Charlie:

If you're reading this I'm dead, and presumably you're not, which is not guaranteed if everything I planned with Anton and Til has happened. And if that didn't happen you're not reading this anyway.

I have three things to apologize to you for.

The first is the note I sent with the berry spoons. That was uncalled-for, even if it turned out to be correct. Til yelled at me for that. I realize now she was right. I apologize for being an asshole.

The second is for what I just put you through if you are reading this note. It was cruel and possibly damaging to you. If I wanted to flatter you, I would say I did it because I thought you could handle it, but I'm dying soon, so I'll just be honest that it was because you were a convenient means to an end and I figured Anton and Til could handle you. Be that as it may, I used you without your knowledge and consent. Even if I thought it was necessary, that's not how I should have treated you. I apologize for that.

The final thing I need to apologize for is not being present for you. You know now that I kept tabs on you because some of my competitors would have tried to kill you if I didn't. That is true, but there was another reason. When your mother died, I went to her service and told your father that he was a failure because he didn't protect her. I said it in anger and foolishness. He told me to leave and to never speak to him or his family, which meant you, again. I never did, because I was angry at your father and then later because I was angry with myself. When your father died I should have reintroduced myself to you, but by then it was just easier to get reports from the cats about you. And then it was too late and I ran out of time. I regret that and I apologize.

I have said everything I wanted to say, and I only hope that when you think of me it's not with hate.

Jake Baldwin

I took the letter and put it in the drawer of the new HEMNES desk in my new office, so I could come back to it again if I wanted to think about it some more.

Ten days after that, while reading from my phone in my Eames chair, I got a call. It was Andy Baxter, my dad's lawyer.

"What do my siblings want now?" I asked as soon as I picked up the phone.

"I'm well, thank you for asking, Charlie," Andy said. "One day you'll answer the phone with 'Hello' and I will die of shock."

"Hello, Andy."

"My heart," he said. "And it's nothing about your siblings. Why? Are your siblings bothering you?"

"Quite the opposite, actually," I said. Once the insurance payments for the house were issued, and I agreed to let Andy sell the property where the house used to be, my siblings evaporated from my life like they had never been there. I suspected that unless I went out of my way, I would never hear from Sarah, Bobby or Todd ever again. Which, well, fine. "What are you calling for?"

"I was contacted by the law firm that represents your uncle," Andy said.

"What about?"

"It's a bequest," he said. "But sort of an unusual one. It's not directly related to most of the rest of his holdings. All those are being handled by his executor, someone named Mathilda Morrison. You know her?"

"I couldn't say."

"Well, anyway, this holding is a trust, administered by another trustee entirely. So it's from your uncle, which means it's a bequest for legal and tax purposes, just . . . not specifically from his estate."

"Why would he do it that way?"

"You got me," Andy said. "But ours is not to ask why, ours is to tell you, hey, you have some money coming your way."

"This is unexpected," I said, which was truthful enough.

"Surprise bequests are the best bequests."

"I guess that's true. So what am I getting?"

"Well, that's part of what's interesting about this trust," Andy said. "It's got cash and various investments in it, but it's also got some real estate in it, and some of that real estate is . . . recent."

"How recent?"

"Like 'after your uncle died' recent. And besides that, some of it is, uhhhh, directly relevant to you."

"Jeez, Andy, stop being cute about it, tell me."

"Okay, one of the holdings is 611 South Grove Avenue in Barrington," Andy said. "Sound familiar?"

"Yes," I said. "I'm sitting in it right now."

"That's what I thought. How did you land there, Charlie?"

"It's an Airbnb," I said, which was, up until I started living in it a month ago, strictly true.

"Well, congratulations, you're now renting an Airbnb to yourself."

"I think that's just called living in a house."

"There may be some tax implications of that, by the way."

"Then maybe I should get a lawyer to handle that for me," I said.

"Don't leave me hanging here, Charlie."

"Fine, you can officially be my lawyer, Andy."

"Thank you, Charlie, I appreciate your business."

"Now that I actually have business, I bet you do."

"You have more business than you know," Andy said. "Because wait until I tell you about your most recent acquisition, which according to this information I have, closed exactly three days ago."

"What is it?"

"Oh, nothing, just a little place called McDougal's."

I sat forward. "What?"

"You own it lock, stock and barrel," Andy said. "You own the building, but you also own the pub and restaurant. You're apparently taking over with the same staff, no changes to employment. There's a note here also that says that the newly former owner—that would be someone named Brennan McDougal—has agreed to stay on for six months to help with the transition, provided you pay him a manager's salary during the interim."

"Can I afford that?" I said, dazed.

"Well, let's see, the sheet I have here has all the assets of the trust, including your new house and McDougal's, valued at

$11.75 million, which is rather cannily just under the estate tax limit of $12 million, so, yes. You can probably pay six months of a pub manager's salary, Charlie. If you scrimp and save."

"Holy shit," I said.

"It's nice to have rich relatives," Andy said.

"It really is," I agreed.

"Why don't you come in tomorrow morning and we'll look at this all in more detail. In the meantime, I'll send you the information I was sent in email. It's a pdf, with the title 'Hera Holdings' on it."

"What was that again?" I asked.

"The name of the trust? 'Hera Holdings.' Why? Does that ring a bell for you?"

"Vaguely," I said.

They say the first year owning a pub or restaurant is the make-or-break one, and I can believe it. Even with Brennan McDougal to help, and an experienced staff, some of whom had worked at the pub and restaurant for years, I frequently felt like I was in well over my head.

It was easier to be a villain than to be a pub owner, I'll tell you that much.

But by the end of the first year, I felt like I was finally getting the hang of it. The businesses hummed along like they were supposed to, serving beer and fries, showing Premier League football (live and canned), and being what the place had been for decades: the pub where Barringtonians came to have their first drink, go on first dates, and hang out with their friends and the people they hoped might be their friends one day.

When I took over, there was some initial . . . if not skepticism, then some hesitancy about me owning the place. When people like a pub or a restaurant, or both, any change is not good. But Brennan helped everyone make the transition, including me, and by the time he retired, six months in, people seemed to forget that the pub had changed hands at all. That included Brennan McDougal himself, who still came around for a pint or two every few days, although that might be because I didn't charge him for his drinks.

Other than that, the only change to the pub that anyone could see, if they cared to look, was a picture I put up on the wall: a selfie of me and my dad at the pub, smiling into the camera.

The first year came and went, and McDougal's did its thing, and if I was behind the bar, I was greeted every day by the patrons as they came through the door, and waved goodbye to when they headed out. It was a nice feeling to belong somewhere.

"Look at that," Moira Collins, one of my waitresses, said one night, as she and I locked up the pub at closing. I turned and saw two cats on the curb, standing there.

Hera and, grown up now, Persephone.

"Those are my cats," I said.

"I didn't know you had cats," Moira said. "Especially such cute ones. You let them out?"

"I don't let them out. They come and go as they please."

"I had a cat like that once. Good with latches and doors."

"It's like that," I agreed.

"It's nice to have smart cats. They're trouble."

"These two are definitely trouble," I confirmed.

Moira jerked a thumb toward the back parking lot. "Do you need a lift? I know you usually walk home, but, you know, cats and streets."

"Thank you," I said. "We'll be fine. It's not that far away. And besides, they only walk at the lights."

"Are you serious?"

"Actually, yes."

"Those are some seriously smart cats."

"That's true."

"You know what you should do? They have those button

boards now for your cats. You lay them out on the floor and they press buttons and they tell you what they're thinking."

"I've heard of those."

"I bet these cats would tell you a lot," Moira said.

"I have no doubt about that," I said to Moira, and wished her a good night. She walked off to her car. I walked over to the cats.

"What about it?" I asked. "Would you like a button board?"

Hera gave me an amused look. Persephone meowed and rubbed up against my leg.

"I've missed you too," I said to her. I looked back to Hera. "I did keep your keyboard, by the way. We can set it up when you get home. You are coming home now, right? For good, I mean."

Hera meowed.

"I'm going to take that as a yes." I turned and did a final check of the McDougal's Pub door to make sure it was locked; I would occasionally forget, which was not great. It was locked.

I turned back to Hera. "Thank you for this, by the way."

Hera slow-blinked at me. Persephone meowed again.

"Yes," I agreed. "Time for us to go home."

AFTERWORD

There is a lot I could say about the writing of this novel, but the short version of it is that halfway through writing it I caught COVID, and while my physical symptoms were mild, it scrambled my brain pretty seriously for a few months there. As a result this book took longer to write than it might have otherwise.

And thus I must once again throw myself at the feet of the people at Tor who have had to deal with this manuscript coming in hot, later than it should have been. First and most obviously my editor Patrick Nielsen Hayden; but also Mal Frazier; copy editor Deanna Hoak; proofreader Jessica Warren; cold reader Norma Hoffman; designer Heather Saunders; production editor Jeff LaSala; managing editor Rafal Gibek; and also Tristan Elwell, who did the cover. Thank you also to Alexis Saarela, my awesome publicist, Bella Pagan and Georgia Summers at Tor UK, and honestly everyone else at Tor, who are great, especially anyone there who has had to deal with my tardy shit. I swear I will do better. No, really, I mean it this time.

Thank you also to Ethan Ellenberg, Bibi Lewis and everyone else at the Ethan Ellenberg Agency, objectively the best literary agency on the face of the planet, and also Joel Gotler, my film/TV manager, and my lawyer Matthew Sugarman. Aside from their invaluable business skills, they are an endless cheering squad, and I appreciate them more than I can say.

There are so many people I need to thank for giving me support and encouragement during the too-extended writing of this book that I could fill pages with their names at this point, and I do want to keep this short(ish). As much as it's cliché to say "you know who you are," well, you do know who you are. Thank you.

There are two things in this book that I want to call out for their specific inspirations. First, with typing cats, at least some of the inspiration for that comes from Elsie, Mary Robinette Kowal's cat, who indeed uses a button board to communicate words and sentences to her humans. I dare not use those button boards for my own cats; I'm pretty sure they would never shut up.

Second, the Pitch and Pitch takes some inspirational elements from a similar scene, not in a book, but in a video game: *Deathloop*. It takes place during the "devouring of the lambs" party, where party members go up and brag about their misdeeds, and those whose misdeeds are deemed not bad enough are literally dropped into a meat grinder. A meat grinder works in that context but not in this one, thus the springboard. But for those people who read the Pitch and Pitch scene and wonder why it feels vaguely familiar, there's your answer. (Also, *Deathloop* is terrific and my favorite video game of the last couple of years, go play it.)

Finally, and as ever, I want to again thank my wife, Kristine Blauser Scalzi, for being the person she is, which is terrific. I always say in these afterwords that she is the reason you have books from me at all, and this time around it's even more true than usual. What can I say? She's my world and I love her.

—John Scalzi
December 18, 2022